GIVE ME GLORY

Linda Wiges

DEDICATION

To **ELEANOR BLAKELY**,
the sweet-natured bloodhound who
inspired the fictional dog,
Murray.

ONE

Tama, IA 2010

Austin Wapiti has never been more nervous. He's given a few speeches in his life and been through a couple of job interviews. But those experiences never produced the anxiety he's feeling on his drive to the Meskwaki Settlement. The home of his youth was the place he wanted to live forever. Until it wasn't. Now he is forcing himself to continue against his will as he did when his Meskwaki mom used to push him through the door of the dentist's office. "Facing your fears will make you strong," she always told him.

He tries to think of anything now except the past. Or even the future. The present moment is all he can manage. He concentrates on the clouds, the other cars, and the fly on the dashboard. Driving below the Highway 63 speed limit is unusual for him, but he chooses to delay his arrival in Tama. So far, four cars have passed his well-used Ford Explorer.

Austin's bloodhound is sitting calm and erect beside him. "Murray, you will soon be entering Indian Territory. I'm betting you'll never want to leave." Murray doesn't reply but looks appropriately serious, his droopy eyes taking in the Tama County cornfields.

Lying on the seat between them is an open letter. It's from Liz Morgan, who was Liz Raines when Austin last saw her. From the sound of it, his natural mom needs his help. He reads her words one more time.

Gray has recently had health problems that have thrown him into a deep depression. I finally found your address online. I hope it's current. I hate to ask you to come back here before you're ready, but I don't know what else to do. I assume you know Gray and I married soon after you left the settlement. We were happy for a while, but recent developments have changed Gray's lifestyle and his attitude. He's in a low place. I think if you could come for a few weeks, it would make a big difference. I'll stay out of your way. This visit wouldn't be about me at all. P.S. The trailer has been replaced by a house. Things look a little different than you remember. And Liz added her cell number.

Austin has never spent much time with his birth father. It's hard to imagine that showing up now will bring Gray out of a low place. That's the place Austin himself is only recently emerging from. He briefly wonders if the *development* Liz speaks of is a terminal diagnosis. Maybe Gray is dying. As if Austin's guilt can get any worse.

His stomach feels a lot like he's coming down with the flu. Several times during the short trip, he considers turning back. He could write a note of apology, saying he can't get away from work. At one point this afternoon, he even drove ten miles back toward Waterloo before he reversed directions and tried again. Evidently, his curiosity is bigger than his fear. He wants to know what's wrong with Gray, and he does hate the idea of disappointing Liz. Her letter sounds a little desperate, and she isn't the kind of female to invent an emergency when there isn't one.

He stops three times to let Murray out. At each pit stop, the dog looks over his shoulder as if to ask, "Again? I can go ten hours without a bathroom break!" But Murray is always happy to scamper in the grass and investigate every insect and twig he encounters.

While watching to be sure his dog doesn't wander too far, Austin reflects on his history with Liz Raines. She was introduced as his mom Ruby's friend, a young white woman who'd just gotten out of prison after being unjustly forced to serve twenty years for causing the death of her mother. From the moment he saw Liz, Austin loved her. Unfortunately, nothing and no one in his life had given him reason to believe the blonde was actually his natural mother. He had no idea he was adopted or that he was not one-hundred percent Meskwaki. While Liz was looking for the right time to tell him these facts, his affections were growing. It wasn't until his Meskwaki mom died and he had confessed his love for her friend that Austin stumbled upon the truth in Liz's journals. The shocking information was more than he could take in. Feeling both ashamed and betrayed, he fled the settlement without saying goodbyes.

After nearly four years of feeling sorry for himself, he finally read the stack of journals Liz had insisted he take with him. Those notebooks written during her incarceration were full of letters to the baby she'd been told had not survived. Her written words answered many of Austin's questions, especially about why she failed to fill him in before he could develop romantic feelings for her. Their relationship was finally clarified enough that he was able to send her a Mother's Day card this last May. Ever since he's been away, Liz has tried to reach out to him, but he's never answered her emails or notes. That one greeting card, sent after accidentally seeing her graduate from UNI, has been the only gesture of reconciliation on his part.

Now Austin's truck is pointed toward Tama and the rural setting where he grew up content to be the full-blooded son of Ruby and Murray Wapiti. Life was so simple. Now he has a hundred misgivings floating around in his brain. He's sure he's over any romantic attachment to Liz, but past experience tells him it would have been safer to stay away. What if the feelings resurface? What if she looks at him like he's a pervert? Can he deal with witnessing her marriage to Gray at close range? Will she and Gray want him to call them Mom and Dad? It's almost a joke that Liz thinks he's capable of helping his birth father when Austin needs so much help for himself.

Today he can't even look forward to the familiar sight of Ruby's dilapidated trailer. The tribe no longer allows members to live in mobile dwellings. He has a moment of sadness because he'll never again see the home of his youth. The trauma of his last day there still haunts him. It was the first time since childhood he'd shed real tears. When he discovered Liz's latest journal in the nightstand drawer, he cried like a baby. The few paragraphs that revealed she was his mother were devastating news. And the idea that Liz hadn't explained everything to him when they first met, seemed to him the cruelest behavior he could imagine.

Austin has forgiven his natural parents but hasn't forgiven himself for developing a crush on his mother. He kept those feelings secret until the end of the summer of 2005 when he came right out and declared his love. There's no way to pretend he didn't say the words or to hope she ever forgot them. But he's trying today to empty it all out of his mind before he reaches her house. Both he and Liz must focus on the present and on Gray's problems, whatever they may be.

As he drives through the settlement, Austin sees the ranch-style homes which are, no doubt, similar to Liz and Gray's new one. Such a building may discourage disturbing reflections. He's never lived in a wooden building, so the Morgan's should hold no gloomy reminders.

"I know they have a big yard, boy. Won't that be great?"

Murray doesn't have an opinion. The dog has been Austin's constant companion since he was a pup, but his conversation skills are lacking. Austin doesn't hold that against him. He's found communication without words to be the most comfortable way to live these days. The folks at work are nice enough, but he hasn't managed to cultivate any close friendships. There are no colleagues, male or female, with whom he cares to hang out in the evenings. Someone who's into psychology might conclude that Austin's past has made him wary of personal interaction. Clint, a Meskwaki acquaintance from college, tried for a long time to draw him out into the world, but he finally gave it up as a hopeless cause.

Maybe it's time now for man and dog to accept the company of humans. And the bloodhound is sure to appreciate the freedom dogs enjoy on the settlement. No leashes or chain link fences. It will be a job to get him back to city rules after this visit.

Austin turns onto White Tail Road, just a mile from the old place. He's startled to see a person on a bicycle coming toward him. The figure appears to be a young Native American woman, bumping along on a no-speed bicycle from another era. She doesn't look his way, but seems intent on reaching her destination. He can't imagine where that could be or who she is. He used to know everyone on the settlement. This woman is totally unfamiliar. He wonders if she's been visiting Liz and Gray or whether she's from town and simply out for some exercise.

As he approaches the house, Austin slows his truck to a crawl. Curiously, a newly built ramp leads from a plank porch to an unpaved driveway. Since Liz and Gray are the first people to live in this structure, they must have been the ones to request it. Why would a healthy couple want a ramp?

TWO

Judging from the urgent tone of her letter, Austin is a little surprised Liz isn't sitting outside watching for him. He texted the time he'd most likely arrive, and in spite of the delays, he's made it on schedule. He won't mind waiting if she's running an errand or something. Her absence will give him a few more minutes to become mentally prepared for their meeting. He inches his car toward the porch. A small girl with black hair to her waist flies out the door and down the ramp. She stands in front of the Explorer, wide-eyed.

He stops before hitting her. The child comes to stand by the car door and gives him an enthusiastic welcome through the open driver's window. "Are you my brother? I *need* a brother." Then she spots Murray and adds, "And a dog!"

In spite of his fears about this visit, he finds it easy to smile at her. "My name's Austin. What's yours?"

The child looks at him like he should know the answer. "Rue ne-*tediso*! But my real name is Ruby."

Austin is completely stunned. It's comforting to hear his native language again, but he hasn't known about his Meskwaki mom's namesake. It's never occurred to him that Liz and Gray might have had a baby since he saw them. He wonders when this little girl entered the picture. "How old are you, Rue?"

"Five. I'm going to go to school!"

"Wow," is Austin's honest reaction. "I bet your folks are proud of you."

"My dad's sick. Are you going to make him well?" Apparently, Rue has been told more than he has about the reason for his visit.

"I'm sorry to hear that," Austin tells her. "But I'm not a doctor."

"Mom says you'll be good medicine."

Austin gets out of the Explorer and immediately finds a tiny hand in his. In spite of his earlier uncertainties, Rue's warm welcome is reassuring. He tries not to stare at her face but can't help looking for signs they're siblings. The little one has Gray's Meskwaki coloring but Liz's features, the same characteristics Austin might use to describe his own appearance.

Rue takes him straight into the front entryway. From there he can catch a partial view of the living room. It's a pretty combination of the white and Native American worlds, skillfully decorated by Liz. And from what he can see, the house is neat as a pin. Of course, Liz has probably been preparing for his visit, but he remembers her as someone who regularly prefers an orderly home.

In spite of her many admirable qualities, Austin was always aware his first mom Ruby had no housekeeping skills. Their small mobile home had been crammed with miscellaneous objects that made it hard sometimes to even manipulate his way from room to room. He'd tried to keep his own bedroom neat but had more or less gotten used to the topsy-turvy condition of the rest of the place. When Ruby got to feeling closed in by it all, she went to the casino. Things like stray pieces of mail and dirty clothes couldn't slow down her quest for the big win. Liz coming to stay in Austin's old room had improved the situation considerably. The white woman tried to justify her presence by cleaning, and in doing so, gave Austin a taste of another way to live.

The most captivating feature of this new house hangs on the wall in front of him. It is the large dreamcatcher made by Ruby.

He saw that work of art every day for twenty-one years when it adorned a similar wall in his and Ruby's trailer. He's glad it found its way to Liz.

Gray is seated at a round table to his right when Austin enters the living room. The man's surprised expression reveals he wasn't told his grown son was expected. Either that, or he didn't believe Austin would actually show up.

Five years ago, Gray was the handsome, athletic-looking guy who had talked football with him after the high school games. The teen-aged Austin didn't know they were related – just that the older man was a former player and a big fan of his. When their paths last crossed in 2005, the fact they were biological father and son was news to both men.

Rather than a welcoming smile today, Gray offers his guest nothing but a scowl. "Guess you couldn't find anything better to do on a weekend than come check out your cast-off family."

Austin is less shocked by the surly words than he would be if he hadn't read Liz's letter. In any case, there's no reason he should've expected a red carpet greeting. Austin must've put this couple through a hard time when he disappeared from their lives.

The man at the table is unfamiliar. This Gray is thin and pale, a sad version of Austin's memories. There's no hint of the strong, confident man he once knew. What kind of illness has done this? Maybe it was something mental, a nervous breakdown.

Gray continues on his mission to embarrass Austin. "Do you have any idea how many nights Liz has cried herself to sleep since you ran away? I bet you never gave her feelings one thought. You tore her heart out, you know, and I was left trying to fix it. The thing was, you were the only one who could've done that."

He finishes by glaring at his son. Who has no defense. "I'm sorry," is the best he can do. He shouldn't have come. It seems so obvious now. Liz asked him in a desperate moment, but she should've known about Gray's feelings. How can Austin be of help to a man who's grown to hate him? Especially, when Austin knows the anger is totally justified.

Rue climbs onto her dad's lap.   She must be used to his grouchy speeches, because she doesn't seem at all disturbed. She brightly changes the subject. "Mom said I can call you Happy. If you say it's okay. Okay?"

Happy is the name Liz used in her journals to refer to Austin. They were written while she was imprisoned and didn't know whether she'd given birth to a boy or a girl. Since reading the many entries addressed to his young self, Austin has begun to take ownership of the nickname. "I guess you can call me anything you want to." And he grins at his new sister. None of his feelings of alienation are the little girl's fault.

He naturally feels it's his place to make an effort at civility. Although Gray is staring at the table top, Austin addresses him. "I hear you haven't been feeling so good."

Without looking up, his father responds gruffly. "Oh, I feel okay. What about you? Been sleeping well the past five years? If not, we have all kinds of sleeping pills around here."

Austin knows he's being baited but doesn't react. Trying to fend off his dad's insults won't get them any closer to the real purpose for Austin's visit. Which is, evidently, to cheer up Gray. *No problem.*

The gap in dialogue is quickly filled by Rue, "You ever see a stump before, Happy?"

If she means the ones in the front yard, Austin himself created those when he cut down some diseased ash trees. If she means an amputated limb, yes, he's seen those, too. He's almost afraid to hear what else the child has to tell him.

"Dad's got a good one. I scratch it for him. Sometimes I rub on lotion. Sometimes I put a sock on it."

Austin looks at Gray for an explanation. The man backs up, and Austin can see he's sitting in a wheelchair. Beneath Ruby on his lap, no left leg is visible.

Austin holds back a gasp. "Oh, wow. I didn't know. What happened?"

"Diabetes." Gray can't look at Austin.

Though he tries not to reveal the sympathy he feels, Austin is sure his dad must sense it. Pity isn't something a proud man wants from his son.

Diabetes isn't uncommon on the settlement. And, in fact, loss of a limb isn't unheard of. But not Gray's. Gray was always so fit. Who would ever have foreseen he'd end up in a wheelchair? One thought comes to Austin and won't let go, *I should've been here.*

Luckily, Rue pipes in, "I'm his nurse. Me and Mom. Want to talk to my mom?" Rue doesn't seem to have put together the fact her brother has the same parents she does. She climbs down off her dad's lap and runs out of the room. Austin is noticing pill bottles on the table within Gray's reach. He wonders if they're for pain or maybe infection. They could be the sleeping pills. He concentrates on trying to read the printing on the labels. Anything to keep from anticipating Liz's entrance.

After a few minutes, she appears at the hallway door. Mother and son look at each other.

"Hello, Austin." Liz speaks with an obvious effort. She's surely imagined this meeting for years and lived it in her imagination. At the same time, she must realize her son isn't necessarily here to make peace with her. He has answered her plea for help because that's the kind of person he is.

Rue's smile shows her pride. "My mom's pretty, isn't she?" Austin nods in agreement. He is reminding himself that he recently sent a Mother's Day card to this woman. Liz must be at least forty now. He thinks he can see a few creases at the corners of her eyes, but she still looks extremely youthful. Austin is seeing a blonde version of himself. He wonders why he didn't notice the similarity when they first met. He probably would have if he'd known to be looking for his birth mother.

He isn't sure he should give away the fact Liz wrote and invited him to come. Begged, actually. Gray might not realize his wife is so worried about how he's handling things. "The new house is nice." A house seems to be a safe topic. Except his eyes take in the fact that the doorways are extra wide, handicapped accessible. Gray is handicapped.

Liz eagerly responds, "Yes. We like it. It's the first adapted one on the settlement. I know others are needed."

"I'm glad you have it."

Gray speaks at the top of his lungs, "Yeah! We live in a house for cripples now! People who are broken and old before their time! But damn it, I can get through the doors. That makes me feel damn normal!"

Austin is struck silent by Gray's outburst. He's never heard the man swear before or even raise his voice. It's as though some evil spirit has taken over his body. Surely he isn't drunk. No one would give a diabetic liquor. Liz's calm reaction tells him she, like her daughter, has become accustomed to such rants. But she must hate her husband to cause a scene today when she's waited so long for their son to come home.

She stands and cautiously puts a hand on Gray's shoulder while speaking to Austin. "You know, Gray usually takes a nap about this time. Why don't you go sit on the porch, and I'll join you when he's settled."

"Sure." Austin gets up and grabs his dad's bicep in a gesture of encouragement. "Life is going to get better. You're a strong man." He turns away before he sees Gray's tears.

THREE

Austin is relieved to go outside, to get away from wheelchairs and pills and wide doors. He sits in a cheery red and white webbed chair and looks out at the lawn he used to mow and the driveway where he taught Liz to drive. In even earlier years, he played catch in this yard with his father, Murray. Thinking of Murray, he motions for his bloodhound to come. He's been sitting quietly at the bottom of the ramp waiting for an invitation. The dog, like the man who was Austin's adoptive father, makes no fuss but is always there for him, a quiet figure of support.

In a few minutes, Liz appears and takes a seat at the opposite end of the porch. She smiles tentatively, and his stomach does a little flip for old times' sake. He can't believe they're here together. He can't believe after five years away from the settlement and her, he has let himself be coaxed back. Is it possible he was just waiting for an excuse to return to the place where he belongs? How long might it have taken if he'd waited until he mustered up enough courage on his own?

"Thanks for coming. I know it...wasn't easy." A little twitch plays around Liz's lips, wanting to burst into a big smile. Austin can imagine she is fighting the urge to hug him and never let go. Reading her journals told him all he needed to know about a mother's love, unfulfilled now for twenty-five years. Here he is, in the flesh, but she's holding herself in check, pretending it's just an ordinary sick call.

Nobody except Gray is anxious to initiate any melodrama by dredging up old hurts.

It would help if Austin was on a more definite mission, if he'd been asked to fulfill a specific assignment designed to change his father's outlook. He'd be eager to get started on that. But Liz's request has been so open-ended. She seems to be leaving the solutions up to him, and he's had no experience with the kind of things Gray's facing. Austin fears he'll only be taking up space or making things worse.

"I want to help Gray, but I can't imagine how to do it." He looks at the ramp which is much sturdier than Ruby and his old steps, even after he tried to repair them. "Unless money will help. I still have Mom's winnings from that last night." Ruby won a large jackpot on her final trip to the casino, and she always said the reason she gambled was to be able to do something nice for her son. The result of her efforts sits in the bank untouched.

"Oh, Austin, don't even think it! I didn't ask you to come because we wanted your money. Those winnings are for you only. You know that."

"Or for what's important to me. This is important. I know prosthetics are expensive and have to be replaced sometimes. That would be a great use of the money."

"Such a sweet offer. But I should tell you that money isn't a problem right now. A couple of years after you left, my attorney filed for me to get compensated for my years of wrongful imprisonment. Iowa is one of the few states that pays. They passed a law in 1997, in time for me to benefit."

"Really? That sure does makes me feel better about things. When I read your journals, I just got madder and madder about all you went through and all you lost. Did they give you a lot?"

"Well, I'd have done better if I lived in Texas, but Iowa paid me $50 a day for the twenty years, so it was a nice chunk. And my lawyer got me lost wages even though I was just out of high school when I was convicted, so I didn't even have a job."

"It's sure not enough but better than nothing. It'll help with Gray's medical bills, right?"

"It will if he lets me pay them. That's why he won't get a prosthesis. He doesn't want me to use my hard-won money on him. But there's nothing else I'd rather do with it. Maybe you can talk some sense into him."

"I'll try but can't imagine he'll do what I say. The tribe has taken care of lots of things, haven't they? Like the ramp and stuff?

"Oh, yes. They've been great to do any work that needs to be done, too, and the police department is continuing to pay him. Thank goodness, finances aren't a serious problem. It's his spirit I'm worried about. It's not like Gray to let anything defeat him, but he seems actually changed. Into a hateful, spiteful man. I want my husband back before his depression makes him do something awful to himself."

Austin stiffens a little at the suggestion of suicide. He's had no idea things are so serious. The whole situation makes him feel out of his league. Liz should be looking for a therapist, not an emotionally confused journalist.

"When did it happen? I didn't even know he's diabetic."

"Neither did we right away. I mean, we both realize there's some in his family. But Gray's always been a healthy weight, and he exercises and eats a fairly good diet. Because he'd gone so long with no symptoms, I forgot to pay attention, I guess. After you moved, he started getting awfully tired compared to when he was younger, but we thought it was just from being busy." Liz pauses, maybe wondering how much to tell their son.

"When was the first time he went to the doctor?" Austin asks. He knows men often resist that, hating to admit something might be wrong. He'd have that same trouble.

"He had a blister on his foot that just didn't heal. It was making it hard for him to wear his work boots. Bottom line, is that he got gangrene, and his toes turned black. They removed four of them, trying to stop the infection. It wasn't enough. The leg finally had to go. Maybe if he'd had a more attentive wife, we'd have caught it sooner."

Austin is quick to reassure her. "You can't blame yourself. He's an adult."

"Well, just so I don't make the same mistake twice, I'm hereby reminding you to get tested. Diabetes is … genetic. Even though you're half Caucasian, you're the son of a diabetic. At the clinic, they can even tell if you're predisposed to getting it. It will pay to keep track. We know Rue is fine so far, but she'll get regular checkups.

Rue comes bursting through the front door. The child seems to have uncanny timing. "I got snacks," she announces. On a tray are three cereal bowls filled with chocolate pudding. She struggles to balance them.

Liz takes the tray. "Thanks, hon." Then to Austin, "In case you're wondering, the pudding is sugar free."

"Well, I do like pudding. But I'm not very good at eating it with my fingers." He winks at Rue.

"Oh! Forgot." And the child hurries back inside. Liz and Austin stare silently at their bowls until she returns.

Austin picks up the previous conversation. "Uh, I think I'm okay, but I'll make an appointment just to be sure. They always checked blood sugar at my college physicals." Austin could remember the last time he'd had his finger stuck with a needle and watched the little vial fill. He'd wondered if the nurse could tell he had impure blood, half Meskwaki and half white. He'd almost expected it to be candy-striped.

"I'm sure you're fine. I just can't help worrying about you. I've done that for twenty-five years." Liz's son knows that to be true from her journals. She thought like a mother even before she was sure she was one.

Rue likes talking with the adults. "I got to get shots for school. I hope they don't make my arm bleed."

Austin can't resist the child's innocent concerns. "Shots don't do that. You won't even feel them." His sister is another half breed, but she isn't worried about it. Why should he be?

Rue gathers the empty bowls and takes them back to the kitchen. She seems to be a born hostess. And caretaker. "Maybe Dad will want some when he wakes up."

"Ruby is such a helper." Liz is obviously proud of their daughter. "Ever since Gray's amputation, she's played nurse. He hardly has to do anything for himself. She doesn't understand that being treated like an invalid is the last thing he needs. I try to explain, but so far, she doesn't believe me. Doing things for somebody with a missing leg just makes sense to her."

"I think the Ruby we used to know would be just like that. I remember how much she waited on me after the car accident." Austin catches himself before he digresses too much into the past. "It's good to see you, but I don't think you need my help. Gray seems to be in great hands with you two. And he definitely doesn't sound glad to have me around."

There's a brief silence. Austin understands Liz wants him to stay for more than one purpose. Just his presence will likely heal a wound in her heart and give her one less problem to think about. The other reason, of course, has to do with his father. But the two men have had so little connection over the years, it's hard for Austin to understand why he'll be any more help than some other member of the tribe. It could be that somebody outside the immediate family would be better able to reason with Gray.

"I feel like you could maybe distract Ruby from her dad's predicament. Also, I know he counts your leaving home as a big loss, among others. He lost his leg, he lost his job or at least the way he knew it, he's confined to a wheelchair and can't do much around here. I feel like he desperately needs a purpose, something to get him going again. A missing leg doesn't mean he's less of a man, but he thinks he is. Another male is probably more apt to understand those feelings."

"I never figured Gray was the kind of guy to feel sorry for himself. If I were the one who'd lost my leg, I bet he wouldn't let me give up."

"You're right. He wouldn't. I don't know. Maybe it's a chemical thing going on in his brain. There's counseling available at the Health Center, but I can't get him to go. He doesn't want my help with anything. Maybe he'll react differently to you." Liz's frustrations are showing. Today might be the first time she's had an adult ear, someone capable of understanding the whole picture.

"I doubt it. I have my own head problems."

She tries a new approach. "Maybe he can get involved in helping you. I think he regrets he didn't try five years ago."

"I didn't give him a chance. I don't know though. I have a job in Waterloo at the newspaper . . ."

"Maybe you can live here and drive back and forth. Would that be too hard? It's only what? Forty-five or so miles? Not too bad a drive in good weather."

A short stay at the settlement will be great, but not if he has to live in the same house as Liz and Gray. He isn't that far along in his thinking. He tries making an excuse. "There isn't enough room."

"You know we can make room. Rue loves having a brother. She wouldn't mind the couch for a little while. But if you don't want to stay in the house, I have another idea. Maybe you can find a cheap camper and stay on the property. The tribe won't like it, but it'd be temporary – just until we can see Gray's spirits are better."

Austin is sure he's going to regret the arrangement but hears himself say, "I'll give the camper idea a try for the summer. And only if I can find one that's dirt cheap. I don't want to invest in some fancy thing I'll have trouble unloading."

Liz breathes a sigh of relief. "The summer. Maybe 'til school starts? I promise I won't badger you to stay longer. That much time could do your father a world of good." She looks in his eyes, trying to impart the urgency of her idea. "If it doesn't, then you will have tried and can go back to your life. With my eternal thanks."

"I'm sure I can get the Courier to let me work on a few feature stories about the settlement and casino, so I won't be totally useless to them while I'm here. I'll have to have internet access. That way I can keep in contact with the paper through email. But I won't ask them about it unless I can find a used trailer. I can spend tonight at Archie's and then look for something tomorrow."

He's glad to see Liz's facial expression relax. "Better not tell Rue," he says. "In case it doesn't work out."

"Thank you so much for even considering it," Liz says. "It gives me hope for Gray."

There is another lull in the conversation. Austin is afraid of saying too much, of making promises he can't keep. He notices his little sister slip out the front door with something in her hand that appears to be a bowl wrapped in a paper towel. Without a word to the adults, she zips down the ramp and off into the trees that line the yard. "Where's she going?" he asks.

Liz smiles as she looks toward the thick undergrowth. "I'm not sure. Lately, she's made a lot of trips into the woods. She always comes right back. I think she's feeding the squirrels. Rue's always afraid some animal is starving. I try to explain that nature takes care of them, but she's giving Mother Nature a hand."

"I don't know if chocolate pudding is good for squirrels, but she sure seems like a sweet kid."

"Speaking of kids … when I caught a glimpse of you after my college graduation ceremony, you were walking with a Native American girl who was carrying a baby. Was that …?"

"No, the lady is just a friend, the wife of my buddy Clint. She was there to see him graduate. I don't have a family." He doesn't add that he's resigned himself to staying single. He's loved once already, and that couldn't have had a more disastrous outcome. His dreams no longer include being a husband and father. He's actually very content with that prospect.

"Oh. That's kind of disappointing. I've spent the last year thinking I had a grandson."

The idea of Liz being grandmother to a child of his is incomprehensible. "Sorry."

The bloodhound nudges his leg, and the old playful Austin speaks. "Murray can be your grandson. He's very well-behaved."

Liz motions for the dog to come to her and scratches his long floppy ears. She and her son must be thinking the same thing. For a short time, a Murray and a Ruby will be living at this address again. Life is a circle.

PRESLEY

The scene is the lounge area of the Anamosa State Penitentiary.

"Hey, Pres! Your time here's about up, isn't it?"

"Yup. Just two days left. I'm keepin' my nose real clean 'til then. Don't want anything to go wrong."

"Whatcha going to do when you get out? Drive a truck or something?"

"No. Probably just bide my time until my mom passes. It can't be long. She's bad off, I hear."

"Then what?"

"Then I'll get the farm. I'll own it free and clear. Three hundred acres."

"Wow. You gonna be a farmer, are ya, Presley?"

"No way. Hate that life. I'm gonna sell – turn it into cash."

"That seems like a shame. Didn't you tell me it's a Century Farm?"

"So what? It's going to the first guy with enough money. Then I'm off to Fiji or someplace far away from Iowa."

"You're lucky you won't have any inheritance fights with your relations. You're an only child, aren't ya, Pres?"

"Damn right I am. And I'm free now to inherit. It should be slick and easy."

FOUR

Archie Buffalo is standing on his porch smiling from ear to ear. "Glad you called, dude! I couldn't believe it was your voice on my phone." Archie is notorious for ignoring his cell phone, so Austin is happy to know his earlier message did its job.

The two young men, friends since grade school, lived in this same small house just before Austin's departure from the settlement. Another circle is complete with Austin's return. If only he could have a redo of the old days. He'd rejoin his friend at the end of the term instead of five years later. At the very least, he'd call him and let him know what happened.

"Hey man! Get on up here!" Austin leaps the two porch steps, and Archie throws his arms around his pal. "Sit down and I'll get us something to drink."

Austin barely has time to find a sturdy chair when Archie reappears with sodas. "When you left, I didn't think it'd take you so long to find your way back."

"I know." Austin says as he pops the tab on the drink. "Sorry I didn't explain myself. I was a mess that day and didn't think I ever wanted to see anybody from here again. Pretty selfish."

"Oh, heck. I'm just glad you're okay and haven't forgotten about me. Can you stay? Drinda Davenport lives with me now, but we can find room for you."

"Thanks, Arch." Austin doesn't remember a girl named Drinda, but he never could keep up with Archie's women. "I just need a place for tonight. Hopefully, by tomorrow I'll have found a camper to use for a couple of months."

"You can stay *here* for that long. No kiddin'. I'd send Drinda away before you." Archie laughs like he's joking, but Austin believes he'd actually do it.

"No need. I'm supposed to be staying with Liz and Gray. I need to be where I can do some good, but I can't make myself sleep in their house. Dumb, I guess."

"Hey, I'm just surprised you're visiting them. I never thought that would happen. Liz tried a few times to get me to tell her where you were living. I didn't even have to lie. I told her I didn't have a clue. I doubt if she believed me."

"I didn't let anybody know. I finished at UNI and then got a job at the Waterloo Courier. Writing feature stories. So I was renting an apartment up there when I got a letter from Liz."

"Yeah. She probably thought she should let you know about the amputation. I wondered if anybody told you when it happened. That was a rotten deal. Gray's a good guy and a good cop. Everybody feels real sorry for him."

A plump and plain Native American girl comes through the screen door. Austin tries to understand what his friend sees in her and concludes she must have a great personality. "Nice to meet you Austin," she says pleasantly. "Why don't you come inside and have some buffalo burgers and bean soup?" She didn't have to ask twice.

While he was downing Drinda's cooking at the small kitchen table, his old buddy filled Austin in on the latest settlement news.

"I had some guy stop by here yesterday. Said he was looking for a place to rent for a while. He said he didn't have a job but would do any kind of work I needed around here. I told him I don't need a hired hand because I myself can do whatever I need done."

"Did he say what his name was?"

"Nope, and I didn't ask. Said he used to live in Tama, but I'd never seen him before. Older – maybe forty-something. Seemed friendly enough, but I didn't feel like taking a chance. You never know what kind of trouble you're in for if you let a homeless person move in. Especially if he's white."

"You were smart. He could be one of the crazies you hear about who shoot people for no reason. Better not take in anybody who isn't from the tribe."

"I shoulda sent him to Anita Kapao's. I bet she'd like a man around to help with all her kids. Have you seen her since you've been back?"

"No. I just got here. Why?"

"Pretend I didn't mention it. Just let me know what you think if you run into her. Some people change." And he grins as though he's picturing the change.

"Well, *you* sure haven't." It's true. Archie looks just like he did when Austin lived with him. He can't be called handsome, but at least he hasn't gotten fat or lost any hair.

"I'm not quite as healthy as I used to be. Got me a little diabetes, and that's put an end to my drinking. Life isn't as much fun as it was before."

"Oh. I wondered about the diet pop. Say, speaking of that, I promised Liz I'd get checked for diabetes."

"Not hard to do. Just go over to the Health Center. They might make you fast for eight hours or so, and they'll take some blood. They can tell right away if you're clear."

"Maybe I'll call now and get an appointment for tomorrow. If I don't do it, I'll forget."

Drinda refills his bowl without being asked. Austin decides Archie doesn't have it so bad. He can remember when the guy lived on hot dogs. He can't help wondering if Drinda knows how to cook for a diabetic. It seems unlikely Archie is very diligent about watching his own menu.

It's good to know nothing's changed between him and his old buddy. Even though Austin has found out he's a half-breed, that fact seems to be of no concern to Arch.

"So how come you haven't married anybody yet, Wapiti?" Archie asks while Drinda is clearing away the dishes.

"Just haven't found anybody up north," answers Austin. "Plus I haven't been looking. I could ask you the same thing."

"Oh, Drinda and me talk about it but just haven't got it done yet. You seem more like the husband type than me."

"Not anymore. I've turned into a confirmed bachelor. Don't try to fix me up, Arch."

"I won't if you don't want me to, even though I've got a couple ideas. Wanna play some cards this evening? It's been a long time." The two passed a lot of evenings playing Pepper when they were teens.

"I guess it'd be fun, but there's only three of us. What kind of cards are you talking about?"

"I can fix the number. I'll just call Portia. You and her can be partners." Archie seems to have the lady's number on speed dial. Before Austin can protest, it's settled. Portia Little Bear is a fourth for Pepper.

The evening turns out to be a pleasant one, and Portia, a girl he vaguely remembers from school, is a nice young lady to be around. She doesn't have a great mind for cards but is friendly and has a quick sense of humor. The Pepper game is actually more fun than if Portia were someone he had a crush on. There's no pressure for Austin to be brilliant or entertaining or to say the appropriate things to impress her.

When they have their fill of potato chips and salsa and no one has lost much money from the quarter-stakes gambling, Portia moves to make her departure. Austin is glad she came in her own car because he doesn't want to take her home. That might give her the idea they've just had a date and he's going to ask her for another one.

"Good night, Portia. It was a fun time," is all he offers the girl.

"You could've walked her to her car," Archie points out when she's gone.

"Why?"

"Because you could use a woman in your life."

"Why?"

Archie rolls his eyes. "If I have to tell you, then you don't deserve anybody."

◆◆◆◆

Austin is going to his truck the next morning. "I sure do appreciate everything, you two. You're a great cook, Drinda. But I plan to get things arranged today so I can live at Liz and Gray's for the rest of my time in Tama."

"Here." Archie hands over a used envelope with some phone numbers written on the back. "I copied down some places you should check about trailers. If one doesn't show up, just come on back here. The door's always open for you."

"Thanks, Arch." Austin starts to his car and then turns around. "You know, you were the only person I told about the feelings I used to have for Liz. Did you … ah … spread that around? I mean, will everybody on the settlement think about that stuff when they see me?"

"Are you kidding? I wouldn't do that. You were beating yourself up enough. I sure didn't want to make it worse. Gossip is only a kick if you're spreading it about somebody you don't like."

Austin should've known. Real friends just sense when something isn't to be shared. At least Meskwaki friends do.

"Oh, and Archie, I doubt if Gray wants everybody to know Liz asked me to come help him."

"No worries, dude."

◆◆◆◆

The first item on his agenda for the day, after doing without breakfast, is to get the blood test he promised Liz. Austin is totally impressed by the state-of-the art health center that has sprung up near the casino. He'd have to be crazy not to make use of it. In less than an hour, he emerges with the comfort of knowing his blood sugar is eighty mg/dl. He has no concerns on that front. One less thing for his mom to stress over.

On his way out of the health center, he runs into an old high school classmate whose name he can't remember. "Wapiti! Where'd you come from? Gosh, it's been years!"

"I know. I've been working up in Black Hawk County. How's everything going?"

"Good. Real good. Suppose you're back visiting Liz Morgan. Couldn't stay away from that sweet stuff, right?"

Austin walks away without answering. His worst fears have come true. People have long memories about some things. And, evidently, even best friends have big mouths.

FIVE

Austin attempts to follow Archie's directions to an RV dealership south of town. Before he gets that far, he spots the back end of a rusted vintage trailer. It is parked behind a shed on a farm near the highway. From what he can see, it might be an old Air Stream or something similar. Its condition indicates it's likely in retirement, not currently being used. Such a situation seems too much to hope for, but it's worth asking about.

Austin pulls into the driveway, passing a mailbox that shows people named Peterson live there. An elderly man in work clothes approaches from the barn and doesn't seem surprised by his visitor's inquiry. "Yeah, we had the thing years ago. It was old when we got it. It's supposed to hold two people, but the wife and I kept bumping into each other. Now that we're both heavier, it'll be even tighter. If we're going to travel around during our retirement, then I think it's going to take something bigger than that old buggy."

"From here, it looks like what I'm needing," Austin ventures.

"Well, I don't want to give it away, but I could be talked into letting it go for a price."

"How much would you want?" From what Austin can see the trailer qualifies as an antique and could be worth a pretty penny.

There's no telling how serviceable it'd be on the road, but as far as he's concerned, it only has to sit in the Morgan yard for a couple of months.

"I usually keep it in the barn out of the weather. Just brought it outside at the beginning of summer to see if there's any interest. Had it parked out front for a while with a For Sale sign on it. Several people stopped, but everybody thought it was too small. Except one young lady who looked like she couldn't afford it even if it was free." Then Mr. Peterson states his price.

Austin recognizes the amount as being fair but not exactly the bargain he's hoping for. "Well, that's a little more than I was thinking. Got to keep it in my budget – which is pretty meager. I'll just do a little more looking." And he starts walking to his truck.

"I won't charge you to look inside it. You might be surprised at how much you'd be getting for your money. Nineteen-seventy model." The man opens the door of the Airstream.

Austin feels sure the man could do much better than his quoted price, but maybe not in Tama. He might have a small chance of success if he does a little dealing. "Just a peek. I actually only have a couple of minutes." He looks inside and is, indeed, impressed. The stuffy smell doesn't hide the fact it's well-laid out and offers all the essentials. There's even a tiny bathroom on one end.

"Before we gave up on it, I did some work in here. Lot of cleaning and painting. You should've seen how it started out. But all that labor didn't make it bigger. The wife can't move enough to cook, and that's pretty important to us."

Austin understands the dilemma isn't just the woman's. Mr. Peterson's large stomach makes it hard for him to turn around in the narrow space, let alone do any tasks.

Austin himself feels crowded even without carrying any middle aged girth. But he doesn't plan to do much cooking this summer nor invite any large friends over, so space isn't really an issue.

"Not bad if I can't find something cheaper. I'll have to have my girlfriend give her approval." A common ploy, pretending he has to check with someone else. The seller often wants to avoid that.

After thanking the man, Austin completes about four steps across the yard before he hears, "I hate you to have to make another trip just to look. What if I knock off two hundred? Will that get it into your range? Maybe you can make the decision all by yourself then. Offer's only good for fifteen minutes."

The farmer did want to sell. "Well...do the furnishings come with it?"

"For fifteen minutes," Mr. Peterson answers.

"One more look," says Austin. He goes back into the camper and gives it a thorough inspection. He can't think of a thing he'll need that isn't included. There is a dining nook, a miniature stove and sink, and a bed, toilet, and shower. Home sweet home. All it needs is a good cleaning and some air freshener.

"Okay. You have a deal." The man shakes his hand, and Austin reaches for his wallet just as a pony-tailed girl on an ancient bicycle pedals up behind his truck. He recognizes the rider he met on White Tail Road. She seems to cover a lot of miles. The lady alights and stomps toward him. He's pretty sure she isn't coming in friendship.

"Are you buying it?" she asks. Her voice is breathless and angry, but her eyes hold fear. She keeps a considerable distance between herself and the two men.

"I'm about to. Why? Were you looking at it, too?" The farmer was right. She doesn't look as though she can afford even the marked down deal Austin is getting.

"I've been looking at it for two days. I'm working on getting the money. Are you sure you need it or are you just buying it so you can deliver drugs?"

Do I look like a drug dealer? "No drugs. And yes, I'm sure. Sorry." He produces a check that he fills out while leaning across his truck's hood. Another glance at the girl reveals her eyes are filled with tears. She's good. "I tell you what. I only need this for two months max. Then I'll mark it down some more, and it can be yours. How's that? It'll give you more time to raise the funds."

"What if I tell you it's a matter of life and death that I get it now?" The question is hesitant, like she expects him to reject the idea.

"I'd say you're exaggerating. And I could make the same claim – life or death." In a manner of speaking, the camper could save Gray's life.

For someone with such a bedraggled appearance, the young woman is quite an actress. Those soulful eyes have probably gotten her what she wanted before.

"Can I have your phone number so I can call you when I'm done with it?" That should convince her he's serious.

"No phone," she mumbles.

"Okay. You can find me at the Morgan place on White Tail Road." He hands the check to Mr. Peterson. Now, he observes, the tears are streaming down pony-tail lady's face. He looks away. The trailer is exactly what he was hoping to find. There's no reason he should feel guilty for beating the girl to it. "See you sometime in August!"

Her facial expression answers for her. He might as well have told her to go jump off a cliff and die. After giving him a few seconds to reconsider, she hops on her bike and spins gravel pulling away. Austin hopes she can see through her clouded eyes.

Those tears have taken away some of the fun of hooking the trailer to the hitch of his truck and driving to Liz and Gray's. But he tells himself the girl will eventually learn life is full of spoiled plans. Nobody knows that better than he. She'll survive for a few weeks. Hopefully, she won't find another small trailer to buy because he's going to need somebody to take this one off his hands as soon as he does whatever he can for Gray.

He wonders how the girl planned to transport the Airstream. He hopes her car is in better shape than her bike. His final thought on the matter is that a grown woman doesn't usually cry when she fails to get her way. *This one must be pretty spoiled.*

◆◆◆◆

A day off from work is spent getting utilities hooked up in Austin's new bachelor pad. Electricity, water and sewer are reasonably easy to secure, at least for temporary use. Doing so is likely against Meskwaki rules, but since he's looking at such a short stay, he reasons that no one on the tribal council will have time to complain. Austin has the required skills but makes sure to ask his father's advice at every turn. A rough ride over the bumpy yard allows Gray to supervise from his wheelchair. He refrains from lecturing about the settlement housing codes, and surprisingly, he doesn't try to talk Austin out of setting up residence in his yard.

Finally, Austin is ready to spend the night a few feet from his parents. "The weather forecast doesn't sound good," Liz warns. "Thunderstorms. Be sure you come in the house if it gets bad. A strong wind will probably blow that thing over."

As it turns out, the weather man was right, and Liz's warning about the blowing was a valid one. The wind picks up before the rain arrives, and the little camper rocks like a boat on the sea. Austin tells himself he may have to stake it into the ground even for a short stay.

When the time nears midnight, flashes of lightening become frequent. Before the storm starts full force, Austin lets Murray outside to do his business. The dog has to be lifted off the step and forced to stand under the raindrops for a few minutes. *What a good watch dog I have.* Though Liz's offer to come in is tempting, he doesn't want to drag a wet dog onto her clean floors, and he can't leave Murray outside alone. Ever since he was a puppy the bloodhound has shivered and whined during thunderstorms. His safe place during those times is under the covers of Austin's bed.

Suddenly Murray springs to life and starts barking. Usually a quiet animal, this noisy display is surprising. He seems to be worried about the woods near the yard. It's understandable. All kinds of animals, including Rue's little friends, live in there, and most of them are likely to be scurrying now to find cover.

Austin grabs hold of Murray's collar and pulls him back into the trailer. He's afraid Liz and Gray might think they have an intruder. Sure enough, the front door of the house opens.

"Everything okay?" calls Liz over the increasing howl of the wind.

"Yeah. Don't worry. Murray's a nervous ninny. I'll keep him in the trailer."

"It's okay. Just being sure you didn't need help." Austin understands that Liz is belatedly playing mother. Her son isn't out late on the highway, but he might be in trouble in the front yard.

A large clap of thunder sends Murray seeking shelter in spite of whatever he heard in the trees. After using two bath towels for drying, man and dog are ready to settle in. Austin takes time to look out the window in the door to view the hackberry trees bending in the wind. Water running down the glass makes it hard to be sure, but he thinks he sees a small round light in the woods in the direction of Murray's concerns. It's near where Rue entered the woods the night before, but she wouldn't be out there now. His impression is that someone is searching through the trees with a flashlight. Maybe a neighbor's looking for his pet.

Austin goes to bed and tries to find room for his feet against a still-damp dog. He thinks again about the light. When he was young, he and his friend Dale would sneak out on nights like this to hunt for night crawlers with a flashlight. It wasn't unusual for them to run into somebody else doing the same thing. *I don't know if people still look for fishing worms, but probably.*

Not inclined to go looking for trouble on such a night, Austin snuggles under his sheet. He's just dozed off when voices awaken him. Loud conversation can be heard from the direction of the house. He can only make out a male voice. "Just stay away from me! I don't need your phony love making. You can get the hell out of this room. Go outside. Getting wet should cool you down!" Not all the words are clear, but Austin hears the gist of the seemingly one-sided argument. Liz is, no doubt, softly trying to get her husband to lower his voice before he's heard over the storm.

Austin debates whether to go in the house and confront Gray. How can he allow him to talk that way to Liz? *Of all people, she doesn't deserve such treatment.* And Gray is the last person you'd expect to disrespect his wife. Austin would've bet the man would tape his own mouth shut before he'd yell at her.

In the end, Austin stays out of the marital battle. Something tells him it's nothing new and that Liz would be humiliated if he came in on them. He's beginning to understand the extent of her husband's anger and why she called for backup.

SIX

Early the next morning Liz is at the trailer door. Her son is relieved to see she has no visible marks or bruises. "It's going to be a sunny day," she declares brightly. "If you have any ideas for getting Gray outside, let me know. Here's some cereal and hot coffee." She hands over a tray that, in spite of his intentions to stay independent, tempts him to accept a handout.

"Thanks. You know, I heard Gray sounding pretty mad last night. I was afraid you might be in danger."

"Oh, Austin, I'm sorry you had to listen to that. It's the way it is sometimes. The frustration just gets the best of him, and I'm the only person nearby to yell at. He always feels awful afterward."

Austin has experience with an acquaintance who's a victim of spousal abuse. As far as he can tell, most abusers do feel awful afterward, but that doesn't stop them from doing it again. "He should see somebody, a professional, before it gets physical."

Liz is trying to work her way outside. She smiles nervously. "It was worse last night because of the thunderstorm. For some reason when there's electricity in the air it sets off the nerve endings in his amputated leg. Sometimes it starts a week ahead of the storm. The pain in his stump gets unbearable and his mood does, too. A lot of times the temper flare-ups happen then. And don't calm down until the weather clears."

Austin puts his hand on his mother's which is still holding the door open to leave. "You've had a lot to deal with. I'm sorry."

"No, Gray's the one who has to deal with it all, and he hasn't quite mastered how to do that."

"I understand about the pain and how it makes him almost crazy. But it shouldn't excuse him for being abusive to you."

"Let's give him a couple more weeks to get things under control. Then we might have to think about getting him counseling."

"Okay," Austin answers reluctantly. "But if he starts to beat you up, come out here. I couldn't stand to know I was close by, and you still got hurt." He puts pressure on her hand. "Promise me."

"I promise. I have to remember Gray's experienced the death of part of his body. He's going through the stages of grief just like we do when somebody dies. Some people cope better than others. Don't worry. He loves me, and, deep down, he isn't a violent man. It's just words."

"You'll never think any man should talk that way to Rue." Then before Liz can get out of the camper, "Does Gray have crutches? Surely he doesn't plan to stay planted in that wheelchair. Too much time in there could make anybody mean."

"He has crutches, but he never uses them. He thinks they're only for temporary injuries. He says his problem is forever, and you can't use crutches forever. He used a walker for a while, but that made him feel like an old man. He says he might as well get used to having wheels."

"Well, nuts to that. I'm going to feed Murray and then take him for a walk. Gray can come with us. Just down to the end of the drive. It'll be good exercise."

"I don't know. He'll refuse. I know he will."

"Might as well find out," Austin says cheerfully. If he works hard enough at this, maybe he'll be able to go back to Waterloo in less than two months and not have to be haunted by what's going on with his parents. "I'll come get him in a half hour. See if you can find the crutches."

After eating the catered breakfast, he rinses the dishes in the sink. Luckily, the drain works, giving him hope the day will go well.

◆◆◆◆

"Come on, Murray. You're going to walk slowly today. Don't chase rabbits, or I'll have to get your shock collar."

Surprising him, Gray rolls out onto the porch. "Good morning," he greets without enthusiasm. "I hear you have plans for me. Sorry to spoil them, but I just now took a couple of pain pills. They make me drowsy. It'd be dangerous to hop around when I'm not clear headed."

"Oh. Too bad. I thought you could help me. I'm thinking of having Murray trained to be a service dog. He seems to have the right traits. You and I can give him an aptitude test."

"Why do you want to make your pet into a service dog? You don't need one. And I don't want one."

"I have a friend who does need one, but he's being stubborn about it. Maybe if he sees how helpful Murray can be, he'll change his mind." Then, anticipating Gray's next remark, "I'm not talking about you."

"Right. I appreciate what you're trying to do, but I don't even like dogs, and I'm awful with crutches. No point in forcing things. The police don't need me anytime soon. They don't have much work for gimps, even on crutches."

"So you're just going to sit and watch TV forever?"

"No. They say I can push papers when I'm ready to come back." It was hard for him to even force out the words. "They'll make a place for me so I can feel useful. Trouble is, I don't want to *feel* useful. I want to *be* useful."

"I get that." The dog is sitting close to Gray, looking up at him. Because of the bloodhound face, he doesn't "smile" like most dogs who are excited, but Murray has a decidedly eager-looking drool going on. He definitely sees a potential friend in the ex-cop as well as a man who can use his assistance. Liz comes out with the crutches. Austin thinks he sees Gray flinch at the sight of them.

Liz says, "Why don't you ride to the bottom of the ramp, and I'll hand them to you."

Gray looks ready to protest but, perhaps because of the relaxation from the pills, he doesn't seem to have the energy. "Well, make it short." He takes the crutches and, without too much difficulty, gets them situated under his arms. Murray waits patiently.

Austin wants to make the walk fun. "Here we go! I remember how much trouble I had trying to back down this old driveway when I was learning to drive. I took out at least two mailboxes."

Gray gives him a recognizable smile. Talk of the past elicits more of those than anything in the present is able to. Murray abandons Austin and stays by Gray's left side. It looks to Austin like his dog senses which man needs him most.

Maybe some conversation will be a distraction. "Which kind of diabetes do you have?" Austin asks.

Gray answers curtly. "Type two. It's the kind you can develop when you're an adult. That's what happened to me. I don't have to take insulin, at least not yet, but I have to be real careful what I eat."

"That's a pain, I bet."

"Sure is. My pancreas can't process sugar like it's supposed to. Not sure why the darned disease picked me. But Liz and Rue police me something awful."

"Well, hope you'll mind them. It doesn't sound like a something to fool with."

"Nope. The consequences of cheating on this diet can be a lot more serious than gaining a few pounds."

"The good thing is you're a sensible, disciplined guy. I can see you getting into all the right habits and handling them like falling off a log."

"Not a very good analogy. I probably will fall. Maybe before we get back to the house."

"Hope not. This gravel would make a rough landing."

Halfway to the road, Austin decides they need a new subject. "Murray spotted something last night back in the trees. It looked like a flashlight."

"No kidding? Where exactly was it? We have neighbors on the other side of that grove."

"Straight over here. Hold on a minute. I'll go check."

"If I can't stand still, I'll move in a circle 'til you come back."

"Stay, Murray," Austin commands the hound, then walks away. He looks around at the variety of paths that have accumulated over the years. None of them seem to lead anywhere, except for one which ends up at an area that's been trampled down. Through a large bush, he notices a tan color obviously not part of the growth around it. He parts the twigs and the leaves to find a pup tent, hardly big enough for one adult. Did someone stay in it recently? There is a flap opening that seems inadequate for keeping out the amount of rain that fell overnight. He looks inside. A thin wadded-up blanket and a Snickers wrapper are all he can make out. Feeling like an intruder, he closes the flap and hurries back to his father.

"There's a real little tent. Could be that somebody was camping. It doesn't seem big enough for two even if they're kids."

"Interesting," observes Gray. "Maybe some child ran away from home." Austin can tell the scene has sparked a bit of interest in the former detective.

"Whoever it was is gone. The rain must've scared him off. We'll have to watch for the light again tonight." Austin has been thinking his sleeping quarters are about as small as any he's ever seen, but someone else must've been even more cramped.

"Our bedroom window faces that direction, and I'm awake most of the night. I'll keep a lookout." Gray sounds almost excited.

"Good idea. At least you won't have to look through a downpour again."

Austin hopes he can milk the little mystery for several days. Gray definitely can use the distraction. How dreary to lay in the dark every night thinking about all you've lost. Austin has done more than his share of that the last five years and doesn't recommend it. Everybody needs something to look forward to, something he wants to get done.

◆◆◆◆

Sometime around midnight, Murray nuzzles his master's face. Apparently, some noise is worrying the dog. "What's the problem, boy?" Sure they are alerting the camper, Austin lets Murray out to investigate. A shadowy figure in a wheelchair sits watch on the porch. Austin motions to Gray to come down into the yard. He can see the man is wearing a .40 Glock, a good precaution.

Neither of them speak as they approach the trees. Gray gestures for Austin to go closer to the tent. He does, being as quiet as possible. *People think Indians can walk without being heard. But since I'm only half Meskwaki, I could be missing that talent.* Murray sounds much like a Clydesdale, following as carefully as his large feet will allow.

Someone is in the tent. He is lying very still, no doubt hoping to be invisible. Austin debates whether to pull back the flap and scare the child to death or leave him alone. The young camper isn't hurting anybody. The moonlight doesn't even show signs of littering. He can't help feeling like he's the prowler as he cautiously approaches someone's resting place. Murray doesn't have such qualms. He goes directly to the flap and works it open with his nose. The large droopy-eyed bloodhound face would be startling, even in the dark. The breed's features do nothing to give away the beautiful personality beneath them. At the same time the dog makes his move, Austin prepares to confront the trespasser. Then he spots something important. Leaning against a tree is the beat-up bike he saw pony-tail girl riding. The mystery is solved.

"Come on out! I'm not going to hurt you."

The form under the canvas remains motionless.

"Truly, I won't. And hurry up. My . . . Mr. Morgan...is waiting for me on the drive, and he gets uncomfortable pretty fast."

Murray obliges by giving the girl space. Her head peeks out. Wide eyes against a tan face and straight black hair sticking in all directions makes the dog jerk back and give a little whine. The lady is a bit of a spooky sight.

"Follow me," Austin commands. "I'm not going to call the cops. Nobody around here is interested in that." He won't mention that Gray *is* a policeman and has a pistol strapped on his belt. Austin is glad for the full moon. Even among the trees, there is ample room for them to be seen.

The girl crawls out and stands up, the grungy blanket wrapped tightly around her. The night is very warm, but the cover must make her feel safer around this outspoken man.

Austin walks back out to the drive. "We have a visitor," he tells Gray. "Harmless, I think. I actually kinda know her."

Gray takes in the girl's bedraggled appearance. "Oh, yeah?"

"We've met before—sort of. But I don't know her name." He looks at her, questioning.

"Glory," is her tentative response.

"Glory? Is that Meskwaki?" He is always hearing given names that are new to him.

"I don't know. Glory and Dawn are my two names."

He thinks it still sounds like she's missing a family name but decides not to pursue the point.

Gray gets right to specifics. "Why were you in our woods?"

She looks frightened but also defiant. She isn't about to apologize. "I was sleeping."

"Oh. *That's* normal." He's being sarcastic. The land doesn't actually belong to him because the tribe owns it, so he can't threaten to report her. "Why are you here instead of at your own place?"

"I'm waiting to get the trailer." She motions toward Austin. "That man might get tired of it, and then maybe I can get it before somebody else does."

"Okay. Fair enough, but the ground is going to get mighty hard before the summer's over."

She doesn't answer, only clenches her mouth stubbornly.

"Go on back to your tent and get some rest," Gray tells her. "And, by the way, if you think you'll just live in the camper when Austin's at work, we *can* press charges. That vehicle is personal property, and you don't have permission."

Austin thinks that's pretty harsh, but Gray's right. Glory probably plans to do just what he's warning her about. The girl pulls the dirty blanket more tightly around her body and trudges off to the tent. Murray escorts her and then returns.

"Am I missing a party?" calls Liz from the front door.

"No. Just hanging out. Neither of us could sleep." Austin knows Liz is probably hoping the two men are bonding.

"Don't let me bother you," she responds quickly, then closes the door.

Before going inside, father and son look at the spot where Glory stepped into the trees. The area is very dark. How could they have sent a young woman alone into that blackness?

"It was her idea to camp there in the first place." Austin says aloud to absolve them of any gentlemen's guilt.

Nevertheless, he spends a restless night wondering about the tangle-haired trespasser lying in a soggy tent.

SEVEN

Austin resists the temptation to look in on their visitor from last night. She's probably already given up her vigil. If not, he'll feel he should take action, and he hasn't decided what that should be.

Hoping the Glory situation will solve itself, he allows himself a morning in downtown Tama, cruising the streets he used to know so well. He isn't expecting improvement. He'll settle for status quo, which is usually a mark of success for a small rural town.

At first glance everything looks the same, but further examination shows significant deterioration. Stores he remembers are closed, the buildings standing empty. Several houses shout out complaints of neglect. No one in the area, it seems, sells exterior paint anymore. Still, it feels good to be back.

In spite of its failure to thrive in the same ways as the much larger cities, he's relieved to notice some of his favorite businesses are still in operation. The settlement and casino being so close pretty much guarantees the little town won't cease to exist any time soon.

He remembers the pride he felt when he learned in grade school that Tama was named after a Meskwaki (Fox) chief named Taimah. Ty-ee-mah in Meskwaki means *sudden clash of thunder*. The Fox leader was known as the *man who makes the rocks tremble*. The town and county of Tama adopted his name because he was such a good friend of the white man and even saved the life of a white Indian agent at Prairie du Chein, Wisconsin.

Hearing such accounts as a young native boy in a largely white school gave Austin pride and an identity. *This whole town and school is named after one of my people,* he told himself. He still has an affection for Tama but not quite the same feeling of ownership he had before he discovered the truth about his bloodline.

A quick stop at the casino brings back memories of his time working at the Blackjack table, of watching Elizabeth Raines walk by, of wanting to know her better. If only somebody had told him then the pretty blonde woman was his birth mother.

He notices several Meskwaki ladies sitting at the slot machines. They will always and forever bring him warm thoughts of Ruby. It seems like yesterday when she'd look at him with the love and pride reserved for a mom. The whole story will never stop being hard for him to digest. At the same time, he feels lucky, lucky he's been the center of the lives of two of the best women in the world. How can he wallow in self-pity knowing that?

The high school is closed for the weekend. It's just as well. The day he and Liz spent touring his old hangout was one he doesn't want to relive. Looking at that day through the eyes of knowledge makes it all seem totally different than it did then. Ignorance can surely color an experience.

He thinks about Glory. *Where did she come from?* If she is Meskwaki, she surely wouldn't seem to be so much on her own. She would have a close family taking care of her, providing her with food and shelter. The beef plant in Tama hires a lot of immigrant workers. Maybe she's one of those. She's probably a Hispanic illegal and is afraid of being deported. Maybe he's seen the last of her and will never know about her background. As a journalist, Austin appreciates a good story, so he'll actually be disappointed if he misses out on Glory's.

When he gets back to his trailer, Rue runs to meet him. Just like Murray, she is as excited as if he's just returned home from a long voyage.

"You came back, Happy!" Rue loves to use that name.

"Hi, Rue! Whatcha been doing this morning?"

"Well…" she is obviously trying to come up with some news. Not easy to do in this wooded hollow in the country. "I played with Murray. He does what I tell him."

"I'm glad you two get along."

"But he growled when the girl came out of the woods. He thought she wanted to hurt me."

"You know about the girl?" The mysterious Glory must have emerged again. Rue doesn't seem very surprised.

"Yeah. She lives there." He can tell by her expression, she's said more than she's supposed to. She must have been told the young lady's presence is their secret.

"She told me she'd have to kidnap me if I told. Don't tell. I don't want to be kidnapped!"

"Does she have any friends? Any big buddies you need to stay away from?"

"I don't think so. She doesn't even have jammies. She sleeps in her nakeds!"

Austin laughs. "What does she eat? I only saw a candy bar wrapper."

"She doesn't have food. But sometimes I take her things. An apple or a cookie. She says, 'Stand back!' so I drop the stuff on the ground and run back to the house."

"Does she say thank-you?" Austin is wondering if the mysterious camper is nicer than the kidnapping threat and the orders for Rue make her sound.

"Yup. But she eats fast. Mom doesn't let me eat fast."

"Hmm. Where is she now? Does she go away during the day?"

"Yup. On her bike."

Maybe Glory Dawn or whoever is still shopping for a used trailer. *She sure is getting her exercise on that beat-up bike.*

"How old do you think she is?" Kind of a dumb question to ask a five-year-old.

"She has a pony tail, but I think maybe she's old like a mom."

Although he'd rather pretend the mysterious camper is none of their concern, he's curious enough by afternoon to check out the pup tent. No sign of life. The pitiful little shelter must have served its purpose. It sags like a cast-off cocoon after the caterpillar has gone. *Well, happy landings, Glory. I hope you find better sleeping quarters by tonight.*

With a good hour of daylight left, Austin decides to find a mower and make himself useful. In the old days, he'd never let the grass in the yard get over three inches tall. It's easy to see some jobs have gone undone since Gray's surgery.

Austin has just finished when a flying ponytail rounds the corner from the lane. Glory brakes and skids to a stop. She appears surprised to find him at home.

"Hello!" He greets her. "Did you go to your house for the day?"

She looks startled, like a fox caught in a trap. "No. I went to find a job. At the Red Earth Gardens."

"I don't remember that place."

"It's just a little ways away from here. I found it. A community garden. They would pay me!" There was something very child-like about the young lady. "But they want identification. Everybody wants identification." She pauses before attempting to explain. "I lost mine," she says with little conviction.

"Didn't see any more trailers for sale, did you? I know you need one soon." He speaks with a touch of sarcasm, remembering the urgency of her earlier plea.

"Don't know where to look. I can't go very far on this bike." The bicycle is, indeed, a clunker, not likely to hold up for a long distance.

"No offense, but it looks like you found that at the city dump." She doesn't deny it. "You know, you'd do better to go back to your place. I give you my word I won't sell the Airstream without giving you first chance at it. But you can't keep sleeping outside until I'm ready to get rid of it."

She appears desperate to change his mind. "I'm not hurting anybody, am I?"

"Well, no. But you're hurting yourself. The weather, the bugs. Don't you have a house?"

"Yes," she replies firmly, almost defiantly. "I have a huge big room. It's almost bigger than the trailer."

Again, Austin is reminded of a child, but he's relieved the girl doesn't always live in a tent. It sounds like she has an apartment. "Well, alright then! Go back to it. You're sure you don't have a phone number or an address you can give me so I can get in touch when I'm ready to move on?"

"No! I'll come here every day and see if you're ready for me to have the trailer." Austin noticed she said *have*, not *buy*.

"Uh, okay. Guess I'll see ya later then." And Austin glances off in the distance as though he expects her to take herself away. She hesitates, like she doesn't want to go but then gets on her bicycle and starts off down the road. He watches her pull up to the stop sign at the end. She gets off the bike and looks both ways as if she's trying to decide which direction to turn.

Austin realizes then that Glory, if that really is her name, is either lost or has nowhere to go. That's why she's standing in the middle of a rural intersection. Who knows how long she's been camped on Gray and Liz's property.

Austin takes off at a run with Murray at his heels. They make a dash down to the stop sign. The lady doesn't try to get away.

"You've been sleeping in the Morgans' woods for quite a while, haven't you?" he asks her. "And maybe in the camper when I'm not there."

She's silent. Again, she's been found out. Having no story for cover, she answers, "Just a few days." He looks at her more closely and sees her clothing is wrinkled and grungy. Her black ponytail hangs oily and straight. She looks incredibly weak and tired, as if she can barely keep her eyes open. "Are you going to put me in jail?"

"Never thought about that. Unless you've been stealing from them." He thinks about Rue giving her apples and cookies. This visitor must be inclined to beg, not steal.

"No! I don't take what isn't mine. The little girl brings me food sometimes. And I use the space on the ground. Not much space."

"You can't be very comfortable living like that. That tent doesn't amount to much."

"That's why I need the trailer."

Oh, boy. Now he's really feeling guilty. This young woman is in sorry circumstances, and he's hogging what might be her one hope of a shelter. How many thunderstorms has she already weathered?

"Are you a member of the tribe? I mean, if you are, you can live on the settlement. You don't have to hide. You can apply for a house or somebody with an extra bed can take you in. Liz and Gray might."

"Nobody can know I'm around. You can't tell!" Her eyes plead with him.

"Well … you should probably know that Gray Morgan is, or was, on the police force. And he's got enough troubles without harboring a fugitive."

"I'm not a criminal. I haven't done anything wrong."

For some reason he believes her, and for lack of another answer, invites her to come back to the house with him. "You look like you're going to drop." He moves to help, but she grabs onto the handlebars possessively. He gives up helping and leads the way back to the yard. She follows, pushing the junk-yard bike.

He talks to the lady behind hm. "I think you better keep out of sight if you're running from somebody. I mean, my little sister seems to know about you. She didn't mean to, but she let a few things slip to me. You can't count on a kid to keep a secret."

"I know … I couldn't help …" Behind him her voice trails off. Austin turns in time to keep her from falling onto the bike that clatters to the ground. "Don't know where to go …"

He isn't sure what to do but knows he can't leave her on the road. He picks her up and carries her, noticing that under more than one layer of clothing, she's very thin. He wants to take her to the house and put her on a full size bed, but Liz has gone somewhere with Ruby, and Gray shouldn't know about this. If his dad has any feelings left for his job, he'll feel honor-bound to report the situation. Maybe that would be the right thing to do, but Austin wants more facts first. And he'd hate to betray the lady while she's unable to speak for herself. He carries her into the camper. Murray seems to approve of his decision. As soon as Glory is curled up on the pull-out sofa bed, the bloodhound climbs in beside her. Murray is keeping watch.

After going back for the bike that hardly seems worth rescuing, he leans it up against the trailer. Inside, Austin surveys the contents of his barely-stocked fridge to see if he has anything to feed a starving runaway. There are mulberries and cheese courtesy of his mother. Also, Glory (he may as well call her that until he finds out differently) desperately needs a bath and clean clothes. He doesn't know a lot about women but instinctively suspects that any of them feel better when they look better—and smell better.

Does he dare go into Liz's bedroom and borrow an outfit? Glory will need underwear. Taking that from his new mother is out of the question. And what if Gray wakes up or if Liz comes home and catches him with his hand in her lingerie drawer? He'd spend another five years living down a new shame.

Seeing no sign of Gray, he sneaks into the living room. He looks around for something that will help the cause. *This must be how it feels to be a thief.* Why is he going to all this trouble for someone he doesn't know? Glory could be a psychopathic killer or an escapee from the mental hospital in Marshalltown. She could be a refugee from another country. The dark skin doesn't have to be Native American, in spite of her claims. She could rob them all blind. Still, watching her sleeping beside Murray, he feels sure she's harmless.

He's on his way out the front door of the house, carrying an afghan, Liz's gardening smock that was hanging on a peg, and a jug of milk, when Liz and Ruby drive in. Liz hops out of the car and stares for a moment at his armload of her belongings. She asks a direct question, "What are you doing?"

Austin can see he's not cut out for a life of crime. Might as well tell the truth and ask for help.

"Well! For heaven's sake! When the girl wakes up, bring her in the house! She'll be more comfortable showering in there, and I'll get her something to eat. Then we can hear her story and do what we need to do."

Austin feels much better with Liz taking control. It's the first time, he's been struck by the reality of what it would be like to have a mother again. A guy is never too old to need one. Even if he's never thought of Liz that way, he's glad they're on the same team.

"Thanks. I expect her to sleep a long time. She's been spending nights in the woods with the mosquitoes, the owls, and the rain. I doubt she's slept much. And she probably lies awake hungry a lot. That old bicycle is how she gets around. It doesn't have any automatic speeds. Makes me tired to think about it."

"Unbelievable. Funny, I haven't heard of anyone from the settlement going missing this week. I wonder who she could be. Did she tell you her name?"

"She said it's Glory." *Glory Dawn, I think. That might not be true. She's set on staying off the radar. There could be people she's afraid of."*

"Well, maybe when she feels safe with us, she'll open up. Don't rush her."

The storm door bangs shut as Rue comes out onto the porch. She must have been listening to Austin and her mom. "Are you talking about Glory? She has a secret, and she won't tell me!"

"That's strange," says Liz, amused. "I'd better go check on Gray. He's going to wonder what we're talking about out here. But I think you're right not to tell him about the girl. At least not until we know more."

Austin isn't sure where to go. It isn't time for bed, but he doesn't want to watch TV and bother the young lady's sleep. A good time to do some writing for work. Then what?

Again, his mom settles it. "You should crash on our couch tonight."

EIGHT

Soon after the sun comes up, Austin is awake and ready to discover more about his guest. He hopes she didn't sneak away in the night. Grabbing his shoes, he makes his way to the trailer and bangs on the door. It occurs to him the farmer didn't give him a door key. Glory has been totally vulnerable inside the Air Stream. But when the wild-haired lady stares at him with half open eyes, he's sorry he panicked. She should've been left alone until noon.

"Are you okay?" he asks lamely. She looks at him like he's speaking a foreign language. "Uh … you can go back to sleep," he assures her. "I'll wake you up when Liz gets breakfast ready. Have a feeling you might be a tad bit hungry."

Glory stumbles back to the bed and falls onto it with her legs dangling past the mattress. Austin uses the time to go for a run with Murray. After a couple of miles, they turn around and come back to find their visitor sitting on the stoop of the trailer. Since she's had no access to different clothes or even a comb, there is no change in her appearance since the last time he saw her. Except that her eyes are now completely open.

"A shower should perk you up. You can go in the house to do that. More privacy than out here."

He takes Glory through the back door and points her to the bathroom. Liz seems to have thought of everything. She's laid out a whole outfit of shorts, blouse and sneakers along with what look like new underthings, comb, toothbrush and toothpaste. "Take your time. Enjoy it."

Several minutes pass without the sound of water. Austin begins to wonder if she fell asleep in the tub. He decides she must be brushing her teeth for a long time. He can't imagine how bad it would feel to go several days without getting to do that.

A faint question is heard from the other side of the door, "How do you get water to come out?"

Austin kicks himself for not explaining how this one works. Who knows whether the girl even has a shower where she usually lives. "Cover up, and I'll come in!" he tells her. Hoping she obeyed, he knocks and enters to find the girl wrapped in a towel, looking embarrassed.

"No problem," he assures her as he adjusts the faucets and lifts the lever. "There you go."

She must be eager because she starts to take away the towel before he can get out the door. He's too startled to register what he can see of her *nakeds*.

Austin tries to watch the Today show while he waits for her to get cleaned up. He doesn't know what to expect or what he should do about the mysterious squatter on his parents' land. He wonders if the same rules apply as when you save a person's life. Maybe he's now responsible for her. Another responsibility is not something he welcomes. For five years he hasn't taken care of anyone or had anyone depending on him. Now Liz is counting on him to perform some life-changing act for Gray, and maybe Glory is going to want something similar. *Time to grow up, Austin. These folks need you to be a man.*

He blinks in wonder when she comes out into the hallway, a changed woman. Scrubbed and freshly dressed, the visitor makes her host want to cry, "Glory!" Under the grunge, lurks a lovely lady of startling coloring. She could be a soap model. "You look great! How does it feel to get freshened up?"

"Good. It's nice. But I feel like people can see me now."
She must've thought the dirt was camouflage.

Liz is watching from the hallway. "Just leave your clothes in
the bathroom. I'll put them in the wash. Now you must have some
breakfast. I called into work so we can do it right."

Austin can't take his eyes off the pretty girl in Liz's old
clothes. Thin as she is, the effect is absolutely alluring. He even
forgets he hadn't meant to eat at his parents' table during his stay.

The Morgans plus two are the picture of a typical family,
sitting down to a larger-than-usual breakfast. Except the man of the
house in the wheelchair looks totally confused, and the black-haired
younger woman is stuffing her mouth with bacon at a reckless speed.

"Glory needed some rest last night, so she slept in Austin's
trailer," Liz says by way of explanation to Gray.

"Well…good." Gray doesn't seem eager to get involved in
what could be another sad story. His own is depressing enough. He
sticks to eating.

"Toast is my favorite," remarks Rue as though she's starting
a conversation with the visitor.

Glory doesn't respond. She's taking bites as fast as she can
get them chewed. Abruptly, she puts down her fork and looks
around the table. "I shouldn't be eating off your plates."

"What do you mean, honey?" Liz asks. "We have plenty of
food. And plates."

"No! I was so hungry I forgot." Her eyes are wide with terror
over some awful guilt. "I'm sick! You could get sick from me. Your
bathroom is probably full of my germs."

Now that she's cleaned up, Glory looks the picture of health.
"What kind of sickness?" questions Gray. He is aware not all illness
is contagious.

"I'm…not sure. I just know I can't be around people because
I'll give it to them. I'm like the lepers in the Bible. I'm so sorry!"

Pulling out her chair, she looks across the table at Austin. "You should wash your sheets and stuff. I know they're covered."

This is a new turn of events. Just when they're ready to hear Glory's story, she shows them she could be mentally ill or a person who invents fantasies.

They've just witnessed the young lady's hearty appetite so aren't convinced she's in bad health. However, Liz comes up with more questions to keep the girl from fleeing. "How long have you been sick? Are you in pain?"

Glory stops at the door and stares across the room as though trying to find the answers somewhere in space. "I've always been sick. No . . . I'm not in pain, but it's a *dreaded disease*." Austin senses she's quoting what she's been told. Something she's always accepted as fact but never understood.

"Are your parents sick, too? Did they catch what you have?"

"No. I don't think so. They always seemed pretty healthy."

"What are their names?" Gray is good at zeroing in on the needed facts. Someone is probably looking for this poor disturbed young woman.

She looks into the globe on the lamp in the corner, as though searching a crystal ball. "Mama and Daddy." She seems to know that isn't the answer they're expecting, but she's at a loss.

Austin concludes she must have amnesia. He's always thought that was an intriguing disease. At least in novels. "Do you have any memories, Glory? Of when you first knew your parents?"

"I don't remember when I was a baby, but ever since I was a bitsy little girl their names have been Mama and Daddy, and I've been Glory Dawn."

Austin is baffled. This beautiful female is somehow flawed. Not only is she child-like, but she is seriously detached from reality. Or she's been raised by apes. "Parents have their own names. Like my father's name is Gray Morgan." He doesn't go so far as to say his mother's name is Elizabeth. "Did you ever see your parents' names on any envelopes or packages?"

She considers that for a minute. "Mamma's Reader's Digest cover says Elsa Becker."

"But you never heard her called Elsa? What does your father call her?"

"He died." Then she seems to regain her thoughts. "I mean it about washing the sheets. You're nice people. I don't want you to get sick. There's no cure." And she runs out of the house, down the ramp, and back into the trees.

"Can I have Glory's bacon?" asks Rue.

NINE

Following the flare-up about the germs, Glory refuses to use Austin's camper. In a way, she's making things easier since Gray has said he'll have her arrested if she tries to stay there.

On the other hand, Austin and Liz are very concerned about her living outside in the elements. Liz borrows a bigger tent from a neighbor and pulls out some clean blankets. The supplies are topped off with two cans of mosquito repellent. She'll survive with those bare-bones accommodations, but everyone knows the importance of finding better answers before they get bigger storms. More than likely, the girl will be back in her own home by then. Her parents or other family have to be out there somewhere. Surely, they haven't abandoned her because of her illness.

The name Elsa Becker should be a huge clue in a small community. There's no one on the settlement named Becker, but there could easily be somebody in Tama. Gray racks his brain. "You know I think Becker might be the name of the farmers that live way back from the highway. At the end of a dead-end road. You can't see the house unless you get right up to it. I remember trying to catch up to some white guy who was speeding, and he led us a chase out that way. Becker. Yeah, I'm pretty sure that was his name. I remember being surprised the farm was back there. It's a big house."

"Well, maybe we should just go there and tell them we have Glory with us," suggests Liz. "They must be worried sick, especially if there's something wrong with her."

"A grown woman doesn't usually run away from home for no reason. It could be an abusive situation. We can't just throw her back into something that was hard to escape from." Gray seems to be getting involved in spite of himself.

Liz insists she'll make contact with old friends who tried to help when she was searching for her own child. The first call is to Barb at Barb's Back Porch Beauty Box. Nearly every woman in town and some from the settlement patronize her business. The ones who don't are likely discussed by those who do. Barb has surely heard of Elsa Becker, and the beauty operator rarely forgets a face. Austin listens with interest as Liz fishes for information.

"Barb? It's Liz Morgan. Guess what? I'm looking for somebody again! No, not a baby. This is an adult. . . . That's what I thought. I even have a name this time, Elsa Becker. I don't know her husband's name. . . .Oh, good. What do you remember?" Liz listens to Barb's story. Hopefully, it's one that will answer their questions. "That's what I was afraid of. Well, do you have any recollection of her mentioning a daughter? Her name's Glory, we think. Glory Dawn, maybe. I thought you'd surely remember because it's unusual. . . . Oh good. You know the son's name? Her husband's? . . . Yes, I'd appreciate it if you would. Sorry to take up so much of your time. 'Bye."

"Didn't sound very hopeful," remarks Austin from the couch.

"Well, she does remember Elsa from years ago but nothing about a daughter. She's pretty sure there was a grown son who came to pick her up. She remembers because he talked loud and tried to be funny. He told some off-color joke that didn't fit, him being in a ladies' shop. Barb was glad they never came again. No name for the son. She said she'd ask around, and I know she means it. She loves an excuse to be helpful."

"She loves an excuse to dig up dirt about people, you mean," inserts Gray.

"At least we know Glory isn't clear crazy. She got the name off the magazine right." Austin feels more positive than he did earlier about Glory's memory and intelligence.

"Right. All we have to do is find Elsa Becker. Shouldn't be hard. If she's alive and hasn't moved."

Austin approaches his father after lunch. "Say, do you feel up to taking Glory and me to that farm you think might belong to her folks?"

"Sure. Just hop on my broomstick, and I'll fly you there."

"I'll drive," Austin offers. "You just point the way. But it will have to wait until I make a call. Glory needs a checkup at the doctor. I have to make her an appointment."

"She isn't your daughter, you know. She's a total stranger. And a trespasser. Not your problem. You'll end up paying the bill. You'd be smarter to find her family and turn her over to them. All I'd have to do is call down to the station."

Austin knows Gray is right, but he's been captivated by the girl. "I guess it can't hurt to do a good deed now and then. Besides, I'm curious about her weird disease and whether we've already been exposed."

"Well, good luck getting her seen. They won't take her at the health center unless we can prove she's an enrolled member of the tribe."

"Oh, yeah. Guess we'll have to take her to the Doc in Tama."

The clinic is able to make a same-day appointment. "Maybe we can trick her into going," Austin suggests to Gray. "She'll already be in the car to go past what might be her home place. We can just take a long way home. That is, if she doesn't panic about filling the Explorer with germs."

"Sounds like you're packing the day with possible trauma for the poor kid. Not to mention the hassle of getting me in and out of the car."

"I'll let you worry about yourself." Austin is determined not to baby his father.

◆◆◆◆

"Glory, I'm hoping you'll go with Gray and me for a drive this afternoon. It'll be more fun than your old bike, I promise."

"I've never ridden in a car before."

Austin tries not to look shocked. *Who hasn't ridden in a car?*

"I don't get to go anywhere. Because of my sickness. I've always stayed in the house and waited for my parents to come home."

"That's crazy. We sure aren't going to leave you behind."

"But it's *for the best*. I'm contagious, remember? I could start a whole epidemic if you take me around people."

"Well, we'll just have to chance it. You've done your part. You've warned us. We . . . uh . . . want to find your house. We won't leave you there. We'll just drive past."

"It's an ordinary house. Why do you want to drive by it?"

"Just interested. Gray wonders if he might know your parents."

"They aren't there anymore. After Daddy died, it was just Mama and me, and then not too long ago somebody came and took her away. She told me she'd come back, but she didn't."

"Do other people live in the house now?"

"I don't think so."

Austin is wondering if Glory has been living alone. If she has, it's a good thing she finally got up enough courage to leave.

The drive is an odd one. Glory is put in back by herself so as not to accidentally touch the men. The part of the seat she's on is covered by a blanket. Gray sits in front with his crutches sticking out the window. Austin tries to follow his father's vague directions remembered from a brief look at the farm many years ago.

Surprisingly, Gray's recollections are accurate. Few people would accidentally find the farmstead. The narrow gravel road leading there from the highway would make travel difficult, at least in the winter. A sign announces a *Dead End*. People out driving probably never choose to venture down the overgrown lane that seems to lead nowhere. The mailman or the police are doubtless the only people who have the persistence to reach the Becker place. The mailbox by the road is missing a name.

The Morgan party pulls up in front of the large house with a wrap-around porch. It and its barn and sheds have existed no more than two miles from their own home without them being aware. The property sits on the first road east of the settlement. The whole collection of buildings is surrounded by tall pine trees.

"Does this look like home, Glory?"

"Well… I'm not positive. I wasn't out of the house much in the daytime. Let me find Mary and Steve."

"Who's that?" The story was getting *curiouser and curiouser.*

"My friends. I think they're on the back side."

Oh, boy. What are we dealing with? Maybe there are dogs tied up back there.

Austin drives down the long driveway and continues on the grass around the side of the two-story. No animals in sight.

"It's them! My dear lifelong friends! Oh, I bet they've missed me." Glory is teary-eyed and immediately fumbles with the door handle. Austin helps without touching her, and the girl runs for her companions and throws herself against one of them.

Mary and Steve are a pair of tall spruce trees about fifteen feet straight east of an upstairs window. Austin and Gray look at each other but don't comment. So what, if Glory has a big imagination? At least, she doesn't have to worry about giving these friends a disease.

They are relieved she's willing to return to the car. Her face is tear-stained, but she wears a smile. It seems the reunion has brought her a measure of contentment.

"So you're pretty sure nobody is living in the house now?" Austin asks, afraid she'll tell him about Mable the table or Ted the Bed.

"It's empty. Unless . . ."

"Unless what? Do you think somebody could be in there?"

"I doubt it. A man was watching the house from the drive one day, but he couldn't get in. The door's always locked."

If only locked doors always keep out intruders.

"Well, I'm glad we found your home. Do you want to stay?"

"No, not today." Her eyes are darting around the yard as though scanning the area for an enemy, perhaps the watcher from the driveway or maybe another fantasy figure like the spruce trees.

"Okay. Fine. We'll be back another time after we find out for sure we're at the right address." Austin knew Gray was probably worried they were trespassing. Mary and Steve couldn't vouch for Glory's story.

Austin makes the call to stop at the Big T Maid-Rite in Tama. To make things easier for his passengers, he elects to order inside, pulling the brim of his cap down as he enters. He doesn't feel like taking any more questions about whom he's come back to see.

After successfully avoiding recognition, he brings the sandwiches back to the car and to the eager folks awaiting him.

Glory eats with gusto. "This is the best hamburger I've ever had!" The girl's been living in Tama and doesn't seem familiar with Maid-Rites. Austin tends to believe she's just gotten off a space ship.

"How long since you went to a doctor?"

Glory is silent. Does she not know what a doctor is?

"Since I was a baby. That's when he told my mom I'm sick."

Just what I thought. Either she went to a quack or the mother diagnosed her own child. One thing for sure – this person named Glory doesn't have the appetite of a sick person.

"Everybody should have an exam every twenty years or so. Especially if they have a serious illness like you do. There might be some new medicine available now. Why don't we take care of it this afternoon while you have transportation?" Austin notices Gray grab his crutches, expecting an explosion from the back seat.

The explosion is only a mild one. "You're going to take me to a doctor? I don't have any money. Doctors cost money." Again, she seems to be quoting her mom.

"We'll take care of that part," Austin assures her. "You don't have to worry about a thing."

"What if he says I'm going to die soon?" She seems remarkably resigned to the idea. Except for one point. "I don't even have a plot. Or maybe I do . . ."

"What do you mean? Did your folks mention a burial plot?" Gray seems to have finally tuned into the conversation.

"Yes. I heard them talking, 'We should get a plot for Glory,' they said. I didn't know what they meant at first, but then they said something about Maple Leaf Cemetery, and I figured out a plot must be a place to put me in the ground when I die. I was pretty young then, so I worried for a while if I was going to drop dead soon or whether they ever bury people *before* they die. Otherwise, why would they be talking about it?"

He keeps hearing evidence her mom and dad didn't explain things in detail to their daughter. She must have been constantly piecing facts together. Not always correctly, it seems.

The name of the graveyard triggers a memory for Austin. He's recently read Liz's account of searching for her baby there. Searching for him, Austin. Wheels are turning in his mind and probably in Gray's. An important clue to pursue. If they can find the deceased Glory of the future, they'll learn more about the live one of the present. The thought is tabled for later.

TEN

"**W**ell, Glory my dear, you seem to be in perfect health, even though you could stand to put on a few pounds. I know it's fashionable these days to be thin as a rail, but you'll be stronger and have more energy if you don't worry about that. I'll let you know when we get your blood work back, but I see no problems at this point."

Austin should probably have asked Liz to come on this visit, but Dr. Brown hasn't objected to him being in the examining room for most of the tests. "Uh, Doc, Glory's been told she has a communicable disease. Did you find any evidence of that?"

"Goodness no. No fever, no indications of anything like that. We'll know for sure when we see her white count, but either someone was mistaken, or she's managed to cure herself." Austin can tell the doctor doesn't believe for a minute the girl ever had such a condition.

Glory looks at him in disbelief. "I think I should get a second opinion." Once more, she sounds like she is quoting something she's heard but doesn't quite comprehend. If she doesn't remember going to a doctor before, she hasn't experienced second opinions.

"Do as you like, but I'm sure any doctor is going to say you're a healthy young lady who should be thankful and not look for problems where there aren't any." His eyes twinkle. It is, no doubt, uplifting for a physician to get to tell patients good news.

Glory can't speak. Her face shows only disbelief. Dr. Brown is telling her something that doesn't calculate with what she's always known to be true. She looks at him with the same expression she'd display if he told her the earth is flat. *Come to think of it, her parents may not have taught her that it isn't.*

Austin puts his arm around the girl. She stiffens but doesn't panic. He knows she'll be happy as soon as the medical verdict has settled in her mind. Her life will be so much fuller when she can be around other people. He can't help wondering if she was truly diagnosed as a baby. And why she hasn't been seen by another physician since then. Most parents of such a sick child would have her under a doctor's care. If not, why not?

Glory's shoulder is tense under his hand. He's sure she wants to run. It occurs to Austin that her parents may have had more than one motive for making their lovely daughter afraid to let anyone close. The fear of spreading germs has probably been as effective as a chastity belt.

Liz is waiting on the porch when they get home. Rue conveniently grabs hold of Glory to show her a fallen bird's nest in the back yard. Austin can't wait to report Glory's medical news.

"Yes, Doc Brown seemed totally sure," he says. "She's fine. Physically, at least. I don't know about her mind. She didn't say a word in the car on the way back here."

"She's probably in shock, poor thing," Liz said. "I wish I'd been with her, but I had to take Ruby to her swimming lesson. I was sure Glory is healthy, but it's still nice to hear it from a doctor. Rue's been around her quite a bit, so I'm glad she isn't infectious."

"I wish a doctor would tell me my amputation didn't actually happen," Gray says in a rare moment of candor. Austin's heart aches for him. Liz gives her husband a hug. Everyone wishes the same thing for Gray.

"Do you ever wake up thinking you still have your leg?" Austin asks. He's heard others describe that sensation.

"Every day," Gray admits. "My first instinct is to hop out of bed. For just a second, I intend to walk across the floor. It still feels like the leg's there. It's like your body's trying to trick you. I know how Glory must feel, like she knows what's true, in spite of the evidence. It might not be so easy to get her to quit avoiding people."

"I'd like to get my hands on whoever told her she was sick in the first place," Austin declares.

Their attention is drawn to an unfamiliar car pulling into the drive. "Be sure Glory goes inside the back way," Austin tells Liz. "We can't blow her cover." Liz nods and motions for Gray to join her in keeping their guest out of sight.

A voluptuous young woman climbs out of the driver's seat and flies at Austin. "Oooh! It's *so* nice to have you back, gorgeous! You should've called me. Had to hear it from my friend Janis." Austin understands now why Archie grinned when mentioning that some people change.

The lady standing before him is Anita, his periodic girlfriend from the past. Actually, *girlfriend* is an exaggeration. Anita is the Meskwaki vixen he used once upon a time in an effort to make Liz jealous. He isn't proud of those days. Anita's crush on him was a fairly serious one, and he treated it lightly.

"I'm not really back. Just visiting. How are you?" He's careful not to sound flirtatious. Anita would like that too much.

"Well, I'm a lot better now that you're here. You're still looking delicious." She sucks in her stomach and smooths her skirt. "I'm a little fatter than when you saw me last, but having three kids in three years does that. Do I look disgusting?" Her wide smile gives the impression she's expecting a complimentary answer that assures her she's still *got it*.

Austin is still recovering from his first glimpse of Anita's chubby legs emerging from her car. It's hard to believe this is the raven-haired Barbie Doll of five years ago. Maybe she's been extremely happy during the last five years. Weight sometimes accumulates alongside contentment.

"You couldn't look disgusting, Anita," he says in what he hopes is a sincere voice. He's pretty certain his facial expression has already given away his initial shock. The girl is easily twice as big as she used to be but seems determined to wear the same size clothes.

"I work at Pete's Bar and Grill in Marshalltown now, and they have real good food." She giggles. "If you come in, I'll give you the all-you-can-eat ribs. Free! Oh, and you should see my kids. Rusty, Dusty, and Stella. They're the best, and we are currently scouting around for a daddy. Hope you'll apply!" Another nervous giggle. "Can't believe you've escaped without getting married." She moves close to him and rubs her hand up and down his arm. "Maybe you couldn't forget me."

"That's it, Anita. You spoiled me." Then before she can respond to his teasing, he says, "Seriously, I've been too busy to think about women. But there's one I need to find out about . . . for business reasons. Ever hear of Glory Becker?" If anybody gets around enough to recognize the name, it's Anita.

"Glory? Nah. I'd remember that. I used to know a Becker guy though. Wesley or Presley – something like that. I think he ended up in the pen. He was a mess, if you ask me. Middle-aged. Smarmy. I wouldn't want to meet him on a deserted street even in the daytime."

"You think he's still locked up?"

"Probably. Haven't seen him around for years. And I'd just as soon he stays lost."

"Do you know if he had a sister?"

"Come on, Austin. Why do you care? Any sister of his wouldn't be good enough for you! Anyway, his parents were old, and I think he was their only child. Sometimes the spirits know what they're doing."

Austin is trying to think of some other information he might get from her, when Anita cuts him off. "Listen, hon, I left the kids alone, so I better get home before they burn the place down. I'll see you real soon." And she kisses Austin square on the lips before she gets into the car and backs rapidly down the drive.

Austin is relieved to see her go. Anita was never on his list of people to visit while he's on the settlement. Still, he's glad she came by. He now has another clue in the mystery of Glory, a smarmy brother named Wesley or Presley.

A guy who doesn't even rate a good reference from Anita probably isn't a sibling Glory should be around. Hopefully, they won't need to connect with him to locate her parents.

◆◆◆◆

Barb from the Beauty Box calls after supper. Austin is nearby so he picks up the phone.

"Just thought I should get back to Liz, even though I don't have much to report. Most people I've talked to think the mouthy son ended up in jail. No surprise."

"At least that will keep him out of trouble. Another source just told me the son's name is Wesley or Presley. Please don't mention that name to anybody, but listen for it in case a customer says something about him being back in Tama."

"Will do. Would love to be able to help you. You know how I enjoy the stuff Liz gets mixed up in."

"I appreciate it, but you can't tell anyone I asked questions. It'd be dangerous if the guy learned somebody was looking for him."

"Oh, no! I won't breathe a word. Uh . . . I mean, *another* word. I already mentioned it to Clair and Dotty. And Janis. But I'll tell them to forget it."

"Right. Thanks for getting back to us, Barb, but now we'd better consider this case closed. Please don't mention another word about it." *If only.*

ELEVEN

The temporary family at the Morgan house has begun a ritual of chatting on the porch after supper. The group isn't without its tensions. Glory, of course, feels self-conscious and usually has nothing to say. She still stays at a distance, presumably just in case the doctor was wrong. Liz and Austin talk around each other. Liz sneaks looks at her son but seems to be walking on egg shells when it comes to speaking directly to him. Austin can tell she's afraid of saying the wrong thing. After waiting so long to have him close by, she doesn't want to risk seeing him pull out of the driveway in a huff. For a while, Austin's father was equally ill at ease. Gray sat in silence, appearing to be in his own world, but for two evenings now, he's entered the conversations. Austin is glad of that change, for Liz's and Rue's sakes. It has to be hard to live with the man's usual gloom.

Little Ruby does her part to keep things light. "I'm a good swimmer! She turns to Glory. "Are you?"

"I don't think so," Glory replies. "I've never tried."

"You should! It's fun!"

It crosses Austin's mind that Glory hasn't had much fun in the big old farmhouse with only Elsa, Mary and Steve to talk to.

Liz still doesn't realize how unusual the girl's life has been. "Do you have a brother or sister, Glory?"

"I have a brother, Presley, but he's pretty old. And he's in jail." It seems Glory could've speeded up their detective work if they'd only asked her the right questions.

"Did you ever meet him? Or write to him?" asks Liz. She's sensitive to hearing about people in jail who are forgotten by family.

"No. He's the devil's own offspring."

Here we go again, Austin is thinking.

"Do you know your neighbors, Glory?" Gray can appear uninterested, but then comes up with inquiries that can actually help.

"Just Wilma," she answers. "She's my aunt. But I don't see her very often. She's sort of afraid of my disease, I think." Austin notices she speaks as if the disease were still a fact.

Gray persists with his line of questioning. "Did Wilma ever stop by?"

"Sometimes. And she came some after Mom was taken away. She never came in, but I'd go out on the porch, and she'd ask me if I needed anything. She brought me groceries once a week. Once there was a geranium in a pot that she must've left."

Austin is relieved to know someone else was more or less looking after the girl and was kind enough to leave her a flower. But who wouldn't tell someone in authority that Glory was sick and living alone?

Gray looks over at Austin and says under his breath, "Tomorrow."

◆◆◆◆

Early the next morning Gray tells Liz before she leaves for work, "Austin and I are going to visit Wilma. If we can find her. She may know a lot about the Beckers. May even point us to Glory's mother. I guess we can take Rue."

"No, Rue can go with me. I've got errands away from the office." Liz is currently employed at her old stomping ground, the Meskwaki Casino. These days she's writing public relations copy instead of taking care of the machines.

Rue has been paying attention to their plans. "I'd rather go with Happy and Dad."

"Soon they'll do something special with you. Today will be real boring," says Liz.

Boring is a dirty word to Rue. "I hate boring." And she picks up her toys and follows her mom.

"I'll want to hear everything," orders Liz as she hands Austin a cinnamon roll on his way out the door. Looking at the large gooey pastry, he feels guilty knowing his father probably isn't allowed such treats.

It takes two extra stops before the men locate the home of Wilma Watson. It isn't near the Becker farm. In fact, the elderly lady lives four miles away, just off the highway. A Buick in the driveway tells them she is capable of traveling back and forth to the Becker's. The small house is set nearly flush with the ground in front, very handicapped accessible. Gray should have no trouble visiting the woman.

"Wilma, so sorry to bother you," Gray says to the round woman with white permed hair. First impressions bring back memories of Mrs. Santa, warm and motherly. Austin suspects his dad's policeman's uniform would have made the woman more eager to give him information. However, a few minutes more tell him any show of authority is unnecessary.

"That's alright. I was just ready to have my morning coffee. Will you join me?" Austin has lived in Waterloo long enough to recognize this small-town trust as a rare thing. Wilma has no idea whom she's opening her house to. He's glad she's more hospitable than Archie was with the drifter who came by his place.

"Well, sure," the guys reply. This woman is going to solve their mystery. She pours cups of coffee and motions for the men to sit at the kitchen table. The room is sunny and nicely decorated. Wilma is an eager hostess. She grabs some home-made cookies from a jar on the counter, places them on a plate along with pretty napkins and sits down, ready for a chat.

"I haven't talked to anyone from the tribe for a long time," she tells them with no hint of prejudice. Austin and Gray are aware their hair and skin color tell the woman exactly where they're from. "Are you just out enjoying the day before it gets hot?"

Gray doesn't want to waste time on the weather. "We recently became acquainted with a young lady named Glory. Would you know who I'm talking about?"

"Oh, yes!" The woman's face brightens. "She's my niece. I'm so happy you found her. I've been sick with worry lately. My sister-in-law Elsa made me promise to watch over her after Elsa had to go into the Home. Then Glory just up and disappeared. I've driven up and down the roads around their place but never saw a trace of her. I thought about telling the police, but they might think I did something to her. I haven't had the heart to tell Elsa I lost her daughter."

"Where does Glory usually like to go?" Austin asks. He's been wondering why the girl picked their house.

"Nowhere. I don't think she's ever been out of their yard. She must be dreadfully scared now if she can't find her way back."

"Actually, she's fine. We're letting her stay at our place just a couple miles on the other side of the highway from her farm."

"She crossed the highway?" Wilma seems genuinely frightened for the girl.

"Oh, yes. We're finding out she's really a pretty brave little lady. Can you tell us her story? How she came to be such a recluse? We can't figure out her situation."

"Well, you won't believe it." The woman takes a sip of coffee and calls attention to the cookies. "Help yourselves, please." They do, so she'll continue her tale. "It started over twenty years ago when Elsa and my brother Burt went to the powwow like they did every summer. The day had gotten to be real drizzly and windy. Elsa and Burt had already feasted on Indian tacos, which was their favorite and really what they came for. So they decided to go back home." She took a bite of her cookie pausing mainly for effect, Austin thought. "On their way off the grounds, Elsa spotted a bundle under a tree. It looked like a bunched up coat. She's the kind who'd want to turn it in to the lost and found. Well, when she picked it up and started to unfold it, she was so shocked she just shouted out, "Glory!" Wilma's eyes get large, just thinking about the moment. "Inside, there was a brand new baby, maybe only minutes old. Darkish skin. Black hair. Had to be Meskwaki or maybe a half breed."

"That's how Glory got her name?" Austin has been curious about that.

"Yeah. Burt thought that's what his wife was calling her at first. They both believed she was a gift from heaven. To make up for Presley who'd been taken off to prison. There was a note sticking out of the pocket of that lightweight jacket she was wrapped in. It said, *Don't want it.* I guess it could've just been talking about the coat, but Elsa and Burt took the note to mean they didn't have to search for the parents. Probably some teenager who hardly understood what happened to her and didn't want anybody to know."

"That's sad. The poor baby."

But Wilma isn't finished. "When Elsa tells the story, she says that as they were walking away, she saw the eye of a girl peeking around the tree. Maybe it was the mother watching to make sure her baby got rescued. I like to think that's what happened. Can't imagine any human being just leaving her child there to maybe get eaten by a coyote or something."

Austin can't believe his ears. He and Glory had very similar beginnings. Wilma's account sounded a lot like what he read in Liz's journals about him being found by Ruby on her doorstep. Picturing the attractive, bright girl who's been staying with them, he thinks it a shame she came so close to dying of starvation or exposure. It makes him feel he should keep his eyes peeled at all times for infants who've been thrown away.

"I take it Elsa and Burt felt like the girl behind the tree must've approved of them."

Wilma nodded. "Elsa thought the whole thing was providence. Her and Burt's first baby had turned out to be the devil's spawn and such a disappointment to good folks who wanted a pure little baby to love. They could've turned this one over to the authorities, but they decided on the spot they wanted to raise her. It was a second chance to get things right."

Gray, always prepared with a tablet, has been taking notes. Surprisingly, he didn't point out that the Beckers broke the law. "When did *you* learn about Glory?"

Wilma seems to like having the floor. She gets up, fetches the coffee pot and pours refills. "That same evening. I just happened to stop by the house and saw her. That was a shock, let me tell you. I was afraid they'd gone out of their minds and stole somebody's baby. They had to tell me then what had happened. I think I'm the only living soul, besides my sister-in-law, who knows there's even such a person as Glory. Well, now you know, too." Wilma smiles lovingly. "She was the prettiest baby I ever saw."

Gray has to ask, "I don't see how come they'd keep her such a secret. I'd have thought they'd want to show her off instead of making her a prisoner."

"It wasn't like that. They spoiled that girl something fierce. Made her a beautiful room with every toy, every piece of clothing she could possibly want. They'd let her out in the yard for short times when they were watching, let her ride a bike on the driveway when it was almost dark out. But they were pretty certain she was Meskwaki. They were afraid the tribe could legally claim her and take her away to live on the settlement. Burt and Elsa couldn't let that happen. When Glory got old enough to wonder why she couldn't go anywhere, they convinced her she had a real contagious disease, and they had no choice but to keep her at home. Everyone outside their house was a threat to the child and she to them."

"That's cruel!" Austin exclaims.

"Some would say so, but you'll never meet two nicer people than Elsa and Burt. They loved Glory more than life and never did or said one unkind thing to her. I don't think they even told that demon Presley they had her."

"Didn't he ever run into her at their place?"

"No, he'd been out of school and on his own for a couple of years and had gotten himself into trouble with the law. He was already serving time in the penitentiary when Glory came along. It's good it worked out that way. I wouldn't have trusted him around her, I'll tell you that. She's always been beautiful, and for a long time now, he's been rebellious and mean. A bad combination. I got word he's going to be freed soon, so it's good Glory isn't still in the house alone."

A noise can be heard outside the open kitchen window. Gray instinctively rises and hobbles over to investigate. "Is there somebody else on your property?" he asks Wilma.

"No. I'm all by myself, and I like it that way. What you mighta heard was Belle and Tinker. I call them my watch cats."

Austin heard it, too, and thinks the felines must be pretty large ones but doesn't comment for fear of getting Wilma sidetracked. "What about school? Has Glory been educated?"

"Not really. Elsa didn't try to get home schooling stuff because she'd have to tell who it was for, so she just did the best she could from second-hand text books. I helped her find some at garage sales and on the internet."

"So she had access to a computer?" That idea gave Austin hope the girl had some contact with society.

"Yes and no. They had one, but she only got to use it when they were watching. And they never told her about email or anything. Couldn't let her identity get out there."

"Guess she doesn't have a phone either."

"No. It's been a lonely life for her, but she seems contented 'cause she doesn't know any different. They meant to allow her out into the world when she turned twenty-one. Just too bad Elsa let the kitchen stove burn the towel."

Gray passed over what promised to be a story for later. "How could you go along with all this?"

There's 'the slightest bit of defensiveness in her tone as Wilma explains. "I love the whole family. I didn't want them to get separated. That woulda made all three of them miserable. I just tried to give Burt and Elsa a little relief when they needed to be away, and I ran errands for them in town. They'd isolated themselves, too, for Glory's sake. I went along with the contagious disease thing because I didn't want to stir the waters, but I was pretty sure it wasn't the truth. I even kept away from her after Elsa left just so Glory would keep believing she was sick. I figured one of us would tell her the truth in a couple of months when she turned twenty-one."

It crossed Austin's mind that the last point sounded like an excuse. Wilma didn't spend any time with Glory and now can tell herself she was only trying to perpetuate the illness deception. There's lots more the men want to ask Wilma, but the woman looks tired and distressed. She must feel guilty for spilling the beans she's kept to herself for two decades.

Glory's aunt watches her visitors walk down the porch steps. "You all come back again. It's been kind of a relief to talk to you. I can see you're good people, not from the newspaper or the police. I thank you for looking after our girl, but hope you won't turn her over to the tribe."

Austin is glad now that Gray didn't wear his uniform. "No, Ma'am. We think Glory is very special, and it sounds like she's ready for some freedom. We don't want to cause her any trouble."

One more difficulty occurred to him. He hated to give the impression they were interested in the girl's money, but they needed to know. "Oh, and right now, your niece seems penniless. Does she have a bank account or any allowance? She's been trying to find a job, but without identification, it's impossible. It takes a little money just to survive in the world. I mean, when she leaves us, she'll have to have a place to live and transportation and food."

Standing in the open doorway, Wilma contemplates the problem. "I really don't know. I didn't ask. She didn't have any use for cash, not getting to go anywhere. But she'll probably get something when Elsa goes. I don't have any extra, so I can't help her."

"Since she isn't a blood relative, and no one even knows about her, she probably isn't entitled to anything automatically," Gray points out.

"I've been wondering about that. Elsa wrote up a will after Burt passed. She wanted to leave everything to Glory instead of that worthless son. But I can't find the paper, and she can't remember where she hid it. Her memory has sorta gone south lately."

"Do you know her attorney's name?"

"There's only one in Tama who does wills, and he don't have it. I already checked. Elsa wouldn't have wanted to give away Glory's existence before she had to. She must've planned to confess to her lawyer on her deathbed and hand him the paper. But then Human Services interfered. I guess we always think we have more time to wind things up than we do."

Gray is still trying to cover all the details. "I might have some questions later for that attorney. Can you write down his name and phone number?"

They wait while Wilma looks up the number in the phone book and copies it onto a notepad on the little stand inside the back door. She hands the piece of paper to Gray. "Bill Hogan's been there a long time, but he probably won't talk to you about Elsa. They have confidentiality rules."

Gray slips the information into his pocket. Maybe if he mentions his connection to the police, he can gain the lawyer's trust. "We'll see. I'm sure Mrs. Becker's grateful for your help. Your being around must take a lot of worry off her while she's in the Home."

"She's family. I do what I can," says Wilma modestly.

"If Glory wants to go home and get some things, will you loan us a key or go in the house with us?" asks Gray. "Don't want to get arrested for breaking and entering."

"I'll let you in over there anytime. I don't have a lot going on."

◆◆◆◆

On their way home, the pair stop by the cemetery. It isn't so important anymore since they've talked to Wilma, but Gray wants the aunt's story confirmed. It's possible she was just spinning a yarn.

Maple Leaf Cemetery is small and laid out to be easily navigated. For people on two legs, that is. The bumpy terrain would be hard for Gray on crutches. "Have at it," he directs Austin.

It occurs to Austin that he'd love to be able to visit his Meskwaki mother and father's graves, but that is a trip for another day. Those good people are buried in the tribal cemetery. His memories of their funeral and interment are blurred by the grief he relives when he remembers. He's sure there's a place for his body to be near theirs someday. Ruby and Murray absolutely considered him family.

Under a young birch tree are the now-familiar names of the Becker family. Beside the modest stone for Burt and Elsa is another for *Our Daughter* Glory Dawn. Evidentially, they don't want Presley remembered. Maybe his parents believed he'd die in jail, and the state would bury him, or that he'd get married and have a marker with his spouse. Glory's inscription shows her birth date as August 13, 1989.

As they look at the engravings on the stones, Austin notices Glory's inscription is missing a last name. Since they never officially adopted the girl, she could conceivably go to her death with a space after the Dawn. *Some guy will fix that,* Austin reminds himself. *A young lady as attractive as she is will pick up a last name.* And a different grave stone.

His thoughts go then to the young mother behind the tree. She'd probably be pleased to know about the monument. By providing that, the Beckers were saying the child is an accepted member of their family. As opposed to the prodigal Presley.

Weird as Glory's life has been so far, she, like himself, has known love, and not every abandoned child can say that.

TWELVE

Every time Austin comes back to the trailer after a day at the newspaper, he finds Gray on the porch flanked by Rue on one side and Murray the hound on the other. If a guy has to be largely confined to home, he can't do better for companionship than those two. Plus he's married to Liz. Austin views that as a definite reason for the man to smile. But Gray goes days at a time without showing so much as a smirk. Presumably, he would rather be pulling in at day's end in a police car and having his daughter and the visiting pooch come to meet him instead of taking care of him.

Austin has been trying to include Gray in his search for Glory's missing life, and the man shows interest at the time he's asking questions. But playing detective doesn't seem to be doing much for his overall depression. Austin notices lapses when his father seems to drift into a deep funk and barely be aware of his surroundings. It's possible, he thinks, that Gray's problems are beyond the help of simple distractions. It could be time to get him professional help before the lapses get any longer or more frequent. However, Austin knows Gray won't be a willing subject. *Maybe I'll give my methods just a little more time.*

Catching the man sitting in front of the television when it isn't turned on, he knows he has to come up with something. "I'm used to working out every day but haven't gotten to do it lately. Is there someplace to go around here?"

He doesn't remember anywhere from the old days, but other amenities have popped up in the last few years. Why not a workout room?

"Yeah. You can go to the gym. They have lots of good equipment."

"Really? Did you used to go there?"

"Sometimes," Gray answers in a voice barely audible.

"I'd like to, but it'd be kind of dull by myself. Want to work out with me?" Austin knows he isn't fooling anybody. He's never before had any problem lifting weights without a buddy.

Gray goes to the window and gazes out at the trees, as if to emphasize his disinterest. "Why do I want to work out? So I can topple off the treadmill?"

"Ah, come on. I'm sure the trainers there will show you how to compensate. You can set an example for other amputees. Build up the body parts you still have. Pretty soon you won't even need *two* legs."

"You should be a salesman. You're so full of it." But Gray finally smiles. "I'll watch while *you* set an example."

"Fair enough."

"I'll do exercises with you, Happy," offers Rue. I want to get more stronger and help Dad walk."

"How does that make you feel, Gray? Your five-year-old is willing to do the work you won't do."

"Shut up and let's go."

The men find themselves signing in at the settlement gym to use the free weights. Austin remembers a few years ago when Gray could've made him look like a weakling, but if appearances mean anything, his father has lost a lot of ground as far as muscle tone. Any definition in his biceps is hard to see. Right now Gray's lack of arm strength looks like it will be more of a limitation for being a cop than the missing lower limb.

While they're working with forty-pounders, Austin continues to challenge Gray. The man he used to know enjoyed any competition. "How many pushups did you do in your prime?"

"A hundred on an average day. But that won't happen again."

"Who says? Have you tried even one in the last six months?"

Gray snaps back. "Maybe you don't get how it works. With a leg gone, your body is lopsided. Your balance in shot to hell."

"Oh, I can imagine. It seems like what you'll have to do is build up your upper body so your arms can hold your torso in balance."

"When *you* lose a leg, you can let me know how well that theory works."

Austin thinks he'd better quit offering suggestions. From then on, the men exercise in silence. Gray does seem determined to make use of his time. When they stop, he's broken a sweat. Austin hopes that doesn't mean he overdid it.

They make plans to return four days a week. Austin has read where physical activity can reverse one's tendency to become depressed. Considering Gray's restrictions, Austin's natural inclination to hit the weights hard will need to be curtailed for the present. It's more important that his father gain confidence in his own endurance than to watch while Austin outdoes him.

◆◆◆◆

Austin approaches Glory who's sitting at the end of the lane on a large bolder. He's noticed her doing that before. Just sitting. She appears to be digesting her surroundings. After a life spent largely inside a single house, even the monotonous Tama County countryside must be mesmerizing. It would be fun to introduce her to other scenic locations on planet Earth. Maybe someday he'll get that chance.

"Are you dreaming of faraway places?" he asks the girl on the rock.

"Not really. I like this place."

"But what if you got the chance to travel – just for a vacation. I mean, if you find out you're well enough. Where would you like to go?"

Glory thinks for a few minutes. *What is she picturing? Scenes from an old National Geographic?*

"I think I'd go to Alaska. It doesn't look like it's as hot as here, and the people look like me."

"Where did you see pictures of Alaska?" Austin asks.

"On my calendar. Mom got it a long time ago from the bank. She got a new one in the mail every year after that, but I left the Alaska one on my wall so I could keep looking at the pictures."

"I've never gone to Alaska but have heard it's beautiful. I know people from the settlement who've made the trip. Maybe I can arrange something for you." Austin himself has never left Iowa. Funny it should seem so obvious to him that Glory is travel-deprived.

His cell phone calls him away from thoughts of cooler climates. "Hey! I think it's a call from Doc Brown. Hopefully, it's good news about your blood tests!"

Glory doesn't seem to share his hopes. Good news from the doctor would mean her parents lied to her. It will be hard to know whether to laugh or cry.

On the phone, Dr. Brown says, "Your new friend Glory is as healthy as anybody in town! I'll put the written outcome in the mail to Gray's address. Will that work?"

"Oh, sure. And thanks, Doc. You've made us all very happy." *With the possible exception of Glory.*

"Am I well now?" She seems to have thought of a way to rationalize the mistaken diagnosis.

Austin resists the urge to tell her she's always been well. That would border on bad news if one considers the needless loss of her childhood. So he goes along with her explanation. "You've recovered. You must've outgrown the disease. You can go wherever you want to!"

She smiles but says again, "I'm fine here."

Austin realizes he shouldn't feel too flattered by her remark. The Morgan grounds is one of the only parts of the outside world she's experienced. Anywhere beyond that must seem as unreal as Neverland.

"And you can touch anybody who'll let you."

"Will you let me?" She gives him a look that from anyone else he'd have considered flirtatious.

"Be my guest," is his quiet reply.

Glory immediately rushes to him and plants a kiss on his mouth, probably mimicking Anita. The act is so surprising, he doesn't even kiss her back. He's barely able to assess his feelings about the contact so resists the desire for a repeat. "That was nice," he tells her.

Even though he hasn't been worried about Glory's health, it is good to have his instincts and Wilma's opinion confirmed. He wonders if Elsa will be surprised about the doctor's verdict. *She shouldn't be,* he thinks, *but sometimes when people live with a lie long enough, they come to believe it.*

THIRTEEN

The upcoming afternoon should tell Austin whether Elsa Becker is a loving woman or a cold-hearted jailer. He has invited Glory to go to the nursing home with him. In all probability, they will get to pay a visit to her mother.

On their way to the Cassidy Care Center, Glory shows signs of stress. "Mama's probably mad at me for not coming sooner. She must be so lonely."

Austin finds it hard to work up much sympathy for Elsa. What could she expect when she's spent more than twenty years convincing her healthy daughter she's too sick to leave the house? *The woman's darned lucky Glory even wants to see her.*

The girl wears a faint smile as they approach the reception desk. At last, she's about to see a familiar face.

After they check in, a nurse approaches. "Elsa just finished her lunch. If she hasn't dozed off, you can go in." And the woman in white leads the way.

Entering the room at the far end of the hall, she calls loudly as if to a deaf person. "Elsa! Someone's here to see you! She says her name's Glory!" The implication is that, even in her current predicament, Elsa hasn't revealed the existence of her Native American daughter.

The lined but attractive woman in the rocker turns toward them with such an expression of wonder and delight it brings tears to Austin's eyes. "My baby!"

Glory lets out a squeal and runs to her mother. "Mama! I thought you might be dead!" They cling to each other for several minutes. The nurse's aide looks puzzled. She's probably assumed Elsa is too old to have such a young beautiful daughter. The woman respectfully creeps out the door, giving the family their privacy.

"Oh, girl, I'm so happy you're okay. I shoulda told Wilma to buy you a phone so we could be talking while I'm away. I didn't want to leave, but when the towel caught fire on the stove and burned my arm, some do-gooders at the hospital thought I shouldn't go back to the house to live by myself. I tried to tell them I had somebody depending on me, but they wouldn't listen. They thought I was just living in the past." She sighs, remembering the frustrations of trying to make the authorities understand.

"I got along. Wilma helped. But one day I saw a man out by a tree looking at the house, and I was scared, so I ran away."

"That must have been Presley. He wrote Wilma and told her he was getting out. I was so worried. He doesn't know about you, but if he did ..." Her face shows fear at the very idea.

"Do you know where Presley is now?" asks Austin.

"Oh, Mama! This is my really good friend Austin. He's letting me live with him. It's a lot nicer than being alone on the farm."

Elsa looks a little worried. "You're on the settlement?" She addresses Austin then. "Your people will want to keep Glory."

"I don't think so, Ma'am. She's just a visitor at our house out in the country. No one except my parents knows anything about her." Then he steers Elsa back to his question. "About Presley ..."

"I don't know where he is, but if he's out of prison, he's probably waiting around for me to die so he can get the farm. He thinks it'll come to him automatically as my only child."

"Is he right?"

"Oh, no. I made a new will. I cut him out. He deserted us and our teachings, so he doesn't deserve anything. He can rob another convenience store if he needs to."

Austin brings a chair around so he can sit facing Elsa. Glory continues to stand by her mom with an arm around her shoulders.

"You made a good call, Mrs. Becker. Where did you put the will?" To anyone listening, he knows he must sound like a money-hungry relative.

"That's what I can't remember. I thought real hard about where to hide it, but for the life of me, I can't think where I settled on. It must be in the house someplace."

Austin pictures the three-story building filled with years of accumulated papers. "Would Presley have any idea where it is?"

"Oh, no. He's probably forgotten what the house even looks like. And he doesn't think he has anything to worry about. Unless he learns about Glory. If he does, I know he'll try to find any forms with her name on them so he can burn them. Nobody can let him know we have another child."

"I can't imagine who would tell him. Unless Wilma—."

"She wouldn't. She can't even stand to talk to him."

A man has to be pretty despicable if his mother and his aunt both talk about him with such hatred. Austin almost feels sorry for the guy who's been locked up for so long only to come home to an ice cold reception. After all, he might be rehabilitated.

"Maybe you should make another will. It would supersede the lost one," Austin suggests.

"Maybe. But Presley would tell them I'm not of sound mind now. I'm scared he could get it thrown out."

"Good point. If you don't mind, Gray and I might take a look around the place for you. We might accidentally find it."

"Go ahead. Wilma has a key. My ticker's weak, so I don't expect to be around much longer. I'd love to know Glory is set before I go. I don't owe any bills so, except for that will, I'm ready when the Lord calls."

"We hope it will be years yet before the will is needed, but it will give you peace to have things in order. If we locate the newest one and leave it with your attorney, you or Glory should have nothing to fear from Presley."

"I'm glad Glory's with you. If she's on her own when Presley gets free, she won't be safe. It's awful to say about your own child, but our boy turned out to be dangerous. He was going to shoot a man!"

"Well, at least you have a daughter to be proud of. And I don't want you to worry about her, Mrs. Becker. She should be fine while she's at the Morgan place." Austin's glad her mom doesn't know the girl sleeps in the woods.

"I can't thank you enough for watching over her. I know she isn't prepared for the world. I'm sorry we had to shelter her so much. She hasn't been trained in any skills so she won't find a job. But if you'll look in my purse on the dresser over there, you'll find some money. If the nurses didn't take it. It isn't much but it might help with her expenses until I die and she gets more."

"Oh, no, Mrs. Becker. You'll need your cash. We can handle Glory's needs. She doesn't eat much." As soon as he's spoken that reassurance, he has second thoughts. Since he's planning to be around for only a few weeks, he should actually have consulted Gray and Liz before volunteering them to pay for Glory's keep.

Gray doesn't protest Austin's offer but asks the logical question, "Did you ever think about adopting Glory? Then she'd be in better circumstances legally."

"We thought about it, but there was no birth certificate or anything, so it would've been hard to do without having her whereabouts come out. The tribe would've fought it tooth and nail, and we didn't want to put her through that. We should've, I guess. The years just get away from a person."

"Glory, do you want to tell your mother about your medical report?" Austin's been looking forward to the woman's reaction when she learns the results.

"Oh, my, don't tell me you're sick, honey." A strange comment from the same woman who's been saying so for years. Mama is quite an actress.

"You tell her." Glory can't bring herself to do the honors.

"Well, Mrs. Becker, I took the liberty of making an appointment for Glory to get a physical. I was hoping she's recovered from that communicable disease she used to have. Otherwise, my whole family would be in danger."

Elsa doesn't answer right away, then, "They probably told you she's healthy."

"That's right. The doctor was puzzled about why she hadn't been out in public all these years."

"You don't understand. We did what had to be done to keep Glory with us. I won't apologize for it."

Austin knows there's no point in trying to show the woman the error of what she and Burt did. It's too late to change the past, and Austin wasn't in their shoes when they made the decisions they made. The couple sacrificed their own freedom as well as their new daughter's.

"You don't have to apologize, but I thought you'd be happy to know Glory is able to live in the outside world now. And she's old enough that no one, even the Native Americans, will try to take custody of her."

Elsa closes her eyes to signal an end to conversation for the day. Throughout the entire interview, Glory has been squeezed into the chair beside her mother, a look of relaxed bliss on her face. Austin is sorry to force her away. "We'd better let your mom rest now. We can come back soon."

Surprisingly, Glory gets up to leave. "We'll bring you some cornbread next time," she promises Elsa. To Austin, she explains, "She loves cornbread. I know she's been missing it."

When they get out to the street, Glory looks back at the nursing home. "Who made her go there? Is she in jail like Presley?"

Austin is sorry for assuming the whole situation would make sense to Glory. No one has explained to her, apparently, what can happen when a person gets old and can't live by herself. In Glory's experience, people are only locked up for doing wrong. Or being infectious.

"There are kind people at the care center. They're taking care of your mom so she doesn't burn herself again. It's a good thing she's there. People sometimes need special help as they age."

"I'm grown now. I could've helped her so she wouldn't have to leave her house."

"You could have, Glory. But the health authorities didn't even know about you. They thought Elsa was by herself."

And therein lies the problem. If there's no proof on paper, does a person count at all? Can one who doesn't officially exist inherit a farm? Austin is glad Elsa hasn't passed on. They are going to need a little time to sort things out. He remembers Glory's statement about a man watching the house. Presley is probably a few steps ahead of them already.

PRESLEY

"Presley Becker! How the heck are ya? Heard you got out. You living with your mom now?"

"Naw. Found out she's in the Home. I'm stayin' at the Golden Moon."

"Too bad. Must be kinda lonesome not having any family left to take you in."

"I have an aunt, but she don't want me around. I overheard some talk yesterday when I was outside her house. She was telling a couple of men about a girl my mother has living with her. Named Glory. Ever hear of her?"

"Nope. I thought you didn't have any brothers or sisters. Your mom was already old when you were sent up, wasn't she?"

"Yeah. Way too old to have a baby or even adopt one."

"Maybe your mom has a past you don't know about, and it just showed up at her door."

"All I need now is some girl trying to pass herself off as my mother's long lost kid."

"That wouldn't be good. Better check that out, Pres."

"Don't worry. Any imposter bitch better be shakin' in her shoes. I'll protect what's mine no matter what it takes."

"I know you will, Pres. Just don't get yourself back in the pokey. Ain't worth that."

"It might be. I don't have a life on the outside unless I get the farm. Without it, I'm just an unemployable ex-con without a pot to piss in. No family, no future. I might as well stay in the slammer."

"Well, when you tell it like that, I think maybe you'd better fight for your rights. I own a gun if you think you might need it."

"Don't know. A gun once got me in big trouble. I'll let you know if I can't figure out some other way. I've got a few ideas."

FOURTEEN

When Austin asks Glory what she wants to do on a Sunday afternoon she answers without hesitation, "Get a Maid-Rite!"

"No kidding? Well, that's easy."

"I want one, too!" pipes in Rue. "Me and Glory are best friends, so we eat the same things."

Glory doesn't confirm that assessment, but she looks pleased. She's had no experience with being a friend to anyone under eighty, so a five-year-old must seem quite acceptable. Rue takes a seat in the booth. She moves close to Glory and proceeds to unwrap her friend's sandwich for her. "Don't use catsup," she advises. "And you can pick out the onions."

Several maid-rites later, the Morgan family and friends decide to drive by Wilma's and borrow a key to Glory's former home. There's no time like the present to see what they'll be facing if they search for Elsa's will.

"Do you want me to go with you?" the woman asks.

"Thanks, Wilma. Another time. Today we're going in as Glory's Sunday guests. She'll give us the tour."

The woman seems disappointed, but Austin isn't sympathetic. She's had years to help Elsa find the will. There's no reason to let her in on the act at this late date.

The first sign of trouble at the Becker place is a broken window near the front door. Some visitor didn't bother with a key. Or flying debris from a storm made the hole. No one but Austin notices, so he unlocks the door without mentioning the shattered glass.

First impressions of Glory's home are comforting. Austin has feared his new friend lived here amid deplorable conditions, but the place is an average old farm house like many he's been in. Not fancy, but very homey if not for the built-up heat and stale smell.

Glory shows little interest in introducing her guests to the rooms on the main floor. But she loses no time leading the way up the open staircase to her own suite. Gray begs off. "I'll just wait for you down here," he says with some embarrassment.

Everyone who's made the trip upstairs expects the young lady to let out a "Ta-da!" when she reveals her room. Instead, she stands rooted in the doorway with her mouth open. "Somebody wrecked it!" And she begins to sob. Austin, Liz, and Rue nudge her ahead. At first glance, they notice a very pink, very ruffled, completely girly room, nothing like they pictured for the rugged girl they have recently met.

Rue is excited. "It's a princess room!" she declares. "It's beautiful!" Indeed, Glory's former quarters look like a fairy tale palace compared to Rue's perfectly fine, but perfectly plain one.

A closer look confirms for Austin that some other visitor has been here before them. He abandons any hope the window was broken by natural causes. This looks like a deliberate trashing.

Every drawer is open with contents spilling onto the floor. Items have been dragged from under the bed. A small closet's clothing has been pulled off the rods. Not one jewelry box, picture book, or stuffed animal has been spared. Even Cinderella's body has been gutted.

"Presley!" exclaims Glory. "He found me, and he hates me!"

Liz sees the extreme disorder as something else. "I don't think he did all this because he hates you. He was trying to find something."

"I don't have any man things in here," reasons Glory through her tears.

The lid on a window seat stands open, revealing many books. The ones Austin sees are for children. A glance out the window gives a perfect view of Mary and Steve. He wonders how many hours she spent over the years visiting with tree friends who never answered her. *I'm surprised she's still sane.*

"We should check the rest of the house," suggests Liz.

Austin is glad to leave the puke-pink room. Granted, he isn't a girl, but he can't imagine spending twenty years in here. For him, it would've been almost as awful as the six by eight foot prison cell Liz occupied for that length of time.

Austin sees Glory snatch a calendar off her wall before leaving. He thinks it says 2000, but he could be wrong. She must want to take something with her as a reminder of home – at least of home before her brother did a number on it. Then he remembers her telling him about the calendar with dream photos of Alaska.

Glory leads her new friends through the house, noting every trace of the evil Presley. They don't understand why the man did what he did, only that it fits with what everybody knows about him. He must've been in a frenzy, outraged at his parents for obviously lavishing so much on another child while disowning him. Looking for a will doesn't have to result in such a mess if no emotion is involved.

Glory tries to straighten things. Apparently, she has been accustomed to a tidy home or perhaps she's only trying to wipe out signs of her scary sibling. "My mom will be *so* upset when she comes back!" she keeps saying.

A thorough exploration of every room tells them the intruder didn't miss a nook or a cranny. If a will was lurking in the house, it didn't have a chance. Austin can't imagine where else is left for them to search, unless they pull up the floorboards, and Elsa wouldn't have been able to hide anything in a place so difficult to reach.

Unless it's now in Presley's possession or been destroyed by him, the will must be in one of the outside buildings. Still, Austin can't picture Elsa going into one of the barns to hide the document.

He regrets not finding out what Wilma knows about the contents of the will. She, no doubt, was present for the signing. Elsa would never have brought in an additional person who would find out about Glory.

They backtrack to Wilma's. In order not to overwhelm the lady, everyone but Gray waits in the car.

The off-duty cop doesn't waste time with niceties. "What have you heard from Presley lately?" He doesn't leave room for her to claim she has had no contact with him.

"Well…I got a real short note about a week ago." she admits. No explanation for not mentioning the note earlier. "But I didn't reply," she adds quickly.

"What did the note say?" Gray is sure the man wasn't simply inquiring about Wilma's health.

Wilma looks like she's trying to recall Presley's words. "I'll show you." She gets an envelope out of the drawer of a cabinet and hands it over.

A messy scrawl done in pencil declares, *I'm finally being released. Will want to see latest will.*

The words imply Presley is aware things may have changed regarding his place in his mother's family.

"How do you think he knows a second will might exist?" Gray asks before the woman can put out the plate of cookies she is assembling.

"I have no idea. I certainly didn't tell him. I wouldn't give that man the time of day!" Glory's aunt is getting irritable about what must sound to her like an interrogation.

"I guess he could have just assumed there would be an updated one. Or you may have let him know accidentally, given him a hint without meaning to. Think about it, Wilma. Oh, and you were the one to witness the writing of the new will, weren't you?" Gray's crutches are always uncomfortable, but he makes no move to sit.

"Well…I suppose I was. It was years ago. I don't remember what it said or where Elsa planned to put it. She wouldn't have told me anyway."

"Think about that, too. Try to picture whether she took it outside or upstairs. Think about what she was wearing, what she said…you might be able to *see* her on the stairs or the porch. Also, maybe you and Elsa think alike. Imagine where *you'd* have hidden important papers. You're Glory's only hope."

Wilma's eyes are filling with tears of frustration. "Oh, my. If that's really the case, I'll try. Trouble is, my memory's not much better than Elsa's. I'm a little more of a sensitive though. Answers to riddles sometimes show up in my dreams."

Austin is not encouraged by the exchange as it's related to him later by Gray. "Wonderful," he replies. "Now we have to rely on dreams. What are the chances she'll remember what she dreamed?"

"What are the chances most of the other stuff she's been telling us didn't come from her dreams? The whole story is almost that hard to believe."

FIFTEEN

Being a recent master of distracting people from their troubles, Austin is eager now to take his new acquaintance's mind off the present state of her family home.

"Glory, do you know something besides Maid-Rites you should try if you haven't? Tacos." He is on his way to the truck with Glory following behind.

"I heard about them on TV but never did see a real one."

"We'll have to take care of that soon. I just thought of them because I passed a taco wagon in Tama this morning."

"What's a taco wagon?"

"It's a little mobile restaurant that somebody sells tacos out of. This one had a For Sale sign in the window."

"Then they probably don't have any more tacos," she reasons.

"Right. But the thing is, the trailer is little, about the size of mine. And a little rickety, so I bet they aren't asking much for it."

"Anything's *much* for me."

"I thought you said you'd been saving for the metal one."

The girl looks slightly contrite. "I lied. I don't have one cent."

"Well, I'd be willing to float you a loan if it's a good deal." He gestures toward the passenger door of his truck. "Wanna take a look?"

◆◆◆◆

As described, Toby's Taco trailer sits in the parking lot of a tire shop on the south side of town. A person can't miss it. The vehicle has been painted a neon shade of orange.

"Oh, glory!" exclaims Glory. "That's bright."

"The color is kind of shocking, but we can paint it."

"Okay." Then Glory offers one of her rare smiles. "We won't make it pink," she states firmly.

Austin laughs. He can understand if she never wants to see that color again. "Aren't you going to check out the inside?"

She opens the door to the vehicle and groans. "It's a mess. It's in worse shambles than my old room! Maybe I can take the silver trailer, and you can have this one."

"Nice try, but I think this rattletrap needs a feminine touch."

After some serious haggling, Austin gets the price reduced to $50 which includes the broken interior items. A real bargain for a homeless girl, who's becoming somewhat picky.

He takes out his phone. "We need a *before* picture so we can take an *after* one later. This eyesore will improve. You'll see."

Glory can barely muster a smile as she poses with her hand upon the customer window ledge of the bright orange contraption that is to become her new home. "I hope nobody's watching."

"Who knew you cared about appearances?" Austin teased. "You need to have faith."

The tire dealer who's just made the sale walks up to the owners of the orange trailer and grins. "When Toby Gomez dropped that thing off, I never thought we'd find it a home. Guess you folks have business plans for it, huh?"

The man must assume that once a taco trailer, always a taco trailer. "No, we're going to retire this little eating establishment," Austin informs him. "It's going someplace scenic and peaceful."

Again, Austin gets to transport a trailer to White Tail Road. Neighbors are going to be wondering if he's starting a roadside dealership.

"Get on some paint clothes!" he instructs Glory. As if she doesn't dare soil her present finery.

It soon becomes evident that, even if Glory had chosen it, pink paint never would have been able to cover the bright orange. A half-gallon of brown found in the garage is barely enough to disguise the neon color. A lot of it shows through, but the final result is a camouflage design that may do the trick. The Chocolate Delight on the little trailer in the woods has little visual appeal but a high concealment rating. As long as it isn't going to be judged in a painted-trailer contest, the transformation should be acceptable.

"That's pretty ugly," Glory comments as she surveys her brown boxcar. She refrains from protesting too loudly, however, to the guy who paid for it. "Maybe it needs some flowers beside the step," she suggests.

"I'm sorry. I know blue or white would've looked better, but you'll be safer in something that can't be seen through the trees. We want you to blend in." Austin isn't taking any chances on her older brother spotting a glowing orange object if he happens to drive by. Glory's new digs get parked in the clearing previously used as her camp site. Flowers can wait.

County health officials will probably be suspicious if they glimpse the camouflaged vehicle sitting out of plain sight. Their first theory would have to be that someone at this residence has something to hide. *They'd be sure to do an inspection though, and that would tell them the owner isn't making meth. They can't arrest us for anything too serious,* Austin thinks. The last thing he wants is for Gray to get cited for breaking the law while he's on leave from the police department.

Later, when the family is introduced to yet another trailer on their lot, Rue decides Murray should inherit the small tent, Glory's first shelter. The dog politely turns it down, but Rue still believes it should stay put, in case some animal gets caught out in the rain.

PRESLEY

"Hey, Pres, what did you find out about the kid your folks had living with them?"

"Not much of anything, really. I've been snooping around the house a little. Even let myself in for about an hour. Didn't see any signs of life but you could sure tell they'd had a little girl in there. A pink room where mine used to be. Maybe they shipped the kid off to stay with somebody else when Mom went to the Home. She's probably waiting for a funeral like I am."

"If your folks took in a kid, there're neighbors who've met her. All you have to do is a little inquirin'."

"Not many people know I'm back in Tama. I hate to call attention to myself by asking questions."

"Well, I never ask questions either, but I always keep my ears open for anything out of the ordinary. Just the other day, I was in the Bradley Tire Company, and Guy Bradley was busy talking to somebody. What he was tellin' was kinda interestin'. I don't know why exactly."

"I'm listening."

"He was sayin', 'I just sold that old taco wagon I had sitting out front. Got fifty bucks for it. It was the Wapiti kid that bought it.' He must be back staying at his old place. I tried to put things together in my mind, but nothing really makes sense. Wapiti don't want to sell tacos. The whole business is just a little puzzlin'. Might be something you'll want to gnaw on."

"Yeah. Not sure what to make of it except the old Wapiti place is just down the road from my mom. Might be worth a look. I've got nothing but free time right now."

"Wouldn't hurt to spread a little fear. If that imposter, is around Tama, she can probably be persuaded to leave."

"That's what I'm thinking. She'll either leave of her own free will or I'll give her some help."

SIXTEEN

Austin and Glory intend to spend most of the following day making the inside of Toby's Tacos livable.

In spite of an abundance of shade, temperatures are climbing, and it's still early. Austin takes off his shirt, and Glory starts to do the same. "Ah ... leave it on! Ladies have to suffer," he teases. Glory obeys but looks puzzled.

The inside of the brown trailer appears to have been through a tornado. Tables and cupboards are broken and piled in all directions.

"It sure isn't much like your room on the farm," comments Austin when they first step inside. "For one thing, this is less space than you're used to."

"That's okay. This will be cozier. And more grown up."

"I guarantee that. Why don't we put all this stuff out on the ground so we can see what we're working with?"

"That's a good idea." Glory appears grateful Austin's leading the project. She looks at a loss about how to create order out of chaos.

"What do we want inside besides a bed, a chair, and a table?" he asks, trying to involve the girl in the planning.

She pauses for a moment. "I can't think of anything."

"Well, if it were me, I'd want a shelf in case I had books. And a rod for clothes. Maybe a couple of drawers for underthings and shorts. You'll have to use the toilet in the house. Their back door is pretty close to you, and they never lock it."

"It sounds perfect, but I don't see any bed or those other things you named."

"Not a problem. I can build most anything if I have some scraps to work with. Wanna watch, or would you rather go in the house where it's cool? "

"I'll stay. I like to watch you. You're my first man."

"No kidding?" That's a surprising idea, but it must be a fact. Elsa's husband passed away when Glory was still a very young child, and she didn't see other men even in passing. Only a glimpse of a fully-clothed Presley in the front yard when she was grown. She must've dismissed the untrustworthy Dr. Brown. Austin is glad he's recently been visiting the gym so Glory's first countable man is, hopefully, a half-way pleasant sight.

"Somebody was here!" Glory calls from outside the trailer.

"What makes you say that?" Austin isn't immediately worried. They only moved her into the spot yesterday. She must be imagining things.

"I can see writing," she tells him. "It's hard to read, but it wasn't there yesterday. I looked at all the outside walls after we finished painting."

Austin proceeds to check out the mysterious lettering, but it isn't clear enough for him to make out. Across the back end of the vehicle are faint words written with a regular ballpoint on the metal siding. After studying the spot, he can see it says, FouNd YOU. He, too, is sure the writing wasn't there earlier. But there's hardly been time for someone to discover the trailer. Unless the writer of the words has been following them or has been camping in their woods.

Not wanting to go there, Austin explores other possibilities. The man at the tire company who took their money might be the culprit. Maybe that guy is Presley. Neither Austin nor Glory would recognize her brother if they ran smack into him. Austin decides not to make a big deal out of the sign. Any explanations are unnerving, and he doesn't want to scare Glory unless he has to.

"We must've missed it before. It'll just take a minute to cover with paint."

Glory seems willing to forget the ominous message since Austin appears unconcerned. But his demeanor hides his real fears. The words weren't a friendly greeting, and changing the trailer color isn't going to deter that person.

While Austin does the paint touch-up, Glory happily goes about making herself useful. She fills a bucket with water from the hose and gives the place a good scrubbing. At one point, Austin hears her say, "Oh, my!" She comes to the door and announces, "Somebody lost a diamond necklace."

He looks at her find but sees at once it's a cheap costume piece. "Not diamonds. Just rhinestones. But it's pretty. You have a nice souvenir of our cleaning day."

She hands over the trinket as though it belongs to him as owner of the trailer. "No. Keep it," he tells her. "Toby's wife should've been more careful with her jewelry." And he fastens it around her neck as carefully as if it's a priceless heirloom.

The lady in diamonds hands Austin nails and tools while he completes the remodel of the brown box. In one afternoon, the place is transformed and awaiting only some blankets and curtains which he is pretty sure Liz will furnish. When all is said and done, Toby's Tacos likely looks better than it has since its original construction.

"Well, you're a home owner now. And a lady with fine jewelry." He gestures toward the necklace which he imagines she'll wear every day in the near future.

"I should really put it in a safe place." Glory thinks for a minute. "I know. Jewels are perfect for my treasure box."

"You have a treasure box, huh? That's interesting. Did I see it when we were in your room?" He thinks of Presley ransacking all her private belongings and hopes the box survived.

"No, and Presley didn't get it. One night I buried it between Mary and Steve so they could guard it for me."

"Smart move! He'd never think to look in the ground."

"Thanks," she says modestly. "Can we go there? I'd like to dig it up. It's been such a long time since I buried it, I can't even remember what I put inside. Probably kid stuff."

"Was the container made of something waterproof? Otherwise, you might find it's all ruined."

"It was an old canister from the kitchen. We never used the one that said TEA on it. It's probably rusty, but I lined it with tin foil. Maybe the stuff inside is okay. You can help me check."

Yet another adventure awaits Austin. He's about to embark on a hunt for buried pieces of Glory's past.

SEVENTEEN

Glory is able to lead Austin directly to the treasure. A rock announcing a dog's grave is midway between her two trees, and a small amount of digging in the dirt beside it uncovers the canister. The word TEA is no longer legible, but the lid seems to have stayed tightly closed. Glory is thrilled to discover this connection with the child she used to be. Austin finds himself becoming more and more interested. He can't imagine what young Glory would have possessed that she felt was worth keeping for the future. He's expecting a few precious rocks and maybe a dog or cat's collar. Those are the kind of items he saved as a little boy. Not the kind of treasure an adult Presley would be interested in.

The two amateur archeologists find a shady spot under Steve to examine the contents of what amounts to a time capsule. Austin is touched that Glory wants to share this private moment with him.

There are several articles inside, and they appear intact. The first is a sizable lock of black hair. "My hair was really long, down to my behind, and then when I was ten, Mama cut it because it was too hard to wash. I loved my long hair. I just couldn't let it all go into the trash. Now it's grown back so guess I don't really need this."

Austin loves picturing Glory as a child with the long tresses. She'd have resembled Rue.

There are a few trinkets that could've belonged to almost any little girl. Then a plastic bag catches his attention. "What's in that?"

"I have to tell you first about the coat," she says, forcing him to be patient. "I found it hanging in the basement." Apparently, Glory'd had free reign of the house. "It's kind of special. It's plaid with a belt." The description doesn't sound like any coat Austin's ever seen, but presumably, this one was a lady's. "I think it would fit me now," she adds, sounding as if the idea has just occurred to her.

Austin remains silent, but he is remembering Wilma's story of how the Beckers discovered a newborn baby – wrapped in a coat.

"When I asked Mama if it was hers, she just said she found it. She didn't even tell me where."

Glory carefully opens the plastic bag and takes out a yellowed newspaper clipping. The heading of the article is TEN YEARS AGO IN TAMA. The Tama News-Herald must have a regular feature that reprints stories from the past. With black-and-white pictures. This story is about an eighth grade class from South Tama School who was on a field trip to the county court house. In the front row of the group is a dark-haired girl in a plaid belted coat. The quality of the photo is too grainy for the student to be easily identified, but the jacket is unique enough to be unmistakable.

"Well," said Austin, unable to decide which way to take the conversation. He doesn't know how much Glory knows about her beginnings.

She explains, "I'm keeping the article because if that girl ever comes here to pick up her coat, she might like to see her picture. She'd be happy she was in the paper."

A faded Polaroid photo is almost hidden under the newspaper story. Glory is eager to show him. "This is a tiny baby. I don't know if it's me or that coat girl, but I like looking at it."

"Why didn't you just ask your mother who it is?"

"Because I sort of stole it. She might be mad and make me put it back. Do you think I'm bad?"

So many secrets for the girl to come to grips with. "No, Glory, I don't think you're a bit bad." And he pats her hand.

"Before I bury the can again, I have to put in the diamond necklace. Even if it isn't real, it looks like it is. Treasure boxes should have something that looks valuable."

Austin wonders what stories she read that gave her that idea, but it's a harmless one, so he helps her remove the costume jewelry from her neck and place it at the very bottom, where "it will be safe from robbers." His touch tells him they've overlooked something. An envelope lies upside down and wedged into the bottom of the tea tin. Miraculously, it seems to be clean and dry.

The treasure can has already revealed a lot about its lovely young owner, and it isn't finished yet. The front side of the envelope shows a handwritten message: IMPORTANT and below that, the words DO NOT DESTROY.

"Where did you find this, Glory?" Austin is beginning to see his new friend as a pack rat. He notices, however, that the envelope is still sealed, so she must be an especially honest pack rat. "Do you even know what's inside?"

"No. I was real young and couldn't read well. I just liked the idea of having something important. I'd found it in Mama's recipe box. I thought it might be her secret cornbread recipe. She must've forgot about the envelope, and so did I."

Of course, Austin has no way of knowing what's in the envelope, and he feels a little ashamed for wanting to open it when Glory has resisted. However, he doesn't feel ashamed enough to keep from asking, "Don't you think you should find out if it's something Elsa will want to see again while she's alive?"

"Okay." And she tears into it with no apparent reservations. The contents look like an official document of some sort. Glory hands the paper to him for clarification. Austin's instincts click in just before he sees the heading, LAST WILL AND TESTAMENT.

"We'll deliver this to your mom," he says.

Glory nods, showing no curiosity about the piece of paper.

They repack the treasure can and rebury it. This time it holds a beautiful diamond necklace. "You need to find a more long-lasting container," Austin tells Glory as he slips the envelope into the glove compartment of his truck when he opens the door for her.

At night when everyone is asleep, he brings out the *important* document and reads it word for word.

I, Elsa Becker, being of sound mind on this 20th day of July, 1995, do bequeath my worldly possessions as follows:

To my natural son Presley, a mother's love and wishes for an improved life. May he use his God-given brain to bring some good into the world during any time he isn't in jail.

To our dear daughter and joy of our lives, Glory Dawn Becker, I leave ownership of the farm, 300 acres in rural Tama, including the house and out buildings.

If I become unable to care for myself, I will end my days at the Cassidy Care Center. My checking and savings accounts will be enough to pay any expenses to them that are not covered by my Nursing Home Insurance. If any money is left in the bank upon my death, Glory Dawn is entitled to it. The burial plot at Maple Leaf Cemetery and stone with her name on it is hers also.

The will shows Wilma Becker and Pastor P. J. Cummings of First Baptist in Tama as signed witnesses.

The surprising item in the envelope is a black and white family photo. On the back side is written *Burt and Elsa Becker with new daughter Glory. Taken on the day of her birth, August 13, 1989.* That picture must have been courtesy of Wilma.

Austin realizes he's very fond of that infant with the full head of bushy black hair, as well as the grownup version now sleeping in the woods. It's hard to believe she grew up only two miles from him.

He'll tell Gray their mission for next week is clear. They must take the will to Attorney Bill Hogan. Glory's future should then be secure. Except Presley won't be happy. And he isn't going to stand by and watch a stray woman live unharmed on *his* farm.

EIGHTEEN

The weekend has passed slowly for Austin. Ever since he heard Wilma's sketchy account of Glory's arrival, he's told himself it will be impossible to track her roots. But after seeing the girl's treasured newspaper photo and hearing about the plaid coat in Elsa's basement, he's been dying to investigate. It looks like those clues could easily lead to Glory's back story. First, he intends to trace the middle school girl in the photo.

He arrives at South Tama School at eight forty-five in the morning, hoping certain staff members work during the summer months. Luckily, the superintendent's secretary is in her office. The name plaque on her desk says *Marilyn McDaniel.* Austin opens with some small talk and then gets to his question. "I ran across a photo from a 2002 issue of the Tama Herald. Do you think you might remember some students from that year?"

"Well, I might, but I have to tell you that my memory isn't what it was when you were in school. I've seen a lot of students pass through."

"Here it is," and he produces the article. "I'm interested in the identity of the girl on the front row, plaid jacket."

Marilyn didn't have to look long. "That's easy. It's Mariel Bluesong. It was when children from the tribe went to school in this building. They have a nice school on the settlement now."

"Did you ever talk to her or know anything about her?"

"I sure did. She was actually a student helper in this office for a while when she was a senior. Very sweet girl. And smart. Missed quite a bit of school at the end of the year, but she kept her grades up."

"Did you know her parents?"

"I never met them, but I heard they didn't like her boyfriend. They were full-blood Meskwaki, and the boy was white. He was older, too, which they didn't approve of. I think she had to sneak around to see him."

"He'd already graduated?"

"Yes, a few years before. He was what we called a townie. Worked odd jobs around Tama. Not likely to ever make much money. Most folks thought Mariel could do better than Presley Becker. Just too bad she had to die."

Austin was rendered speechless. He'd received two shocks in two seconds. Mariel Bluesong dated Presley, and she's dead. He hopes the two facts aren't connected.

"Did you know her?" asks Marilyn, taking his silence for grief.

"Not really. I'm looking into something for a friend. She'll be real disappointed to hear Mariel passed away. Was she sick?"

"No. It was late in the summer or early fall. Soon after she graduated. She was on an outing with a few friends to the Tama County Lake. She went in swimming and got a cramp or something and nobody noticed in time. Real sad. I don't know why the good kids always seem to be the ones to go."

"Do you know much about the Becker guy?"

"No, I started here after he was out. I know he was a farm boy. He was pretty nice looking if I remember right and seemed friendly. Then, I think it was soon after Mariel graduated when he got jailed for armed robbery. Emptied the cash register at Casey's and shot at the clerk on his way out. Didn't hurt the man, but the attempt made the crime more serious. It pretty much put an end to

Presley's romance with Mariel. I doubt they ever saw each other again."

"What about Mariel's mom?"

"I don't know. Someone told me Danee Bluesong had some kind of breakdown when she lost Mariel. Got into alcohol. She hasn't been in Tama for a long time now. Don't even know if she's still living."

"That's a sad story," managed Austin. It was sad for so many people.

"Yeah. A tragedy is what it was."

On his walk down the school corridor on his way out, Austin passes the large composites of all the graduating classes. Curiosity raises its head, and he finds himself looking eagerly for South Tama's most unlikely sweethearts. First, the Class of 1985. Presley Becker grins at him. The photo makes the boy appear mischievous and likeable, a charmer by the looks of it. Nothing like the man Austin's pictured after hearing him so often compared to the devil. It's easy to imagine this graduate as a man with a future – husband, father, community leader. Such erroneous impressions make him lose all faith in high school yearbooks and wall photos.

Further down the hall is pictured the more recent Class of 1989. That date rings a bell. It was the year Glory was born. The year a Meskwaki girl abandoned a baby wrapped in a coat.

As a healthy male, he's good at scanning a group to see if there are any attractive girls. It takes only a second to pick out the most striking of this bunch. She's obviously Native American and proud of it. Her dark skin and hair set off a gleaming smile. She looks like a happy person. What made her want Presley? Maybe he was good to her. Maybe she thought he loved her.

"People always like to look at those pictures," comes a gruff voice from close by. Austin looks over to see a man pushing a broom. The school janitor, from his memory, is usually the guy who knows everyone and can tell you all the gossip.

"Yeah." Austin replies. "It's hard to walk down this hall without stopping. I used to be one of them, but I like to look at the older classes. Do you remember a lot of these kids?"

"Sure do. Some of them leave impressions that don't go away – some good, some bad. Lots of them I still see all the time 'cause they stayed around Tama."

Austin can't pass up the opportunity to ask, "Do you remember Mariel Bluesong and Presley Becker?"

"Oh, yeah. Funny you should pair them together like that. Most folks didn't even know they were a couple."

"But you did. How was that?"

"Well, sometimes Mariel would hang around after school. I'd talk to her a little bit before Presley showed up. He'd stop by after he got off work, and she'd leave with him. If she'd been my daughter, I'd have forbid it, but I barely knew her. She always gave him a little kiss when she saw him, so I didn't feel like she was going anywhere against her will."

"What kind of reputation did Presley have?" He kept hoping somebody would say a good word about the guy.

"Well, I don't really know. He was older than the students around here, so I never did hear anybody talking about him. He had an unusual name. Always wondered if his mom was an Elvis fan and how Mariel got mixed up with him in the first place. She wasn't a big talker, so he must've been the one to get things started."

"Suppose he gave her a ride somewhere once," Austin guessed. "Twenty years ago, not all girls knew how careful they should be about getting in with guys they didn't know."

"I do remember one particular date of theirs, come to think of it." The janitor props his broom against the wall like he's getting serious about telling his story. "It was the night of one of the proms. Must have been when Mariel was a junior. I think she was out sick for her senior one. I had to stay here and work because the dance was in the gym. It was my job to make sure no kids came .through any doors except the one where they collected money. The school had a rule. You couldn't invite a date who was out of school or from another town. Well, I guess that didn't make Mariel too happy because the only guy she wanted to ask had graduated several years ago."

The janitor sits on a nearby bench, so Austin joins him. "I remember Mariel in this hallway that night, just standing around. She seemed to be waiting on somebody. Presley, a'course. The banquet was over, and it was dark outside. The dance was getting ready to start, and she just kept standing. I tried to make conversation. Felt sort of sorry for her. Don't know sometimes why the school makes the rules they do. Still, if Presley showed up, I knew I couldn't allow him to come in. And if Mariel left with him, she couldn't get back in, even if she wanted to. Then I saw his old pickup in the parking lot. 'I've got to go,' she told me."

Austin finds himself listening to the tale with as much interest as if it happened yesterday. "Did you let her leave?"

"I'm just the janitor here, so didn't think I should be making any judgements. I went ahead and opened the door to let her out. 'You can't come back tonight,' I told her. She said she wouldn't want to. Well, I watched her go to that old pickup and get in wearing her long shiny formal. They just sat there for a while. Of course, I couldn't see what they were doing. Figured if he tried to assault her, I'd hear a scream. But all I heard was music blaring from the car radio. Pretty soon they got out and danced together in the parking lot. Guess they decided to have their own prom. I have ta tell ya, it seemed like they were having a real good time. Maybe if two kids are in love, they don't want a bunch of teachers and other people around. They left in the pickup after a while. I worried a little about what all they did then. You hear all kinds of stories about prom night, most not good. But at least Mariel and Presley didn't get in a car accident. I'd have felt terrible. Like it was my fault."

"And I thought a janitor would have a boring job. Makes you wonder if those two would've gotten married if she'd lived."

"It's possible. They kept going out all through her senior year. But I'd bet her folks would've fought marriage, him being older. I figure they wanted Mariel to maybe go to college and come back and marry somebody from the tribe."

Austin is glad he didn't rush away from the school without hearing what the janitor had to say. The mental picture of Mariel and Presley dancing to his radio is a touching one for some reason. He's learning that even the nastiest person can have a soft side. It seems to him like some folks are born bad, but some can go either way. Life circumstances decide what course they'll take. Presley's decision to carry a gun and to commit robbery must have turned him into the scorned outcast he is today, somebody different than the young man in the class photograph. Someone whose mother doesn't even claim him.

◆◆◆

After the schoolhouse visit, Austin is set for an attorney one. It is important to hand Elsa's will over before it gets away again. He feels sure Presley is willing to go to great lengths to locate it so it needs to be in a secure place.

Luckily, he catches Bill Hogan in his office. "Thanks for getting this to me," he says when Austin presents the badly creased document from the treasure box.

"It contains some family secrets," Austin feels obliged to mention. "It's important they stay secret until the will is read."

"Don't worry, Austin. Confidentiality is our business, and there's no need for me to read the will before the time comes. I'm just glad Elsa's found somebody to assist her with these matters. The poor woman has ended up pretty alone in the world."

NINETEEN

None of the previous day's revelations at the high school are shared with anyone in the house. Unless he learns there's a reason for the others to know, Austin will keep the Presley/Mariel relationship to himself. Glory is being bombarded with all kinds of new discoveries. It seems to him she has enough to deal with without dredging up the truth about Presley. How can it help her to know the devil's spawn could be her father?

Austin spent five years blaming his natural mother for keeping the facts of his birth from him *for his own good.* Now here he is, doing the same thing to Glory.

◆◆◆◆

The time has come for Glory to pay Elsa another visit. Much has happened since the last time. Austin decides to play it by ear when it comes to talking about the will. Elsa, like her daughter, has had a lot thrown at her in the past month. So far, she seems to be hanging on to her coherent thought, but just barely. More surprises might have a damaging effect.

Liz was good enough to make fresh cornbread in the morning. Austin judges it to be the best he's ever tasted so, hopefully, Elsa will appreciate it, too. Both he and Glory start to worry when she takes the container and comments, "I wonder if I'll like cornbread."

Glory isn't discouraged. "I think you will, Mama. It's just like you used to make. I even brought a bottle of syrup. Sorry it's cold."

Austin sits in one of the two chairs in the room and lets Glory prepare the snack for her mom. He can't stop himself from testing the waters, from attempting the conversation about disposing of Elsa's assets, even though indications are that today isn't one of her most lucid. "We've made some progress since we saw you last, Elsa. With finding the new will, I mean."

"You found a new will?" she asks with interest. "What did it say?"

"That you want to leave everything to your daughter when the time comes."

Elsa looks baffled. "Do I have a daughter? I thought Presley was a boy. A sweet little boy."

Austin and Glory exchange a look. "This is your daughter Glory who's standing by your bed. Don't you recognize her?"

"Oh. . . yes. I . . . just woke up from a nap and can't think straight. Sometimes I dream Presley is still my little man, Burt's and my pride and joy. I don't know where he went."

Glory patiently brings her mother back to reality. Austin can imagine she's done so many times in the recent past. "Mama, Presley has been in jail, but he's out now. Do you want to see him?"

"Uh . . . no. Somebody changed him. He robs and shoots at people now. He'll take my farm. Might even shoot me."

Austin is very glad they found the will. Today's confusion might be temporary, but Elsa no longer seems of sound enough mind to compose a new one.

"Mama?" asks Glory. "Are you saying Presley used to be a good person? Somebody I'd like?"

"Oh, my. He was, my darling girl. Presley was loving and kind. Not mean at all. But that was when he was still in school. " She looked straight into Glory's eyes. "You don't want to let the devil get hold of you. He'll suck out all your goodness."

The nurse's aide came into the room. "We've been a little concerned about Elsa lately. Her mind goes in and out. Some days she's her old self, and other days she's what you've probably been hearing, pretty muddled. We're trying a new medication that might clear the air."

"If we leave, can you give her another chance at the cornbread?" asks Glory.

"I sure can, honey. And I'll call you when she's thinking better so you can come back. It's all just a matter of timing."

"Thanks," Austin replied as he got up to leave. "Glory and I have to run some errands. We'll see you again soon, Mrs. Becker."

Glory leaves the room before Elsa's parting words. "Okay," the old woman says pleasantly, "And you can ask Mariel if she wants to come."

Dementia talking? Or does she know more than we think?

◆◆◆◆

The drive back and forth to Waterloo has been taking far too much time away from Austin's objectives in Tama. It's time he finds a way to marry his day job with his family obligations for the summer. Hence, he is at his computer composing a pitch to present to his supervisor in the Courier Lifestyles section. This proposal is for a five-part series of articles, a project that will not only *allow* him to spend time on the settlement, but will *require* him to.

He has made no secret at work of the fact he's Meskwaki or that he's been living for several years away from the tribe. His decision to do that has been a unique one and one that many Courier readers might find interesting but won't be hearing. His reasons are highly personal and, naturally, won't appear in the paper. However, he can make use of the homesickness that has been the result. He may not be so honest as to describe how many nights he cried himself to sleep, but he can, hopefully, tell some of the sights and sounds and people who have occupied his dreams since he jumped ship in 2005.

Throughout his years in northeast Iowa, he was a mere forty-five miles from his childhood home. But culturally, he was a world away. A series of stories entitled *What I've Missed* can involve interviewing several members of the tribe and taking colorful photos. Hopefully, he'll be able to convey how much he loves the place where he spent his early years and make his readers appreciate it also. He's working hard to use his best writing to present the idea.

"What's shakin', dude?" A head peeking in the door of the trailer disturbs him until he sees it's only Archie.

"Not much," is Austin's usual reply. It isn't so much that he doesn't have news. He just knows Archie wouldn't be that interested. When he talks about his work, his friend's mind appears to wander. Austin admits to sounding boring sometimes. The two young men don't have as much to talk about as they did in high school. Nobody's fault. Their worlds are just different now.

"I've been thinking," Archie says with a grin.

"Ha. Never thought you'd be wasting your time doing that," Austin replies in fun. Actually, his curiosity is peaked. Arch doesn't usually appear to have much on his mind. "Sit down and tell me about it." Glory is in the house, so the two guys are free to chat about anything, even girls.

Archie doesn't even hit the couch before he begins. "I have a big decision to make."

"Aw-oh. Are you thinking about asking Drinda to marry you?" Austin thought he saw that coming when they were playing cards at Archie's place.

"No . . . I mean, maybe. I know that's what she wants, but I really don't make enough money to do anything like taking on another person. I've decided to look for a job that pays better."

"Good for you. Hope there's something around here like that."

"There isn't. Nothing I'd be good at." Arch has apparently given the situation some thought. "I might have to move out of town."

"So do it. A bigger city would give you more opportunities. You might even want to go to some kind of trade school."

"I did some lookin', and I met a guy in Des Moines who said he'll help me." Archie takes a deep breath and looks dead serious. "I'm just scared to leave the settlement."

He has Austin's attention. "What are you scared of? That you won't find anything? Or that people around here will give you a hard time for going?"

"Both. I've never lived anywhere else. I've barely been out of Tama. Drinda neither. And we might make a few enemies around here if we desert the tribe."

"You wouldn't be deserting anybody." Austin thinks he understands what Archie is expecting. "If the other guys make cracks about it, it's just because they'd like the do the same thing but don't have the nerve. You'd be showing them it's possible to get away, so you'd be doing them a favor."

"Maybe. But Drinda says she stayed in Marshalltown once for three nights and didn't sleep a single wink. That might happen to me. And I need my sleep."

Austin is silent for several seconds. He's contemplating his friend's dilemma and wondering if he thought the same way a few years ago. If he hadn't had the problems with Liz, maybe he'd never have gone anywhere, never become a writer.

"Just tell your family you'll come back a lot to visit them. They'll get used to it, and you'll all value each other more after you've been living apart for a while."

"I's hoping that's what you'd say. But I may have to ask you to explain that to my folks. They're not going to get it."

"When you go to tell them, you'll find the words. And believe me, getting away for even a short time will be good for you. Look at it as a vacation. It'll give you a whole new appreciation for life here. Everybody needs a change of scenery every twenty years or so." *Just ask Glory.*

TWENTY

The hour is nearing midnight, and Austin is wide awake. Again. One would expect sleep to come easily. Here he is, hanging out in the country where there are no bright lights or emergency vehicles interrupting the peaceful atmosphere. Nothing but the sounds of nature which were his lullaby for twenty-one years of his life.

Austin's boss at the Courier no more than read the pitch for his series than he called Austin to give him the go-ahead. Plenty of work awaits him now, but at least he doesn't have to worry about losing his job. Unfortunately, making decisions in one area of his life doesn't help other areas. His current restlessness has been brought on by internal conflicts unrelated to the paper. So many family problems are still unresolved. After all, he isn't Superman. He isn't even a man with life experience – just a regular guy who has a desire to help out but no real idea how to do it.

One issue is new. He's seen it coming for a couple of weeks. Glory. Even though he closed the book on romance a while ago, he didn't count on Glory. Tonight, for instance, he wishes she were in the trailer with him. No matter where he is or what he's doing, he needs her beside him. Is it love or just some sort of protective instinct?

Thoughts of a protector remind him of Murray. He looks out the door then to see if the dog is nearby. Gray has been taking him along on his late-night walks and tonight is no different. Austin could have been jealous of Murray's affection for another guy, but he knows it's a blessing. Gray has a companion now who doesn't preach to him about what he should and shouldn't do, who doesn't worry about him or show disappointment when Gray has a meltdown. Murray just accepts the man and does his best to help where he can. Fortunately, blood hounds have extremely sensitive noses. Though he has no formal training, Austin is pretty sure his dog will recognize trouble if Gray's blood sugar drops. At least, the animal would be more apt to than any human, including Gray himself.

Austin misses his canine friend being with him but knows he will soon be scratching at the door when the man with the crutches is safely in his house.

Having finally dozed off, Austin is awakened by a frantic barking. *Oh, God, is Gray having problems?* Austin grabs moccasins and is out of the trailer in one second flat. But there's no sign of Murray, nor of Gray. The blood hound's howl is coming from back in the trees, in the direction of the taco trailer. A heavy cloud of smoke drifts toward him. *No wonder Murray's upset!*

To his immense relief, Glory is standing just outside her door enveloped in a quilt. Liz is trying to get her to move further away from the smoking trailer, but she won't go. *Where's Gray?* In order to get inside, he'd had to navigate two steps and a high door jam. It would've been difficult, but judging from Glory's words, that's exactly what he's done. "Make him come out! Let it burn!"

Before Austin can do that, his father appears in the doorway of the trailer. The smoke is dissipating, but the traces make it obvious there's been some sort of fire inside. Gray descends the step on his rump, and Austin helps him stand on his crutches. "What in the world happened?"

Gray calmly reports, "Murray smelled the smoke right away. There never were any real flames that I saw."

Austin thinks Gray is avoiding the question, so he gives it another try, "Could you tell what started it?" Glory doesn't cook and doesn't even have a heat source. He doubts she owns any matches. She can't afford cigarettes even if she knows what they are.

Gray can see Glory is occupied talking to Liz, so he says softly, "It was a match, in the sink under the open window. There was nothing for it to catch right there, so it apparently just burned for a few seconds and then fizzled out. Someone must have thrown it through the window and run away. He might be close by right now." Both men look among the trees trying to spot any suspicious movement.

A rustling noise catches Gray's attention. "Somebody's running through the trees! That fool Presley is still around, and I'm going to track his ass down." And Gray starts to run like a man with two legs. Except he doesn't have two legs. He falls hard on the rocky ground. "Damn!"

"Dad! Are you hurt? I'll help you!" Rue is eager to come to his rescue even though she weighs only thirty-six pounds.

Austin realizes his father is probably as embarrassed as he is angry. Despite knowing the man wouldn't want his assistance, he automatically reaches down to help. Gray predictably slaps his and Rue's arms away. He wants to get up on his own power, but all who are watching realize that won't happen unless he has something to hold onto. Murray calmly stops in such a way as to offer a bench in front of the one-legged man. Gray immediately understands the dog's thinking. He puts his hands on Murray's back and pushes himself up. Rue is ready with the crutches.

Everyone feels like cheering, but there's a collective sense that Gray wants no celebration. He failed to catch the arsonist so isn't feeling very proud at the moment.

Stupid, stupid, stupid, Austin chastises himself. To think, he took for granted Glory was safe in a place totally open to any demented person who wants to cause trouble. "I guess we're lucky the guy didn't go inside and do something awful to her."

"The fire *could've* been awful," Gray says. "There were no lights on. The trailer would've burned down with Glory asleep inside, and no one could've proved who did it. Or she could've been overcome with smoke. Murray's nose saved her life."

"Along with you. You beat me here. And you didn't stumble around like a crippled man. You reacted like an able-bodied cop. We don't need proof. There's only one person who has reason to hurt her. And he's just desperate enough to risk starting a forest fire."

"Wish I could've caught up with him. The weasel is lucky I'm disabled. But I'll think of something. You and I will make him sorry he ever terrorized a lady. We aren't going to put up with this kind of thing again."

Austin is flattered his dad includes him in his plans for Presley. Gray has the mental training of a cop, and Austin has the legs. Maybe together they can outsmart a scrawny ex-con.

Liz takes Glory into the house for the rest of the night, but Austin is already making plans for the future. He can't set traps around the trailer clearing because Murray will probably step on one of them before the prowler does. Two things are certain. Glory isn't safe alone at night in the woods, and the family has to be able to sleep nights.

The day following the fire is taken up by another camper-cleaning. Austin and Glory work together to scrub and disinfect the place. Liz provides a different set of curtains and finally, the place smells fresh and inviting. They all know it's an illusion. Even locking the door wouldn't have prevented last night's arson attempt. And most nights are too warm to keep the windows closed. The only way to insure no one tries to harass Glory is to have her spending nights near Austin or Gray. Even if Rue didn't sleep in a single youth bed, he wouldn't want to put Glory in with her. There is no way, he'll endanger his sister by placing her in the path of Presley.

Aloud, Austin volunteers, "Well, Glory, I guess you're going to get to stay in the Airstream for a while. Along with me this time. I'll make sure we can both fit, and then you'll have free accommodations. You might as well get used to sleeping in there since I promised you can have it when I go back to Waterloo."

"I keep forgetting that. I was just getting used to Toby's."

"You can still hang out there. During the day you can spend time reading or whatever in the brown trailer, but after dark, you'll be with me."

"What about Murray? Will he be there, too?" Glory has become very fond of the dog and always looks for him when he wanders out of their sight.

"I've been thinking he should sleep at Gray's feet instead of mine. This will be a good time to start it. If you and I have a dog that size lying with us in bed, we won't be able to move." Austin likes the sound of "lying with us in bed".

The temporary family visits on the porch until almost eleven o'clock. Finally, they adjourn to their bedrooms. Murray goes with Gray and Liz, and Glory with Austin.

"Uh . . . one thing we better talk about," Austin begins when his trailer mate starts to remove her clothes. "Rue mentioned you sleep in your nakeds. That's really not going to work out while you're staying with me."

"Does it get cold in here?" she asks in all innocence. "I'm pretty warm blooded. We didn't heat the upstairs at the farm."

"Well, you see, the thing is . . . you're a girl and I'm a guy, and it just wouldn't be a good thing." He has the feeling he might get to be the person to explain the facts of life to this young lady. But not tonight. He wants the rest of tonight to be uneventful. "I'll give you a t-shirt. It's thin. You won't get too hot."

"Well, okay. I saw Liz has a pretty nightgown. You can see through it, so I know I wouldn't get too warm if I had one like that."

Just what I need. He answers her with as much vagueness as he can. "Someday. Here, you can undress behind the shower curtain. It's kind of like a little closet."

When she steps out of the shower wearing a proper pair of sweat pants and a t-shirt, Austin is disappointed. His old clothes do very little to disguise the girl's sex appeal. He has dressed himself in a similar outfit. They are both going to be sweating before long.

"Why don't *you* have to change in the shower?" Glory inquires. "Because only girls have to hide? Mama always turned out the lights to change for bed. But I don't think Daddy did."

Austin has no answer to that mystery. "Let's see if we can get comfortable. I don't have a fan, but I can buy one tomorrow."

"Do you have a radio?"

"No. Are you used to going to sleep with a radio playing?"

"No, but I always thought it'd be nice. We had one, but it was in the kitchen, and Mama didn't want me to take it upstairs."

"I have a CD player, so I can get that going for tomorrow night."

"We get to sleep like this tomorrow night, too?"

"Oh, yeah. As long as Presley's on the loose."

"Better not touch me," warns Glory. "'Some germs may be left over from all the years I was sick. I don't want them to get on you."

"No worries. Germs don't live outside the body that long."

Glory sighs and closes her eyes. She's asleep almost instantly and, in spite of the germ concerns, her right arm is involuntarily thrown over Austin's chest. He is afraid to move so stays immobile as he often does when sleeping with Murray. It isn't unusual to awake with a cramp after a night of insuring the dog's comfort.

He remembers watching a real old movie where Clark Gable hung a blanket between him and Claudette Colbert so they could sleep in the same bed. He is wracking his brain to find a way to duplicate that idea. *I must be a throwback to a different era. But not because I want to be.* If he were with a girl like Anita, it wouldn't be a problem, but Glory is a whole different matter.

After a few minutes, Austin lays his left hand over hers. Even if he could have figured out how to do it, there isn't room for a blanket to hang between them. *How long can I live like this?*

He hopes Presley is sleeping on the hardest and buggiest ground around.

TWENTY-ONE

After a largely sleepless night, Austin is more than ready to work off some of his frustrations at the gym. When he and Gray are finished, they drive over to the casino for a cup of coffee or, in Gray's case, diet soda.

Chatting with his natural father is a treat. Murray, his Meskwaki Dad, as kind as the man was, wasn't very talkative. Hence, he and Austin didn't share much conversation. In Murray's defense though, most young boys don't like to sit and visit with an adult for more than a couple of minutes. If the man had lived longer, he and Austin might have had some good talks.

Anyone watching today from nearby probably can't guess the relationship of Austin and Gray. Only sixteen years separate them, and when Gray is in a good mood, as he is after a workout, he looks very youthful and handsome, like he could be a peer of Austin's. Today's good mood doesn't last long.

"Did Liz ever mention a guy named Skyler?" he asks when his soda arrives.

"No, but we haven't talked that much since I've been here. Is Skyler somebody I ought to know?"

"Not unless you've heard her talk about him."

Austin thinks for a moment. "Not a word. Does he live around here?"

"No. Oklahoma." Then Gray adds with little enthusiasm, "He's my younger brother."

"Really?" *My uncle.* "See him often?"

"Not since before I moved back to Tama. He's single and girls fall all over him."

Austin chuckles. "Those Morgan brothers are hot, huh?"

"*He* is. Just ask him. People got us mixed up in school. We were just a couple of Indians who looked the same to the whites, but Liz could always tell us apart."

"She never dated him, did she?"

"No, but he tried. He had a big crush on her. Maybe just because I did."

"I'm surprised he hasn't come here for so long, especially when you had your amputation."

"It's a long trip. Plus, he couldn't be bothered. And he might be kind of embarrassed he hasn't done much yet with his life. He was always the smartest of the two of us. I was the jock; he was the writer."

"Oh, yeah? What does he write?" Austin is thinking he inherited his love of writing from both his uncle and Liz.

"Novels. But I've never read any of them. He'd have probably come around sooner if they'd hit the best seller list and made him rich. That would be something that would really impress Liz."

It seems to Austin that Gray is being pretty hard on his brother. And Liz. *So what, if they both like to write?*

"He's going to be stopping on his way to Illinois though, for some reason," Gray continued. "Called me yesterday."

"I get the impression you don't want to see him."

"I don't. We've always been rivals but pretty evenly matched. Now I feel like I'm the definite loser. He'd be the kind to take advantage of something like that, too. He'll see my handicap as his big chance to make a move on Liz."

"Let him try. I don't care if Brad Pitt came by. She isn't in the market for anybody else. She loves only one Morgan guy."

"She used to. But why wouldn't she be interested if there's a man who looks like me and talks like me but is whole? Switching to him would be like making a trade-in for the same make of car without the wear and tear. Plus he'd probably write her a poem."

"I don't want to hear that kind of talk. It's insulting to your wife. You make her sound as shallow as Anita."

"You don't have any parts missing, so you don't know what things can run through a man's mind."

"It could still happen to me or to Skyler or to any other person. We don't have any guarantees. But if I ever have to lose a body part, I just hope I have a partner like Liz to see me through it." Austin has just surprised himself by admitting he does have some positive thoughts about marriage. "You don't know how lucky you are."

Gray is staring out the window, lost in thought. "Lucky. That's me."

◆◆◆◆

The evening conversation on the porch has slowed, and the group is about ready to go inside away from the mosquitoes when an older model Cadillac approaches. No one speaks. Maybe tribal authorities are here to check on Glory. Austin rises from his chair and gently guides her inside the house. At least no one is going to physically remove her on his watch.

First to alight from the car is a golden retriever, a beautiful animal wearing a blue vest. Murray's ears twitch, but he otherwise, reacts calmly.

The dog is followed by a tall man, Native American. Austin stands watching out the screen door, waiting for the visitor to introduce himself. Before the words are uttered, it becomes apparent the gentleman coming up the ramp is Gray's younger brother, Skyler. They look remarkably alike except the younger Morgan has two legs. Facial expressions are contrasting also.

Skyler's pearly white grin seems fit for the paparazzi. Gray is looking like a thunder cloud.

"Skyler!" Liz is the first to greet him and give him a hug. She may be thinking it's about time he showed up, but her little laugh gives nothing away.

"Hey, Liz! You look great! And Gray, old man, you look better than I expected." Gray receives a man-hug, but Austin can feel his father's tension from the other side of the screen door. He brings Glory outside then to join the family since the visitor doesn't seem to be a threat to her.

Rue, always the greeter, offers a "Hi! Are you my uncle?"

"Yes, I guess I am. You must be Rue. Haven't seen you since you were a baby. You're as pretty as I remember."

"Did you steal my dad's face?" she asks, staring at him.

"No, I wouldn't do something like that. We just look alike because we're brothers."

"I look like my brother, too," declares Rue as she takes hold of Austin's hand.

Rue's words initiate more introductions, including one of Austin and of their *guest* Glory. It probably doesn't hurt if this man from Oklahoma knows her name.

Skyler addresses Gray when he explains, "I'm sorry it took me so long to get here, but I have a good excuse. For the last couple of months anyway." The retriever is still sitting beside the car where she's been told to stay. Obeying a gesture from Skyler, she walks confidently up the ramp and plants herself in front of the man in the wheel chair. "Meet Neka."

The dog sits looking up at Gray as if to say, "Here I am, at your service."

Gray is taken aback but can't help but be intrigued. "Is she yours?" he asks his brother.

"Nope. She's yours. We have a training school for service dogs back home, and I took it on myself to have them get one ready for you. She's specific to hypoglycemia. She'll be your best friend and protect you from the ups and downs of your blood sugar." Skyler looks pleased with himself. He's arrived to save the day.

Austin immediately feels bad for the replaced Murray, but after a second thought, he's happy about the new dog. If this Neka is what she's supposed to be, he'll get his beloved hound back. Murray seems to understand and moves to stand very close to his former master. *Let the female take over if she's up to it.*

Skyler is just what Gray described. Handsome, confident, a beautiful male specimen. If he has one visible flaw, it is that he, himself, believes he's a beautiful male specimen. It's subtle, but a little conceit is evident. "I'm on my way to Chicago, actually. Going to dance in a powwow there. Lots of old friends have asked me to come, so I finally gave in."

Austin is wondering if the brother who's narrowly escaped death would've rated a visit if not for Skyler's command appearance east of Tama.

"Don't you have a wife, yet?" Gray asks, as though to point out the fact that his brother hasn't found a woman who can appreciate perfection.

"No. Have come close a couple of times but managed to escape. Nobody's as special as Elizabeth. And you beat me to her." He gives Gray's wife a look designed to melt her heart. She pretends not to notice.

Austin's sympathies for Murray grow to include Gray. Both are being made to feel like cast-offs. "How long can you stay?" he asks.

"Just overnight. I want to get out of Neka's life so she can bond with Gray. Also I'm expected to dance tomorrow evening, and I'm cutting the time pretty close."

It isn't his exact words that bother Austin. It's his overall attitude. He hasn't once inquired about the state of his brother's health. *I'm glad Liz had the good sense to pick the oldest Morgan guy, leg or no leg.*

Austin is a little surprised his dad hasn't disputed his need for a new service dog. After all, Murray has proven himself to have superior natural abilities. Why does Gray need two animals watching over him? But then, Neka has eyes that would be hard to reject, and Gray will be able to stop feeling guilty for monopolizing his son's pet.

"How much do we owe you, training and all?" Gray asks.

"Forget it," is Skyler's cheerful reply. "You have enough expenses these days, and you're not even able to work. Neka's the least I can do."

"We can afford her. We have the money, and I'll be working again soon," Gray insists.

"No discussion. Everything's paid for."

Here it is. Male pride, sibling rivalry.

"All that's left is a possible visit from the place where I got her. They may want to give you some training and look around to see if the environment here is a healthy one for Neka. I told them there's no problem about that."

Austin wonders how Sky can be sure, since he hasn't been around for so long. Assuming his father has had enough of little brother for the evening, he tries to get everyone organized for the night.

"Okay, Liz. We'd better figure out how we're going to sleep. Murray can come to the trailer with me and Glory."

"I can take the couch," volunteers Sky. Nobody fights him for the privilege.

When everyone is settled, and Murray has had time to run around the yard, Austin again lies in bed, eyes wide open. He feels protective of this household, of Gray's feelings, and of Liz's loyalties. He's counting the hours until the long-lost uncle will be gone. Hopefully, by the time the man comes again, he and Gray can meet on equal terms. He is sure Gray will someday be his old self and not so easily intimidated. It was encouraging to hear him tell

Skyler he is going to work again. Of course, that could be something he came up with on the spot and didn't actually mean.

The walls of the trailer are thin and the window is open, so when a conversation begins on the porch, the words are nearly discernable. But not quite.

"I've thought about you a lot over the years . . ."

"It's been hard lately . . ."

". . . want to help . . ."

". . . can use email . . ."

Little snatches that can be interpreted several ways. Austin has to believe Liz has her reasons for consenting to talk privately with Skyler. But she's human. It's probably been a while since she's had real romance in her life, and she could be weakening. Like Gray said, Liz could trade him in for a new model. Skyler gives the impression he'd be very willing to be the replacement.

Austin doesn't strain his ears to detect a long pause that might indicate a kiss. If that happens, it's better he doesn't know. He just hopes Gray is sleeping and didn't hear his wife slip out the front door. Judging from the fact his father has lain awake during many less stressful nights than this one, the odds are good he now knows all about Liz's rendezvous with Sky.

It is an hour later when the bang of the front door tells Austin it's okay to give up his watch and go to sleep. Surely, the couple he's been listening to aren't going to do anything intimate in the house where Gray and Rue are.

At the end of two hours of backyard instruction and supervised bonding with the golden retriever, Gray is pronounced official master of Neka. It is clear there's a powerful understanding between man and dog. By the time Sky is at his car, ready to make an unremarkable exit, Austin can see his dad is happier and more relaxed than he's appeared all month.

Sky has tears in his eyes when he looks at the dog a last time. "Take care of yourself, man," he tells Gray, "and let me know how you like Neka. If you don't, I'll help you return her. Actually, I think I'll stop again on my way home from Illinois just to be sure."

"Thanks." Gray manages from his wheelchair. He must hate having to look up to see his tall brother. It puts him at a disadvantage. "It was good of you to bring her."

Everybody always says what's expected when it's time for one of them to leave, thinks Austin. *Most people just want the moment to be over without any conflict. Even if you can't stand a person, you'll probably say, "Great to see you again!" When the time comes, I hope my farewell to Glory is more honest.* But he doesn't like to think about it.

Since overhearing the late-night dialogue between Liz and Sky, Austin hasn't stopped stressing. During the evening of Handsome Uncle's departure, he realizes there is nothing that will clear the air except to confront his mom. There's no sense letting himself draw unfair conclusions. Leaving his little sister and Glory watching TV in his trailer, Austin prepares to have a serious talk with Liz. He finds that Gray has gone to bed, and she's on the phone in Rue's room. From outside the door, he hears Liz say, "I've been trying, but it's harder than I expected. Check your email, and we'll talk in a few hours."

Austin quickly goes to the kitchen for some milk. He feels sick. He used to know a ten-year-old kid who was afraid his parents were going to get a divorce because his mom fell in love with another guy. Austin isn't ten, but he knows how that kid felt. Why did Skyler Morgan have to show up just when Austin's almost ready to use the words Mom and Dad again?

From the sound of it, Liz is finding it hard to tell her husband about her and Sky. *I hope it's so hard, she doesn't do it.* Gray is definitely not ready to handle such news.

◆◆◆◆

From that night on, Austin pays close attention to Liz's activities. It's disheartening to have such suspicions about the woman he's always thought was perfect.

Many times over the next few days, he catches her away from family, talking softly on the phone. The name *Sky* is usually uttered often enough he has no doubt who is on the other end of the line. They never seem to run out of things to say to each other. Sometimes the subject sounds deadly serious. Sometimes Liz laughs with delight. The laughter is the hardest to listen to. He has barely heard her laugh around Gray since he arrived.

At other times, he's noticed her texting. That hasn't been something he's seen Liz doing before Skyler came on the scene. He's tempted to borrow her phone when she's sleeping and find out once and for all what she's been typing. However, his mother Ruby was known to say that if you eavesdrop (or read other people's emails or texts) you should be prepared to learn more than you want to know. That is surely the truth. There is nothing Liz could be writing to Skyler that wouldn't be more than Austin wants to know.

TWENTY-TWO

Glory appears to be checking her schedule on Liz's kitchen calendar. "What day is today?"

"August thirteenth. Why?" asks Austin. He's noticed her checking the calendar before like she expects something interesting to appear there. Maybe she's always wished she had some event written down to look forward to. He couldn't imagine twenty years of nothing coming up.

"I thought so," she says with a big smile. "It's my birthday!"

"No kidding? That's great. Is this the big one?"

"I don't know if it's big, but it's number twenty-one. I'm getting pretty old."

He feels a little awkward about it, but Austin assumes a hug is in order. He can't just brush off an occasion like this. Glory laughs with pleasure at his embrace. "I need to have more birthdays," she teases Austin.

He lets go of her to ask, "How do you usually celebrate? I'm sure your folks must have made a big fuss over you even if you did have to stay at home."

Glory enthusiastically describes her past parties. "Mama tried hard to make them nice. She always made a chocolate cake and put the right number of candles on it. We always had spaghetti, because that's my favorite food. And they always gave me a present, usually something nice to wear even though I had nowhere to go to show it off. And they always took my picture with the cake and the present. The one difference from year to year was the way I looked in the photos. I kept getting bigger like I was supposed to, I guess. But the people and place never changed – not even the kitchen wallpaper. The big difference was after Dad died, there were just two of us left."

"A pretty small family," comments Austin, but he's thinking how he would have had a family of two, except for the bevy of relatives and friends who always came for a birthday feast. He remembers his own twenty-first party five years ago as a big occasion on the settlement.

"When I was little," continues Glory, "I'd ask why my brother didn't come. 'He's locked up,' Mama would say. I always wondered if he had spaghetti and chocolate cake where he was, and if he knew his sister was growing up."

Austin avoids pointing out that Presley didn't even know of her existence at that time. "How do you want to celebrate this year, Glory?"

"Well . . . I think we should go see Mama in the Home. And you and me should go someplace together, someplace fancy so I can wear my diamond necklace."

"Those things sound easy except digging up your treasure box to get the necklace doesn't seem like a good use of your time today. We do need to eat out though. The casino is about as fancy as it gets in Tama."

There is really no danger anymore in letting other people see the girl. A person can't be identified as Meskwaki just by the way she eats her lunch.

"Do you think they want a sick person eating there?"

"I don't know, but you aren't sick, so it doesn't matter."

Glory looks uncertain. Her mind must be telling her Austin is right, but she's spent a long time thinking she's an untouchable. The idea doesn't want to die. Austin may as well get used to her doubts.

He sends Liz a text informing her about the special day. Rue should forgive him for whisking the birthday girl away if she will be around the house that evening.

It would be fun for the staff at the Full House Cafe to be aware of the momentous event they are hosting, but Austin decides not to turn his friend into a spectacle. He is pretty sure she'd rather blend in.

He chooses a table for two and lets Glory sit where she can see the entire room. Other people will offer excitement for her, and she can mimic how they act. As expected, she picks up the menu and begins to study it.

"See what sounds good." Austin isn't sure how sharp her reading skills are but figures the colored pictures should help. "Somebody will come and ask you what you want."

"What are you going to get?" she asks, sensing that copying Austin is probably her safest bet.

"I'll just get a sandwich, but it's your birthday, so you can get the most expensive thing they have if you want it."

Glory's eyes scan the menu, but Austin is pretty sure she hasn't decided, when a young man comes up to them and asks, "Can I get you anything to drink?"

"Do you sell milk?" she asks him.

"Of course. Would you like a glass of water to go with that?"

Glory looks at Austin, and he nods affirmative.

"Yes."

"Ice?"

"Ice?" she echoes.

"In your water."

"No?" And she looks at Austin to see if she responded correctly.

When he's gone, Glory predictably asks, "Am I going to get water and milk both?

"Yeah. But you don't have to drink it all."

"I was always told not to take more than you want."

"Yeah. Well. It won't matter today."

A young woman stops at their table. "Have you folks decided what you want for your entree?"

"I'm sorry. I only speak English. Where did the man g—?"

Austin interrupts. "Have you decided what you want to eat, Glory?"

"You can have a few more minutes," offers the waitress.

"I've decided on . . . spaghetti."

"Do you want a side with that?"

Glory looks at the waitress blankly and shakes her head *No.*

"She'll just have the garlic bread and a small tossed salad," adds Austin. "I'll take the tenderloin basket."

"Do sides taste good?" Glory asks when the waitress has gone.

"Some of them do. Sides are salads or something to go along with your main course."

"Like corn or cooked carrots?"

"Yeah. Kinda like that." Austin was enjoying Glory's first restaurant experience. "You never got to go anywhere to eat besides your kitchen?" *I guess nobody did in the old days, but she hasn't even had a school lunch for variety.*

"Once or twice Elsa went to Marshalltown for something and stopped at a place called McDonalds. She brought me food in a sack, but the meat and potatoes were cold, so I didn't think I wanted her to do that again."

"No wonder. Marshalltown is over twenty miles away."

Their food arrives at the table then, along with company. "Hi, ya!"

Austin can't stifle a groan. Anita Kapao still has her old way of showing up just when she is least wanted. This important lunch with Glory is not a good time.

"What are you doing here?" he asks ungraciously.

"I stopped in to see if they can use another waitress. I kinda need a second job, and the casino has always been good to me."

"What happened to your position in the spa?" The last he knew, she gave manicures and pedicures just down the hall from the cafe.

"Oh, some snooty whites moved in and took my place when I got pregnant."

Austin doesn't really want to hear the details. "Well, good luck. Better go ahead and find the person in charge."

"Yeah. I'd better." She's looking at Glory curiously. The girl is showing interest only in her plate of spaghetti. "Next time, baby, I want to meet your girlfriend!" And Anita walks away, attempting to swing her hips like she used to, but the effect of her exit has changed with her size.

Glory gives Austin a puzzled look. "She called you *baby*."

Before he has to think of an explanation, Anita returns with an afterthought. "By the way, that guy Presley Becker you asked me about? I just passed him when I walked through the machines. He was busy throwing his money away— the creep. Second row from this end." And she leaves again with a cheerful little wave.

"She saw Presley?" Glory is immediately on alert. "I didn't know he comes here. We have to leave!"

"No. We're going to eat our lunches. He can't get by with anything here. Besides, I don't think he knows either one of us. And I wouldn't recognize him, would you?"

"If he looks like the devil, I probably would." She's set her fork down, having apparently lost her appetite.

"I always heard the devil disguises himself as a prince." Austin lowers his voice ominously. "The Prince of Darkness."

Glory isn't amused. "His offspring isn't a prince. At least Presley wouldn't look like one. You heard your friend. He's a creep."

Austin spends the rest of the meal trying to steer the conversation to pleasant things. Thankfully, Anita doesn't check in with them after her interview.

It is time for them to find their way among the gamblers to the front exit. He tries to explain the world of gambling, the world that took his Meskwaki mom away from him. "The people sitting at those machines are playing games that can win them money."

Glory smiles mischievously and exclaims "Cha-ching!" Apparently, she's watched TV commercials from other casinos.

Austin laughs. "Yeah, everybody loves the sounds of winning a jackpot. Of course, most of the time people are losing more than they're winning."

To his right in about the location Anita described, is a thin guy with bad posture, hair running back, and a sparse mustache. Austin has to admit, he could play the role of the devil's son. The man is watching his machine work with as much intensity as if he were able to control the outcome. There's no obvious resemblance, but instinct tells Austin this is Glory's no-good relative.

Austin steps between Glory and the mustached man. Her eyes are taking in the room, but her view of Presley is blocked. "I don't see any creepy looking men," she whispers.

"Me either. I think he must've left."

As he makes that statement, someone behind him in the aisle greets the hidden gambler in a quiet voice. "Hey, Pres! Havin' any luck?"

The sitting man doesn't even turn toward the speaker. "Naw. Savin' my luck for later."

Austin picks up his pace and practically pushes Glory toward the front doors of the casino. She doesn't seem to have heard the men's comments but is, instead, fascinated by the humming of the many slot machines. "Can we play, Austin? Or watch for a while?"

He hates to deny her wishes on her birthday, but memories of his mom's addiction and fears about letting Glory be near Presley make him say *no*. "We'll come back another time," he promises as he takes hold of her arm and presses forward.

He fears she'll continue to protest and draw attention to them, but Glory shows herself to be mature and accepts his refusal quietly. "Is my birthday over?"

"Oh, no. There are other ways to have fun besides letting a slot machine eat your money. We can . . ." but nothing comes to mind right away. It will be good if they can stick close to the slots and be able to follow Presley when he leaves, but the guy might be settled in for several hours.

"Want to check out the gift shop? I haven't bought you anything for your birthday."

"You don't have to buy me anything. You paid for my trailer."

"That was a loan."

"And you let me keep the diamond necklace."

"That doesn't count. It wasn't mine to give. Let's just see what's in the shop."

The two turn toward the opposite end of the building. As they pass his row, Presley can be seen out of the corner of Austin's eye. The man still looks determined. Austin is afraid he's going to be just as unwavering when it comes to getting his hands on the farm. Presley gives the impression of being a lot more ruthless than Glory. Austin knows he should be focusing on Gray's troubles, but can see he's also going to have to help this girl fight for her inheritance.

The gift shop is a spot to pick up useless overpriced souvenirs. If he didn't have time to kill, he'd have steered clear of the place. One thing he doesn't need are knick-knacks to remind him of the Meskwaki Casino.

"These are nice! What are they?" Glory is looking at a display of dreamcatchers, the traditional Native American decorations familiar even to whites. Austin's first mother, Ruby, furnished those for the casino shop years ago. He sees these as being inferior to the ones she made.

"They're supposed to catch your good dreams and hold them and let the bad dreams drift through the web and disappear. Maybe you noticed the big one Liz and Gray have in their living room."

"Yes! I like that! If you really want to buy me something, that would be my pick."

The item brings back humiliating memories of giving a dreamcatcher to Liz as a token of his love, but Austin is still glad to have a gift idea that will make Glory happy. "Great! Pick out the one you like best and save it for when you get a permanent place to live."

She makes a big task of choosing her favorite, but finally they're able to leave the shop, Glory with a big smile. "I have bad dreams I want to go away. But I have some pretty fine dreams, I'd like to hold on to."

"Me, too, Glory. Pretty fine."

Outside, Austin's eyes scan the long rows of cars. Even in the middle of a sunny August day, it looks as if no one has a thing to do except go into a dark casino and play games. The parking lot is full. He can see the chances of tracking Presley are slim.

"No, I can't give you a ride," comes a familiar voice in the next row. "I have to get straight home to my kids."

Anita is standing with her car door open talking to the star of Glory's nightmares. Austin doesn't draw Glory's attention to the conversation she isn't listening to. She has her dreamcatcher out of the sack and is examining it as she walks.

"Suit yourself sweet cakes," Presley is saying to Anita. "Appreciate the info. I got things to take care of myself." And Presley Becker disappears among the cars.

Austin is wondering what *info* he got out of Anita.

TWENTY-THREE

Hours later, Liz comes up with an especially tasty late supper, and everybody sings "Happy Birthday" when the chocolate cake is brought out.

Gray is a little livelier than usual and congratulates Glory on being a legal adult. She seems surprised at the idea. Twenty-one hasn't been of much significance to her until she hears the word, *adult.* She sits a little straighter and smiles at Austin as if to tell him, "Please notice I'm not a kid anymore." He takes hold of her hand under the table and gives it a squeeze.

Rue presents the birthday girl with a picture she's drawn of an unclothed girl beside a trailer in the woods. "It's you!" she declares, and it's good she did because the portrait is a little hard to identify. Liz and Gray give Glory a pair of properly baggy summer pajamas, which Austin is glad to see.

There's plenty of daylight when the celebration ends, so Austin proposes a trip into town to the Cassidy Care Center. Elsa shouldn't be left out of Glory's twenty-first birthday party. She's the reason it's happening.

The nurse tells them the woman didn't eat her evening meal. "She seems depressed," she explains. "We're not sure why."

Austin knows why as soon as Elsa sees her visitors.

Her facial expression goes from tragic to triumphant. "Oh, Glory! I thought you forgot about me."

"I could never do that, Mama. I even brought you a piece of chocolate cake. It's really good but maybe not quite as good as the ones you made me."

"Oh, this is wonderful! But I don't have a present for you."

"I don't need anything," Glory assures her. "I just wanted to see you're doing alright without me here."

"Well, I'm fine, but I think about you all the time. About the good times we had at the farm."

What an understatement, thinks Austin. *She makes it sound like Glory used to visit on weekends.*

After eating the cake, Elsa starts looking weary. Her bedtime has arrived. She makes an effort to offer a proper good-bye by giving Glory a kiss on the cheek and a big hug. "I hope you had a nice birthday, Mariel."

Austin isn't extremely concerned about the woman's confusion. He remembers his Meskwaki mom substituting her husband's name for his. He answered to *Murray* almost as often as *Austin.*

Out in the hall, Glory is looking distressed, but doesn't seem to want to ruin the day by speaking of her mother's mental difficulties. "I hope she liked the cake," is Glory's only comment.

That night Austin and Glory lay side by side in his trailer with only the moon for a night light. She is wearing her new pajamas, and a blanket is rolled up between them. Austin has been trying everything.

"My birthday was nice," she says quietly. "Except for the very end. It was the second time Mama mentioned somebody named Mariel."

"It's been a good day for me, too. Don't worry about what your mom said. People get names mixed up when they get old and when they're tired. She really does know who you are."

"I hope so. But I wonder where she got that other name. I've never even heard it on TV."

"It could be somebody who popped into her mind from when she was young." But deep inside, he's wondering the same thing. Elsa must have known about Presley's girlfriend, after all.

After several minutes Glory poses a question. "Now that I'm twenty-one, I can have a baby, right?"

Austin is caught off guard. Again, he's startled at the lack of life learning the girl has had. "Don't worry about that yet."

"But if I *wanted* to be a mom, I could." The idea seems to stir up feelings of awe in the birthday girl.

"Oh, yes. You could've been a mom several years ago, but you wouldn't have been ready. You aren't even ready now."

"I wouldn't mind begetting a baby. Mama told me she'd explain all about it when I was grown, but I think she forgot."

Austin thinks it was pretty irresponsible of Elsa not to have had the *talk* when her daughter reached puberty. What must be Glory's understanding of the reason she bleeds every month? Surely Elsa could've found a book that explained things. A book besides the Bible and all its *begets*.

Glory continues, "I know you better than anybody. You can tell me everything I need to know, can't you?"

Oh, my gosh. "A woman can give you that information." There's no way he is going to tread into that territory. No way.

"Okay. Maybe I can ask that lady in the cafe. The one who said she has kids."

"Anita? No, not Anita. There're lots better people for you to talk to about woman things than her. I'll get back to you about it." *How's that for skirting the issue?*

Glory's had a big day so dozes off amid talk about *the talk*. Austin doesn't have to face any more questions tonight.

For him, his mom Ruby had put the story of the birds and bees into a few plain sentences. But Austin can't remember what they were. Could he possibly enlist Liz's assistance? It could be a practice run for her before Rue reaches the age for explanations. He imagines the embarrassment involved but asks himself, *If I don't find someone for Glory to confide in, who will?*

In the shadows he can see the silhouette of her dreamcatcher hanging from the mirror over the sink. He hopes her birthday dreams are happy ones.

◆◆◆◆

Liz comes to the trailer the next morning bearing a pile of clean sheets. "Laundry Service here!" she says at the door. "I finally got caught up from the fire."

"Oh, hi. Come on in. Where's your shadow? Haven't seen her since supper."

Liz enters and sits herself and the clean clothes on the bed. "Rue tagged along when Glory went for a walk. I hope she isn't getting on Glory's nerves. For somebody who's spent her whole life mostly alone, that young lady is taking the chaos around here real well. Still, I wish we had a female her age so she can kind of catch up."

"Yeah, me, too," Austin agrees. "Glory's been asking me stuff a girl normally asks her mother or a girlfriend."

"Do you mean, about . . . sex?"

Austin plays with the band on his wrist watch. He is definitely uncomfortable hearing that word from Liz. "Yeah. Kinda. And having a baby."

"I never thought about that. These days the schools give the kids most of the facts when they're real young. Or they just find out from talking to their classmates. But Glory hasn't had any of those opportunities. Poor girl. No telling what kinds of theories she's concocted by piecing together the little she knows. Did her parents farm? Some kids learn about reproduction from watching animals."

"I think they did, but her dad died when she was pretty young, and they must've sold everything then. I haven't heard her talk about animals much."

"You and Glory are getting close, aren't you, Austin?"

"In a way. We're pretty comfortable together. I seem to be about all she has right now."

"I was just thinking that. You know, it's none of my business, but she could easily think she's in love just because she probably craves that. You may be the only man she knows who isn't a relative. She's really vulnerable right now."

"She told me I'm her first man. I guess she forgot about Gray and Dr. Brown. There's no romantic competition for Glory's feelings." And Austin gave Liz a little smile. "Guess I can't be too honored if she falls for me."

"Well, just don't rush anything. Even after she sees more of the world, she might very well decide you're the best there is." She returns the smile. "She will if she's smart, and I think she is."

Liz's words have lifted his spirits. Though he knows she speaks through the biased view of a mom, it's still good to hear. If she thinks he's a good catch, Glory might someday think so, too. He only hopes some other guy doesn't come along first and take advantage of her innocence.

"I wonder how she's been getting her monthly supplies. I'll try to catch her alone and check on that. And I'll see what I can do about her sex education," Liz offers. She became pregnant with Austin just before her high school graduation. "But you realize my own mother never gave me any information on that subject. If she had, you might not be here."

TWENTY-FOUR

After searching for a few minutes, Austin finds Glory sitting on the large rock at the end of the driveway. "You know Anita, that woman you met at the Full House Cafe?"

"The one wearing a tight skirt?"

"Yeah, well. I was thinking of stopping by her place today if you'll go with me. I want to hear what Presley said to her at the casino."

"Why do you care what that awful man said? He tried to burn my trailer."

"I just want to find out what other stuff he's up to and where he's living. He might've told Anita something."

"I don't mind going with you. I don't have anything else to do. And she can maybe tell me how to make babies."

"No! Don't ask her that. At least not when I'm around. You don't have to say anything. I just need you to keep Anita from thinking I'm there to see her."

"I thought you *were* going to see her."

"I am. But not really to *see* her. Uh . . . never mind. Let's just go. First I have to find out where she lives. I guess I don't even know her last name now. Don't know if she was ever married." If not, Anita isn't going to be much of an example for Glory.

He catches up with Gray who's out behind the house doing something with Neka. Austin is glad to know his dad is taking an interest in the dog. That will be something, even if she turns out to be worthless at diabetic service.

"I don't have Anita's cell number anymore, so I thought I'd just stop at her place and ask her a couple of things. But I don't know her married name or where she lives. Do you?"

Gray smiles. "I don't think you need to worry about her name. As far as I know, she's never been married. She's still a Kapao. I'm just glad she's old enough now I don't have to watch over her for my old partner. She was always too much for me. I was a lousy guardian."

"Anita is Anita no matter who's looking after her. Anyway, when she stopped by the other day, she said she's looking for a daddy for her kids, so I thought she might be divorced."

"Not Anita. I think she lives in the same house she used to. With her parents. You sure you want to get started with her again?"

"Definitely not! That's why I'm taking Glory with me. I'll be sure Anita gets the idea we're a couple."

"Ouch. You're ruthless."

"I thought Glory might like to check out the kids. I doubt she's ever seen any live ones besides looking in a mirror when she was little."

"Well, I'd be surprised if Anita's are very well-behaved. They might scare Glory."

"She'd never seen a dog, but she hasn't been scared of ours. She seems to just accept everything as being interesting and normal." Neka is looking very normal as she sits waiting patiently for her master to get back to her.

"Good luck," Gray tells Austin. "I won't mention to Liz you're going there. You know she's never been a fan of that woman."

Saturday must be Anita's laundry day. She's lugging a basket of wet clothes outside to hang on the line when Austin's pulls in. She recognizes the truck right away and immediately drops the basket and rushes in his direction. Three small children, one a toddler, come around the house and follow their mother.

"I'm so excited you came!" is Anita's cheery greeting. "I told the kids, 'You'll all love Austin!' They kept asking when you'd be here!"

Austin and Glory manage to get out of the car, but he can already see he's made a mistake by coming here. He had no idea he's a household name at the Kapao's. "Hi!" he greets the little ones. If they've been looking forward to meeting him, the least he can do is be friendly. "I'm Austin, and this is my friend, Glory."

Glory is staring at the children in awe. "They're so little!" she says softly.

Anita hears the remark. "They aren't really. They're all big for their ages. The twins' daddy is a gigantic guy, but I'm not sure about Stella. She's too young for me to tell which boyfriend she looks like."

Austin has no response to that information and hopes he isn't going to have to explain it to Glory. Now that they've been introduced, the children feel comfortable around their company. They proceed to drag the wet wash out onto the ground and spread the pieces all over the sparsely grown grass. Anita just appears happy they're occupied.

"Is there something special ya need, sweetie?"

"Well, yes. I noticed the other day at the casino that Presley Becker followed you to your car. It's none of my business if you talk to him, but I was just wondering what he wanted."

"Are you jealous?" She gives him a suggestive look and reaches for his arm.

Of course, Anita would interpret his words to mean that. How dumb could he be? "No, like I say, I don't care if you talk to him or go out with him. I just need to know what he meant by thanking you for the info. What kind of information did you give him?" He doesn't mean to sound accusatory, but he's getting impatient.

"I just told him the name of Ralph's Rentals and also told him about a guy I know who has two vehicles. Presley had stopped me in the parking lot to ask if he could borrow my car. Guess somebody sold his while he was in jail, and he's had to walk or hitch transportation since he's been out. I told him I need my car all the time. I work in Marshalltown for land's sake, and I've got little kids who can't be walking all over the place."

"Yeah. He had a lot of nerve to even ask you."

"I think he might've tried several people. And he probably remembers me as kind of a push-over in some ways. Well, not when it comes to my job and my family." Anita glances at Glory as if to be sure she's straightened out any misconceptions the girl might have about her.

"He didn't say where he's living?" Austin was almost as good as Gray at digging for answers.

"No, and I didn't bring it up. Didn't want to seem interested in him. He told me he's going to be coming into lots of money, so then he'd be sure I was well paid if I loaned him my car. Right. He'd use my gas and not get the car back to me on time. And if he inherits money, I'd never see a penny. I can just imagine how he'd take advantage of my kind heart."

"You don't sound like a pushover at all, Anita. Pretty wise, actually."

"I'm a parent now. I *haveta* be wise." The twins are currently having a tug of war with one of their mom's blouses, and the smallest is digging a hole in the yard and eating the dirt.

Austin wants to get away before Glory thinks of female questions to ask the *wise* woman. "Thanks, Anita. We'll let you take care of your washing now. Sorry to bother you."

"Oh, you're never any bother, lover boy!" And she throws her arms around him in her usual way and gives him a smooch. The lady is a little much, but she means well, and Austin knows she tells things as she sees them. There's no guesswork about Anita. He's glad she resisted Presley's selfish request. Austin's old girlfriend seems to have enough problems without some jerk taking her car.

Dusty – or Rusty – gives Glory a proper sendoff by throwing a handful of grass he's pulled up just for her. She brushes the grass away without smiling or commenting. She just glares at the boy until he runs for cover behind his mother's leg.

In the car, Austin begins to feel guilty he didn't give Glory a chance to say anything. "We can come back again soon just to let you have your girl talk," he promises reluctantly.

"No. I'm thinking you're right. I'm not ready to have babies. Hers seem like a lot of trouble. Dogs are easier as far as I can tell."

Austin is somewhat relieved at her conclusions. For today. But later, he's sure she'll be a wonderful mother. He hopes he still knows her then.

"She gave you a pretty big kiss," she comments. "Did you like it?"

"Not really. I just counted it like a handshake. Kisses can mean different things."

"Oh."

He can see the wheels turning in Glory's mind. Who is going be receiving a "hand shake" from her? Hopefully, not the attorney or the doctor.

TWENTY-FIVE

"**Y**ou know what Anita said about Presley not having a car?" Glory is riding with Austin to The Trading Post and has been deep in thought for the first several minutes of the drive. "I have to tell you that the bike I used really belongs to him. At least I think it does. I found it in the barn in a pile of old stuff. I think he probably had it when he was a kid back in the old days. I should probably give it to him since he's been walking everywhere."

"That's a nice thought, but I don't want you to have to meet up with him to do it. Anyway, he'd probably just use it to do more mean things to you. I think he's trying to scare you away, make you leave Tama before anyone knows about you."

"I reckon. But I don't think I want the bike anymore, so we can put it back where I got it. If he wants to use it, he'll know where to look." She already seems to have the situation all worked out in her mind.

"I doubt if he'd like being as visible as he'd be on a bike, but we can put it in the barn if you want. We can do that today." Glory looks relieved. She must've been feeling guilty for leaving Presley to beg people for transportation.

For the life of him, Austin can't understand Glory's concern for a troublesome brother she's never met. *The bond of blood is mystifying,* he concludes.

When they arrive at the Trading Post Diner, Austin offers to buy Glory something called *brunch*.

"It's a little late for breakfast and a little early for lunch. You can mix it up if you want, pancakes with a sandwich or something."

Glory laughs. He loves to hear her laugh. He has the feeling she hasn't had much reason to do that in her life. Elsa is a kind woman but probably not a barrel of fun.

"I think I'll have two eggs with chocolate ice cream," Glory announces.

"Okay. Great." Austin orders her request. If she were his daughter, he'd have nixed the combination. But he figures Glory has a lot of bowls of ice cream to catch up on.

"Last night I happened to think of other good things about you turning twenty-one, besides being old enough to have a baby."

"I'm glad there's another reason to get old," she admits.

"You'll be legal. You can buy alcohol."

"Why would I want to buy that?"

"No reason," Austin says. He has to be honest. Mostly, it's caused problems for the people he knows. "Just telling you. Buying beer is something a lot folks like to do. Not me."

"Mama said Presley drinks beer, and that's something else about him she doesn't like."

"Well, it isn't generally a good thing to do, that's for sure. A better thing about being an adult is you get to vote. Actually, you could've when you were eighteen, but you wouldn't have been registered. Now you can help pick the President of the United States, the Governor, and lots of others. You get to have a say-so in how the country is run."

"Oh, I doubt any of those men will ask me what I think."

"No, but you have a little control over whether they get the job in the first place. Do you know who our President is?" He feels like Jay Leno on the street, trying to make passersby look uninformed.

"Sure I do. It's Barak Obama."

"Very good!" Austin is surprised.

"And Joe Biden is Vice President."

"Whoa! Now you're scaring me. Did Elsa tell you all about the government?"

"She did. She didn't go vote, but she always talked a lot at election time. It was interesting to hear what I was missing. She told bad stories about Bill Clinton, and she was almost in love with George Bush."

"Well, that makes me feel good that she paid attention and taught you some of what she knew."

The food came then, and Austin had to ask, "Do you risk the eggs getting cold while you eat the ice cream first or risk the ice cream melting while you eat the eggs?"

Glory smiles. "I'll eat them together." She picks up her spoon. I'll eat fried eggs with ice cream on top." And she proceeds to assemble her brunch.

There is silence for a few minutes while Glory revels in her delicious concoction, and Austin munches on his toast. "Did Elsa teach you things like reading and math? I mean, did you have some sort of schooling? Wilma said she loaned you some books."

"Yes. I learned to read early. My folks bought me a few baby books at garage sales and kind of helped me read those until I had them all memorized. Mama and Daddy asked Wilma to bring some from the library, but I think she was scared to take them back after I touched them, so she said no to that. I had the Reader's Digests that came in the mail and a set of Britannica encyclopedias my folks kept in the basement. They didn't smell too good because they'd been there a long time, but I read them all."

"I'm impressed. You probably know a lot of stuff I've never even heard of."

"Oh, and I had the Bible. I read that through about four times. The print was real small, and it got to be hard for me to see. I was starting to get headaches. Mama didn't dare take me out to an eye doctor because of my disease. Finally, Wilma brought me some glasses she calls *readers*. They helped a lot."

Austin remembers the Becker house with its shadowy rooms and pictures young Glory squinting to read an old encyclopedia. It's enough to make him angry.

Glory is finished with her food, so Austin gets coffee for both of them.

"Mama didn't like me to drink coffee. She said it would turn my toenails black." Glory takes a sip of the steaming liquid Austin has brought her and seems to savor it.

"I don't think it will now that you're twenty-one," Austin says playfully. His words win him another smile. "I'm impressed you read so much. Did your folks help you with math at all?"

"I can add and subtract and multiply and divide," she answers proudly. "If there's more things than that, I don't know about them. And I can diagram a sentence."

"Geez. I never figured out diagramming. Sounds like you spent a lot of time having school. Not a very fun life, huh?"

"Oh, I thought it was fun! Everything new that went into my brain was better than the sameness of my room and the view out my window. I had a lot of hours to fill during twenty-one years!"

"You know, if you'd gotten to go to school, I'd have known you a long time ago. Though I would've been a few years ahead of you. I have to admit I didn't pay much attention to underclassmen."

"I'd have noticed you. I know I would've."

Austin is uncomfortable talking about might-have-beens. Doing that only makes him depressed. "Your folks owned a computer didn't they? Lots of people spend hours and hours online. But I guess you didn't have Facebook or email or any of those things."

"Nope. Mama thought I'd learn sinful things by being on the internet. And, besides, our computer was real old, and we didn't pay for any connection."

"Too bad. Google could've given you a whole new life. But the radio must've helped."

"I know Rush Limbaugh real well, but mostly I liked to listen to music. I know the words to every country western song in the world!"

"Good! You'll have to sing for me sometime!"

"No. I couldn't do that. The only ones who've heard me besides Mama were Mary and Steve, and usually I had the window closed when I sang to them. I know they're wondering why I stopped."

Austin is speechless. Just when he starts to think of Glory as a regular girl who hasn't gotten out much, he's reminded of the serious after-effects of living like she did. The difference between trees and humans is probably forever blurred for her.

"Refill?" he asks. He'd like to keep the conversation going. It's nice not to have the whole family around when he's trying to get Glory to open up about her life.

She nods *yes*, and he goes to the coffee pots in the corner where customers are expected to help themselves. On his way back with the full cups, he sees his friend has company. Three young men from the tribe are encircling her, and she appears to be trying to catch Austin's eye.

He crowds in front of the intruders and takes a seat beside her. "What are you guys up to?"

"Nothing," they say quickly and start to leave.

"You can keep saying whatever you were saying. This young lady and I don't have any secrets." And Austin smiles an insincere smile at the two guys he doesn't remember from the past. They were probably only bratty kids when he lived in Tama.

"Just sayin' hello," one of them answers, and they hurry out the door of the diner.

Glory is left wide-eyed and shaken. "I'm so glad you came back. They were too friendly for strangers. And the short one squeezed my shoulder and told me I'm cute!"

"Idiots," replies Austin. "Some guys think a girl is just a chance for them to make a pass. Especially a pretty girl like you. You can't encourage them at all or they take it the wrong way."

"I only said, *Hi! How are you*? Was that encouraging?"

"To that kind of guy it is. It's best to ignore them even if it seems rude." *The poor girl. She finally sees new people, and I have to tell her not to talk to them. I'd make a pretty strict father.*

They get back to their conversation about education, and Austin has an inspiration. "You know, at some point, you'll have to have a high school diploma if you want to apply for a job. Everybody needs that piece of paper."

"It would take a long time to go to school enough years."

"Right. But you can take tests that prove you know as much as most graduates. If you can pass, they'll give you a GED."

"What's that?"

"Good question. It's an Equivalency Diploma, meaning it's the same as the real thing. You'd be like a graduate."

"Okay. Where do I get one?"

"I'll look into it. You may have to do a lot of studying first, but we can get some practice tests that will tell you what kind of stuff you'll need to know."

"Will you help me?"

"Sure, but you should think about whether you're truly interested. It needs to be something you want to do for yourself. Not just for me."

Glory looks at him straight on. "Why can't I do it for you? I like to do things for you."

Austin can't decide if she's really that forthright and innocent or only a good pretender. At any rate, it's very disarming.

"Because. Anyway, I'll get you some information about it." Austin has no doubt Glory is bright enough to pass the tests, but finding her place in the world is still going to be an uphill climb. She actually needs a mentor to guide and encourage her. He can feel himself dangerously close to making long-range promises.

TWENTY-SIX

Friday afternoon finds Gray at the round table in their house entertaining two other members of the Meskwaki Nation Police Department. They are a delegation sent to find out his intentions. Gray is more than welcome to return, they say, but they need to know how long it's going to take him. Should the department keep using the substitute for a while more or advertise for a permanent replacement?

Austin, in the kitchen, is trying to be a fly on the wall. Only an island separates the two rooms, so it isn't hard to listen in. He can understand why the officers are here. Gray has been postponing his reentry into the work world, but crime has kept on happening and overloading the tiny force. It must seem to them Gray is taking an unusually long sick leave.

"We'd be more optimistic if you were wearing a prosthesis," they told him. "We don't see you being very effective in a wheelchair or even on crutches. And we have to consider how safe the members of the tribe would feel under the protection of a handicapped officer." That is the police chief, sounding as though he's reciting a prepared ultimatum. The words are meant to be firm but realistic.

Austin thinks they could've left off that last point. Gray will be more apt to want to go back to work if he thinks his people are missing him than if he gets the idea they're nervous about his competency. Honesty is usually good, but here a white lie might have had better results. The men could have said, "The tribe feels unsafe without you on the force."

Gray squirms in his chair, aware he has to make up his mind before they leave. And what they're telling him makes sense. He glances over at his son and silently asks for his opinion. Sensing his father's indecision, Austin gives him an up and down nod. If the man wants his views on the subject, Austin is all for the prosthetic route. Gray is free to ignore that advice, but it's hard to imagine why he'd want to.

Gray's response to his friends isn't wishy-washy. "If I can, I'd like to come back to the office right away just to get back in the groove. I'll get fitted for a new leg and work with it until you think I'm ready. I know I'll have to pass some agility tests. But I miss working with you guys, and I want to give it my best shot." It all comes out in one breath as though he's afraid if he pauses, he won't get it said.

"Glad to hear it," the younger of the two men answers with a smile. Paxton Bear has always looked up to Detective Morgan and is sure to be extremely let down if his hero wimps out.

When all plans are in place for a Monday start, Gray is left sitting alone at the table looking stunned that he let the men talk him into something he's been resisting for weeks. "I forgot to ask if they mind a service dog in the office."

"I don't think they have a choice," Austin answers as he looks at Neka lying on the floor beside his dad. "The dog stood by you in plain sight when those guys were here. Officers are supposed to be observant, so they should've noticed her vest that told them who she is. You'll have to keep them from petting her though. And talking to her. Her job is to be loyal to one man. She can't be the police force pet."

"Yeah. Guess I'll have to make that clear."

TWENTY-SEVEN

Standing in for Liz, Austin prepares to drive his dad to Iowa City to see a prosthetist. Gray needs to be evaluated and fitted. Liz must have opinions on the subject, but it doesn't take much to figure out Gray isn't ready for her help. Austin can see his father's pride is a big reason for him being so abrupt and cold around Liz. Gray was taught, growing up, that the husband is the stronger half of a couple, and the wife relies on him. Somehow Gray's situation has been reversed, and he doesn't know how to handle it. Austin tells himself his father has to learn to be a different kind of male, one who can allow himself to accept his wife's help when it's needed.

When Austin and his dad are getting in the car to leave, Rue gives her final instructions. "Dad, tell them you want a foot that can do the Pipe Dance."

"Well, I can ask, little one, but I'm pretty sure they don't sell dancing feet. I'll have to settle for a walking-running one."

Austin is glad he's along for this important meeting. He observes, while the doctor does tests to determine Gray's K-level. That measurement is the rating between 0 and 4 that tells Medicaid how his physical and cognitive skills are. The number will indicate how much he is likely to benefit from the prosthesis. Gray is top-notch in all categories so is apt to have great results. The trick will be to keep his mental energies operating.

Austin senses a spark of excitement in his father. He must see that patients in the clinic seem to be navigating very naturally. The atmosphere is not at all a dreary one. At one point, they strike up a conversation in the waiting room with an older farmer who declares he needs an adjustment for his leg before harvest starts. The implication is that it's a routine precaution to take to get ready for a busy season.

Gray is fortunate his amputation was just below the knee. Attachment will likely be much easier than if it were higher on his leg. He chooses the top-of-the-line model. If he is going to attempt police work, he'll need all the help he can get. Liz has reminded him more than once, "We have the money. Get the best." Even the best will probably need to be replaced in three years, so he certainly doesn't want to start with an inferior prosthesis. At the last minute, he decides to go for broke and get a cosmetic cover that will make the limb look more lifelike.

"If it were me, I'd have a tattoo of the Meskwaki Nation symbol put on it somewhere. Dress it up," suggests Austin.

"Why not?" says Gray. "Though nobody's going to see it."

While they await the construction of Gray's new limb, Rue dutifully nurses the stump. Austin wonders if she believes a leg and foot will grow back if she tends them diligently enough.

"You're getting your dad in great shape for his new *fake* leg!" he assures her.

"It will be good as new," she informs her brother as she picks up the lotion bottle to take to her dad's bedroom. Austin imagines Liz has used that phrase when Rue has taken a tumble outside. "Let's give you a band aid. That will make the owie as good as new."

"Well, the stump will heal, but the leg and foot won't grow back. That's why he needs a make-believe one. It will be one that can't get diabetes in it. It'll be better than his first one."

"I want a new leg too!" Rue is sure she doesn't want a diseased limb like the one that made so much trouble for her dad.

"You don't need one, Rue. But you'll like to help your dad with his. He might even let you sign it." He isn't sure whether a five-year old can sign her name, but figures she'll have some way of giving her autograph.

"I can make R-U. I can't make the last letter."

"Your dad will know Ru is you. He'll love it."

Rue seems pleased to think her father will love something. He tries every day to smile for Ruby, but she can still see his depression and probably half-believes she caused it.

Liz is closing her laptop when Austin comes in at noon. "Need some help with lunch?" he offers. His mother hasn't been paying much attention to household matters lately. Austin and Glory can do okay from the food supplies in the trailer, but Gray and young Ruby aren't able to fend for themselves as well. Rue can't even reach the kitchen counter.

While he's taking sandwich fixings out of the fridge, he asks in what he hopes is a casual tone, "What is it that's been taking so much of your time these days?" She's either taken a leave of absence from the casino or is doing her work at home. She hasn't given any explanation that he's heard.

"I wondered how long it was going to take you to ask me that. Can't imagine why Gray hasn't said anything."

"We're just trying to respect your right to privacy."

"You're sounding like the cop of the family. All I can tell you is that I'm using some vacation time from the casino to work on something with Sky. He's writing and I'm editing. We'd like to finish as soon as possible, so that's why the push."

"I didn't know you and Sky were so close," he ventures.

"Oh, it doesn't have anything to do with being close. I barely know the man, really. Gray thinks he knows him, but he's going to be surprised by this. Please don't tell him."

"I don't know anything to tell. But I'm sure he's worried about the calls and texts to Sky. His confidence is pretty low these days, so I'm sure he's imagining an affair between you and his brother."

"Do you think so? I suppose that's why he keeps making cracks about me moving to Oklahoma. That's so crazy, I usually don't even answer him. I could explain I guess, but I hate to blow Sky's surprise when it's almost done. I keep thinking Gray can hate me for now, because it'll be okay later."

"Well, you might want to speed things up or try harder to hide the signs you're in touch with Sky. Right now Gray hears just enough for him to think he can fill in the blanks." *I do the same thing.* "And I doubt if the stress is very good for his diabetes"

"Thanks for telling me. I'll be more careful, but I hope he can trust me for just a few more days. The whole idea is to make Gray feel *better* about things in the end. Oh, and Austin, I have to apologize to you. I haven't forgotten your birthday. I will never do that, but I just don't have the time to organize a feast this summer."

"I was hoping you wouldn't. I'm not ready to do the party thing. I'm a big boy now. My birthday isn't a huge deal, and I don't want to have to make small talk with a ton of people. Other things on my mind right now."

"Thanks, sweetie. I feel the same way. We'll make up for it later."

Austin finishes making the sandwiches, and Liz clears papers from the dining room table. The rest of the family come in to find lunch ready by noon. The table conversation centers on Rue's upcoming first day of school. She's feels very grownup about the fact she'll be starting to "work" soon.

"I get to ride the bus," she tells Glory proudly.

Liz, knowing Glory probably can't identify with the school experience, interrupts. "We'll go to town next week and shop for supplies. Glory can help you pick them out. It will be fun for you to look at them every day until school starts."

"Yay!" responds Rue.

Gray speaks up. "I don't know how you're going to work that into your busy schedule. Won't you be typing and calling and texting Skyler? I can take Rue shopping for school. I'd better get used to doing that kind of thing."

Austin isn't sure what "that kind of thing" means, but the man must be referring to *mother's work*. He's probably still convinced his wife is going to leave him and Ruby, and he'll have to be a mother as well as father. Austin hopes Liz's secret project is worth all the misunderstandings. Some things can leave a bad taste even after the truth comes out. He tells himself, *I'll be out of it after August*. He can't fix everything before then. But at least while he's away this time, he'll be in constant touch and will know what's happening in the family. *If they tell me the truth.*

TWENTY-EIGHT

The melodious pounding of drums across the powwow grounds brings back wonderful memories for Austin. Years of celebrations that included friends from other tribes across the Midwest. Wearing glorious regalia fashioned by Ruby, his Meskwaki mother. Watching Ruby proudly sell her dreamcatchers and other beaded creations. Everything about the powwow was magical. Until that last summer.

It was just before Austin's big dance, the one he was so anxious for Liz to see. He and his Meskwaki mom's best friend found themselves alone together, and Austin couldn't wait another second to profess his love. It wasn't something he would ever do lightly. He was sure of his feelings. Never would another woman be so right for him as the blonde Caucasian he'd known for only two months. But the moment the words were off his lips, he could see Liz didn't feel the same way. He experienced then the most devastating disappointment a young man can fathom. His survival, his very life, depended on changing her mind. Surely he could make her see he was the man she should spend the rest of her life with. .

The more he thinks about it, the more he now realizes Liz's reaction to his declaration of love was nothing other than motherly. She lectured him on what was wrong with him caring for someone so much older than he was. That night he didn't sleep a minute. He went over and over the signs he'd seen throughout the summer that told him he and Liz were on the same page. In his mind, he couldn't be wrong.

He was actually very wrong.

Today, he's back at the scene of his humiliation. And now there's a little girl, the daughter of Liz, named for his first mother. A little girl who looks at him like he's her hero. He vows to help make this powwow special for her.

Several years have passed since he's been in the arena, several years since he let himself think about dancing. But it's still inside him, the desire to move to the rhythm of the drums. This time it will be more pleasurable than ever before because he'll be sharing the experience with his new sister. The Friendship Dance will be their debut. If they don't realize it already, the rest of the tribe are going to see Rue is a dancer to beat all Meskwaki child dancers. Her father has never danced to speak of. Even before losing one, he claimed to have two left feet. And her mother is white, so the two of them never have put much emphasis on traditional dancing. Austin has noticed though, when the child dances around the house, she has a natural rhythm and grace that many older tribal members should envy. And she displays soul, an essential ingredient for every dance. With practice and Austin's encouragement, Rue can be better than he was when he was young. And he was considered exceptional.

The plan is to meet Rue at one o'clock in front of the announcer's stand. The grand entrance will kick off the afternoon program, and Rue will be part of the Tiny Tot's category, always a visitor favorite. After the entry, when the drums have stopped, there will come the usual prayer, flag song honoring the country, and victory song honoring the veterans. The stands are full of spectators, including white tourists from around the state. It is one time when Native Americans get to shine. And this afternoon Rue is sure to be the shiniest.

Austin is dressed in his outfit from five years ago, a work of art from his mother Ruby's hand. He's happy it still fits perfectly. The clothing makes him feel strong and proud just as it always has. Ruby's love is touching him, assuring him nothing can go wrong with the upcoming number.

He hasn't seen Rue's dress, but she told him earlier it is the *beautifulest* because it has jingles on it. Luckily, her mother constructed the dress early in the summer, before the mysterious Skyler project took all her time. Their last minute plan is for Liz to braid Rue's hair.

He wishes Glory could've come but knows it wouldn't be safe for her among all the people. Her sinister relative might be lurking in the crowd, ready to ruin everything.

Austin's eyes sweep the scenic grounds beyond the arena. *I wonder which tree was the one baby Glory was found under.* He will have to ask her mother soon to describe its location. Hopefully, Elsa's memory still holds that important bit of information. Someday he'll get to bring Glory to the powwow and allow her to come full circle.

His watch shows ten minutes until the grand entrance. Dancers are getting lined up. It isn't like Liz to wait until the last minute. And he's surprised Rue hasn't badgered her to hurry. *Maybe something went wrong with her outfit.* Liz insisted on making it by herself although she has little sewing and beading experience. She might still be trying to get the jingles to stay on. Also, the hair braiding may be taking longer than planned. Perhaps Rue is the reason for her own tardiness. This morning she declared,"Ne-metagi mitti nenoteivi takoani!" Little sister likes to eat Indian tacos and might be trying to down one of those before the dance. Surely, though, her folks would've made her wait until later.

Looking again toward the entrance to the grounds, he sees Liz running toward him without Rue. Maybe the child's nerves have gotten the best of her, causing her to back out. It wouldn't be the first time one of the little ones lost her courage. Though their dancing isn't done chiefly for the benefit of the audience, just knowing a crowd is watching can be very intimidating, even for Austin. He'd at least like the chance to give his sister a pep talk.

When Liz gets closer, she is breathing hard, and her eyes are red as if she's been crying. "What's wrong?" he asks, trying not to sound frightened. "Where's Rue?"

"I don't know! We were on our way over here from the car. I turned around, and she was gone. I called 911 then went home and got Gray. We've been looking everywhere! Now Security is involved." Liz looks terrified. Austin regrets not having any answers.

An announcement comes over the loud speaker. "We are interrupting the ceremony because a five-year-old girl is missing. Please join the search for Rue Morgan. She is three feet-six inches with her hair in braids. She is wearing a white jingle dress. Report any information to the desk at the west end of the arena. Dancing will resume as soon as Rue is found. We repeat . . ."

It doesn't take long for the powwow to turn into a crime scene. The Tama police come from town and are soon joined by patrols from other departments in the county. Everyone is hoping the child will appear and tell them she's been playing with friends. Members of the Meskwaki community know Rue and her parents, so they are extremely concerned. The drummers are silent. Everyone is on the lookout for a little girl, a little girl who has been counting the minutes until her turn to dance.

It's still early to assume Rue has been taken, but Liz and Gray explain to the officers questioning them that a man named Presley Becker should be looked at. No one at the powwow admits to seeing the man since his release from prison, and, unpopular as he is, he has no known motive. Most people don't think of the Morgans as having money to pay a ransom. Nevertheless, as far as Rue's family is concerned, the whole alarming situation has Presley Becker's name written all over it.

When every inch of powwow grounds has been covered, Liz, Gray and Austin head for the Explorer. It's time to return home to Glory and have their own powwow. If they put their heads together they might come up with an idea the other searchers have so far missed.

As they are clamoring into the truck, a large note taped to the inside of the windshield shouts at them. In childish printing are the words GIVE ME GLORY AND YOU'LL GET YOUR DAUGHTER BACK.

Liz and Gray stare at each other. Someone is after their young friend from the brown trailer. Rue is just a pawn. They find themselves wishing Austin had never met Glory. Her presence is what took away Rue.

After seeing the note, going home doesn't seem to be called for. They know little Rue didn't merely wander off. And there aren't many individuals who could've written the note. Two elderly ladies are the only people besides their immediate family, and possibly Presley, who are familiar with the name *Glory*. The list of suspects has become very short.

Austin gets dropped off at the trailer to tell Glory what's happening. He should've let her come with them in the first place. The girl has been left at home alone enough in her life.

They hate to alarm Wilma, but Liz and Gray stop at her place simply to find out if she's seen Presley. The golden retriever is beside Gray when he knocks on her door.

Assuming she's being suspected of something, Wilma won't let them in her house. She sticks her head out the door as though greeting a vacuum cleaner salesman. Her entire demeanor is on-edge and irritable, nothing like the first time Gray and Austin came calling. "Why are you here?"

"We aren't singling you out, Wilma. We're just very scared for our daughter. She disappeared at the powwow, so we have to look at every possibility. You're one of only a few folks around here who remembers Presley, and we wonder if you've seen him since he got out of prison."

She still looks scared stiff. Mention of a child gone missing doesn't even seem to arouse her interest. "No. Why would I? He isn't a friend of mine. Just because he's my dead brother's boy, doesn't mean I have anything to do with him."

Gray tries to sooth her temper. "I didn't mean you'd deliberately contact him. Just thought he might have come to you when he found out his mom isn't living at the farm."

"He isn't here," she announces firmly, as though daring him to say anything different.

It's awkward carrying on a conversation with a head, but maybe she's trying to keep her cats from getting outside or trying to protect them from the vicious-looking service dog.

Gray tries to keep his voice casual. "Do you judge him capable of kidnapping a child? I mean, does it sound like something he'd do?"

Still holding tight to the door, Wilma responds, "I think he's capable of any crazy thing you can think of but don't know why he'd want your daughter. What would he do with a child?"

"We're not sure. The note he left in our car sounds like he wants to make a trade. Rue for Glory. Glory may be in his way when it comes to inheriting the farm."

"I told you before, I don't know nothing about that," Wilma snaps. And she closes the door in their faces.

Rue's parents aren't just disappointed and panicked. They are puzzled. The Wilma that Gray talked to earlier would've been worried herself, and eager to give helpful advice. He feels sure of that. Especially if she heard Glory might be involved.

"Presley must have gotten to her," says Gray. "The woman is terrified. And she obviously knows something. I need to get a search warrant."

PRESLEY

A police officer from Tama approaches Presley at the tavern.

"Did you hear there was a kidnapping on the settlement today?"

"Naw. I don't keep track of the Indians and their troubles. Got enough of my own."

"The little girl who was taken belongs to Gray Morgan. He used to be on the Meskwaki police force. Pretty good guy, I think. Lost a leg, so he isn't working now."

"Sad story, but policemen sometimes have enemies. Guys out for revenge. They'll probably never find the kid alive."

"I was hoping you could help, Presley."

"Why me? You think I go around snatching little girls? I've got limits, you know."

"You might've had your reasons. Something you wanted from Officer Morgan."

"What does a one-legged guy have that I want?"

"Probably nothing, but we need to know where you were at one o'clock this afternoon.

"I was right here. Ask the bartender."

"We'll talk to him. You can count on that. Even if your alibi checks out, you still might be able to help us. You must know some dangerous types who might do something unlawful."

"I don't think I like what you're saying. That just because I served time, I'm the person who knows every criminal in these parts. All bad guys don't hang out together. I don't know any kidnappers." And with that, Presley rises from his stool at the counter and starts for the door.

The police officer lets him go with, "Call us if you think of somebody. There might be a reward."

TWENTY-NINE

No one is going to get any sleep. After searching all afternoon and evening along with the groups deployed from the sheriff's office, the Morgans take a break to meet on the front porch and consider their next move.

"Alright," begins Gray. His voice is tight and tells the family he is stressed beyond belief. It does help that he's used to functioning under pressure during his days on the force. He seems to operate on two levels, the father who is devastated and the cop who is efficient. The husband who's crippled isn't on display during this crisis. "What do we have so far?"

"Nothing," answers Liz tearfully.

"Not correct. We have a note. It should be a big clue." He digs it out of his pocket. "Give me Glory," he reads.

"Do that," Glory says. "Give me to him. It doesn't matter. I can take care of my brother, and you need to get Rue back. I mean it."

"Don't even talk like that. We want you both. No trading." Gray is absolutely firm in his resolve not to make deals with the ex-con. "I don't think Presley will harm Rue because that would only get him more prison time. He wants you, Glory. It's nothing personal. It's just because you're in the way of him getting the farm. He wants to be the only heir standing. Nobody even knows you exist, so he thinks he can . . . dispose of you and not be caught."

"Ew! You mean he'd kill me? I'm his sister! He can have the old farm. It doesn't matter. I have the taco trailer."

"Yeah, that's almost the same thing." Austin wants a lot more for Glory after all she's done without until now.

"Do we know for sure the note was from Presley?" asks Liz. "Didn't the police say he has an alibi for the time Rue was taken?"

Gray acknowledges his wife's point. "That's right. He must have had help."

Liz is beside herself with fear for Rue. "There was a crowd of people around us at the powwow. Someone should've noticed a struggle. Who could've come along and calmly persuaded Rue to go with them? It must've been someone she recognized or someone who didn't seem frightening. Where was my head that I missed it? I'm the one to blame. Tama has always seemed like such a safe place. I was worried about the time, but it never occurred to me to worry about Rue's safety."

Gray continues to be understanding about his wife's worries. "Whatever happened, happened very fast. No one blames you at all. It would've been the same if I'd been there with you."

His newspaper experience inspires Austin with ideas for spreading the word. "We should put an ad in the paper with Rue's and also Glory's photos. And I can put it on the Meskwaki Nation Facebook page. It can explain who she is and that she's missing. That would take away Presley's intention to do away with a person no one knows exists. Everyone will be on the lookout for her, and he'll be the first suspect. He'll have to change his mind about killing her to protect his financial interests. Convicted killers don't inherit farms." Austin is already on his way inside to use the computer.

Those still on the porch are silent. The Facebook idea is a good one, but as far as it deterring Presley, he probably won't even know about it. He has no access to a computer. They need to do more. Then Gray speaks. "Wilma acted awful strange. We have to get back out there. I don't think the police have any reason to look into her alibi, but I'm sure she's guilty of something."

"By the way," he continues, addressing Liz, "do we still have the piece of paper she gave me with the attorney's phone number on it?"

"I think it's by the phone, but he's Elsa's attorney. He can't do anything to help."

"That isn't why I want it. I'd get the note, but I'm slow."

Liz gets up to go inside. "And bring the note from the car, please," her husband adds.

Austin can see now where Gray is headed. He wants to compare the two pieces of paper. *But why? Wilma isn't a kidnapper. Maybe his father has lost some of his investigative instincts. Maybe we're all sitting here listening to a man who's finally cracked under all the stress he's had this past year. We're losing time!* Austin stands up. "You guys can go back to Wilma's, but I'm going to the Becker farm. Anybody we need is probably somewhere around there."

Liz is back with the two written notes before Austin can leave. She hands them to Gray. "Anything?" It's easy to see that, in spite of his recent rants, his wife has faith in Gray's ability to find Rue.

Austin pauses in his intended exit. He does want to hear what is significant about the notes.

Gray looks quickly at the two pieces of paper. They are the same size. Austin peers over his father's shoulder and sees the sheets of light blue note paper are identical, at least to the naked eye. "Ah-oh."

"I thought so!" exclaims Gray. "I can't tell by the handwriting because one is longhand and one is printed, and the ink is different, but I watched Wilma write the address down. She got the paper from a pad under the phone. The message taped to our windshield was on one of the same papers. How do you suppose that happened?"

"Presley is at Wilma's house! That's why she wouldn't open the door. He must have had a gun pointed at her."

"And maybe he's holding Rue inside!" Liz is on her feet.

"OR the notes could both have been written by Wilma. Maybe she's got Rue."

"That doesn't sound logical," Austin points out. "She wouldn't try something like that by herself. Rue's probably stronger than she is."

"Wait a minute," Gray says. "Since Presley has an alibi, he might not have been around for the whole operation. Rue might be with his accomplice. Somebody we don't even know."

"Maybe Presley has a friend he met in prison. Probably promised him a cut of the inheritance. It would be worth it to Presley to keep himself in the clear. The guy who did it is probably long gone, but he wouldn't have wanted to drag a kid with him. I think Wilma's or the Becker farm are our best bets."

Then Glory says what no one wants to think about. "I know Rue's so scared! She probably thinks she's going to die and wonders why nobody's coming to save her!"

That does it. All four of Team Rue are off the porch in record time. And, in spite of all the law-enforcement in the area, no one arrests the one-legged, on-leave cop for flying over gravel roads at eighty miles per hour.

THIRTY

Having by-passed the search warrant, the self-appointed militia arrive on Wilma's doorstep with no weapon except Gray's pistol which he's seldom seen without. He has it in a holster in plain sight when Wilma answers the door.

"We're coming inside, so move it," he demands.

Wilma does as she's told, looking as guilty as if she's been caught with a bank sack full of money.

Her voice is shaking, and her eyes plead for Gray not to shoot. "I didn't hurt your daughter."

The fact she seems to know why they're here is telling enough. "Then where is Ruby?" screams Liz. In her distress she is using her daughter's given name.

"Ruby who? I don't know who you're talking about," protests Wilma in a shaky voice. Austin can tell the woman is out of her element. She's done something wrong, and she is very near the point of confessing. Who would've thought Glory's aunt would be a person involved in a federal crime?

Liz spots something shiny on the floor by the pantry door. "It's one of her jingles! I didn't sew them on tight enough!" And she begins crying.

The fallen jingle is actually evidence they are in the right place. With that encouragement, Gray concentrates on wearing down Wilma.

"We're going to have to search your house. We'll trash every inch of it if we have to. Rue could be here. If you want to keep us from wrecking the place, then tell us where she is." Gray is so intimidating Austin himself is inclined to blurt out some answer, any answer, just to satisfy his father.

Wilma evidently feels the same way. Just as Gray pulls her antique bureau over on its side, nearly causing himself to topple to the floor, the woman gives in. "Stop! I didn't know things would go this far. Presley told me I deserved some money, too. I do, I really do. I kept their secret for twenty years, and I helped take care of Glory, and—!"

"Shut up or I'll give you exactly what you deserve. Now where's Rue?"

"She was in the pantry for a while. I thought she was safe in there, but Presley came and took her with him. I don't know where!"

"How was she? Was she crying?" asks Liz.

"She never did cry. She just seemed real worried about not telling you she was leaving. Cute little thing."

Austin and Gray both believe Wilma is telling them what she can about Rue's fate but think she might know more than she realizes. "Have you had any dreams that could help us?" He might as well give her an excuse for what she knows.

"As a matter of fact, I did dream last night that a child was in a dark scary place. Tied up, I think."

Why wouldn't Wilma have mentioned that sooner? "So do you remember anything else about the place … in your dream? Was Presley there?"

"No. The girl was alone."

"Does Presley have a car?" Gray can see Wilma's through the window so knows he hasn't taken that one.

"No, he doesn't. That's why he needed me. Earlier."

"Then he probably hasn't gone far. It would be hard to travel on foot with somebody Rue's size. He may have her hidden somewhere outside. Maybe in the garage or a tool shed."

"He did say something about the fruit cellar. Asked me if I had a key. I told him no. I call it the *cave*. Never needed to lock it. I can't even get down the steps anymore. And there isn't any light."

All of Rue's small search party react with horror. What a gruesome place to store a five-year-old, even a brave one.

Austin drags Wilma along as they tromp out to the large hump of earth near the back porch. He lifts the heavy wooden door to reveal total blackness. "Rue? Are you down there?" She could be tied and gagged, so he listens for a grunt. Nothing. "It's your brother, Happy. We're all here to take you home." He still doesn't pick out any definite sound except movement of leaves by something like a rat or a cat. Maybe Bell and Tinker hang out in the cellar.

"I'll get her," says Gray.

"But the stairs…" No one wants Rue rescued more than her mom, but she also doesn't want to see Gray tumble down into that dark musty unknown. He might break his other leg. Crutches just won't work.

Everyone is wishing Gray's prosthesis had arrived. But, even if it had, he wouldn't be used to it and ready to tackle stairs.

"Get back. I'm going down. You guys can be figuring out how to get me up." He puts his hand on Neka's back. "Stay, girl."

It's obviously futile to think of talking Gray out of his rescue mission. He's the father and the cop, a double responsibility. No one exhales, not even Wilma.

Gray moves slowly and carefully. The hours of working on his biceps are paying off. He can lower his body to the ground without letting himself drop. From a sitting position at the top of the stairs, he rises as though doing a form of push-up, then lowers himself, step by step. The good leg is stretched out in front of him, and he bumps his way down eight levels. Each time the stump hits the cement, Gray emits a low moan of pain. To his spectators, the descent seems to take an hour. Neka shows signs of anguish at not being able to be with her master. Austin thinks the dog should've been allowed to go along.

When he reaches the damp floor of the cellar, Gray calls up, "Made it. Can't see anything." He can be heard then scooting around on the dirt floor, looking for a breathing person—or a body.

The awaited words finally come. "I found her! Hang on until I see what's what."

No one can speak. Austin, Glory and Liz are huddled together listening for a further report. Liz holds tight to Neka who instinctively wants to be with Gray no matter the dangers. Gray hasn't said if Rue's alive, but his tone reveals excitement. Each person is mentally preparing to go down and help the two people out of the darkness. Even if Rue is okay, she might be hurt or too scared to move. Gray isn't up to finishing the rescue unassisted.

More shuffling and voices can be heard. And little jingles. The jingles could mean Rue is alive and moving. Or that Gray is moving her. Patience is wearing thin outside the cave.

"I knew having you back was too good to be true," Liz said to Austin. "Maybe losing my daughter is the payment for recovering my son. I'm not permitted to have you both."

"That's crazy," Austin answers. "Think of all the folks who have two or more children. You aren't expected to sacrifice one for the other. You'll see." And he makes up his mind to quit humoring Gray and go help him.

Liz is showing more and more anxiety. Her entire family will be in the cellar. "What if Presley is hiding down there, waiting for us?"

That would be okay thinks Austin. *He'll be outnumbered. He'll be the one to be scared.*

Before going down, Austin stands at the top of the cellar steps straining to see a glimpse of something, anything. The damp earthy smell almost makes him hope his sister is somewhere else. Then he can see something white coming into view. A bedraggled Rue is very slowly climbing the stairs while her father follows, his

179

hands on her shoulders in the same way he'd grip a walker. With Rue's body for balance, he hops on his left leg up the stairs. Luckily, the height of the steps is shallow and Gray's strength is such that he can hold his own weight and avoid putting it fully on Rue. When they are almost to the top, Austin reaches his father and pulls him past the door frame.

A clamor of joy engulfs the pair. Gray has succeeded in spite of his handicap. Rue is safe and able to smile and hug her mom. "You didn't make a noise. I was so afraid you weren't okay." Liz can't help voicing her anxieties now that they're in the past.

Wilma is gone. She has fled in her car. Her whereabouts is of concern but not as much now that they can see and touch Rue.

Gray is half lying and half sitting on the ground, catching his breath. "She was tied up and gagged. She could've grunted or something but probably assumed she couldn't with a sock in her mouth."

"The bad man said if I made a peep he'd kill my mom and dad." explains Rue, her whole body shaking. "I didn't make a peep even when I could feel the spiders."

Liz is hugging her daughter so tightly the child can barely breathe. "He didn't hurt you, did he? I mean, he didn't *touch* you?"

"Nope. Just when he was tying me up. Is my dance over?"

Liz hates to tell her. "I think we missed it, baby. But I'm sure your dress will still fit next year."

Fortunately, Rue is even more concerned about Wilma's pets. "We couldn't find Belle and Tinker. They ran away, and I was helping the lady look, and she told me to get in her car. I couldn't see where you were!"

So that was how Wilma got Rue's attention. A tried and true method. All children are vulnerable when it comes to pets. "It's okay, honey. We'll talk more about it later." She remembers having the stranger-danger talk last year, but Rue probably assumed they were talking about a scary man with a mean face and not an elderly white-haired lady who looks like Mrs. Santa.

THIRTY-ONE

While the others take Rue to the police station to be questioned and checked, Austin and Glory go to her house to see if there are any signs of Presley. According to that man's thinking, the farm belongs to him. The farm he hasn't set foot on since high school. It might be his safe place now. They're thankful they don't have to think of Rue being with him.

A surprise awaits in the driveway. Wilma's Buick tells them she's come to tell Presley his hostage escaped. The woman isn't showing very good judgement. She's probably still hoping to be paid for luring Rue into her car. Doesn't she know she was nothing to Presley but a convenient minion, and now he doesn't need anything more from her? If he's still around, he may want to eliminate the only person who knows he's guilty.

Austin is realizing too late he should've sent Glory with the others. Even though it's her house, there's no reason she needs to be here. After all, she's Presley's target. "Stay in the car with the door locked," he tells her. "I'll find out what's going on."

At the kitchen door, he runs into Wilma who now seems relieved to see him. "I was supposed to meet Presley here, but I can't find him. Who knows where he's gone to? I was supposed to help him look for the will I signed. He plans to burn it so everything will come to him. He *is* Elsa's real son, you know, so it would be fair."

"And how will that benefit you, Wilma? He's not going to give you any of his inheritance. He has no reason to do that. Not in his mind."

Wilma looks frightened. "I guess I haven't been thinking straight. Presley used to be so sweet when he was little. I think I saw a tiny bit of that boy when he was asking for my help."

"That boy is gone, Wilma. And you're wanted now for kidnapping. The best thing you can do is give up and cooperate. You know you couldn't live knowing you helped hurt your niece. I'm calling the police now and telling them you're on your way there. They'll probably meet you on the road and give you an escort."

He proceeds to dial the station while the old woman gathers her purse and makes sure Elsa's gas stove is turned off and the kitchen window is closed. She has tears in her eyes when she walks to her car. Hopefully, she's headed to the police station. Her parting words are, "Tell Glory to take care of Bell and Tinker. They're in my back yard."

Sure thing, he's thinking. *As thanks for almost getting her killed?* He hates to count on Wilma to turn herself in, but Presley is in the house, and he's the one Austin most wants to get his hands on.

As soon as Wilma's car starts up the road, he concentrates on listening for any sound that reveals he isn't alone in the house. The quiet is unnatural. It's as if the window frames and loose boards are holding their breaths.

He spots one visual sign that puts him on alert. The door to the basement is barely ajar. *Why didn't Wilma look for Presley down there?* Perhaps the door doesn't ever close all the way, so she didn't notice the crack. She should be glad she didn't have to meet up with the man who got her into so much trouble. Austin, himself, isn't looking forward to confronting him. Twenty-one years ago when

Presley felt trapped, he shot at a store clerk. Elsa's son isn't good under pressure.

No sound can be heard from the direction of the basement. Hopefully, Presley isn't playing with matches again. Perhaps he thinks he can wait it out, that Austin will give up and leave. Maybe he's still looking for the will. Or perhaps he's already climbed out a downstairs window and taken off across the fields. In spite of the logic of that last possibility, instinct tells him the man is close by.

"Come on up, Presley! The will isn't anywhere in the house. Glory found it, and we took it to Bill Hogan. It's too late for you to take the farm. Your mother disinherited you!" All his words are probably doing is making the ex-con more angry and desperate. Suddenly, Austin feels very vulnerable without a weapon. He looks around for a makeshift way of defending himself.

Above the back door in the kitchen hangs a rifle, probably put there by Burt Becker. Who knows if it's loaded? *Better than nothing,* he thinks as he removes it from the wall. At least he'll look somewhat intimidating when he makes his way down the stairs.

He uses his Indian tread again, but the steps are old and creaky, so a kitten would've made a noise on them. The dim light shows a single bulb has already been turned on, another indication he will find Presley down there. Standing at the bottom, he looks around at the boxes, trunks, and clothing hanging from one of the many pipes. His eyes fall on a thin figure, crumpled on the floor, holding something plaid and sobbing. Presley isn't even aware anyone else is around.

"Austin!" Glory cries out from the top step. "I can't stand being by myself out there. What if my bro—" She, too, sees the devil's son, in a heap beneath the hanging clothes. Her concern for what he's holding is stronger than her fear.

"My coat! What's he doing with my coat?" And she descends the top four steps.

"Yours?" croaks Presley. "It isn't yours!" And he tries to stand, never taking his eyes off Glory.

"I found it. And it fits me. And I have a picture in my Treasure Box." She must know who she's talking to but feelings for the coat are making her reckless.

For several minutes the man stares at her. He sounds almost accusing as he says, "It belongs to Mariel. *My* Mariel."

Glory knows no one named Mariel but does remember her mother calling her by that name. She remains still, hoping Presley will reconsider.

Austin is remembering the photo in Glory's treasure box and his visit with the school janitor. "What do you know about the coat?" he asks without giving Presley any hints.

"Mariel's mom made it, so it's one of a kind. Why is it here? She's dead!" and he starts crying again.

Austin decides the conversation is getting into territory best not heard by Glory. "Go on back to the car. I need to listen to what's bothering Presley."

"I know about the coat girl in the picture. I want to hear!" she protests. "I've looked at that coat for years."

Austin keeps his eyes fixed on Presley as he tries to protect Glory. "Please wait for me outside! I'll fill you in on our way home. Right now I want you safe." So Glory reluctantly goes back up the stairs and, presumably, out to the car.

The short dialogue between the other two has given Presley a moment to think of more questions. "Was Mariel at this house for some reason? Did she die in this crappy basement? They told me she drowned. Did my folks do something to her?"

"Presley, the drowning was the truth. And you're on the wrong track about your parents. They did you a huge favor. They raised your daughter. But I don't think they knew it."

The man was speechless. He paced back and forth among the boxes, still holding the coat. He appeared to be putting the facts together in his head. "Glory?" he asks finally.

"Yup, Glory Dawn. The girl you've been wanting to hurt." Austin almost pitied the man. It would be a lot to take in.

Presley sinks down on a large trunk, forgetting for the moment he's wanted for kidnapping and should be getting out of town. "But Mariel said she was going to give the baby up for adoption. For twenty years, I've thought—"

"Maybe she intended to, but then changed her mind. She wrapped the baby in that coat. And the Beckers found it under a tree on the powwow grounds."

Presley goes from tears to talk. "The baby was the reason I robbed Casey's. I was trying to get some money before she was born. Prove to Mariel I could at least pay for the doctor. I didn't want her to give the kid away."

Austin walks closer to Presley and tries to defend the dead girl. "I'm sure she didn't want to, but by the time she had the baby, you'd been sent away for a long time. And she couldn't have coped by herself. I doubt if her parents or friends even knew she'd been pregnant." Austin remembers the note left in the jacket pocket. *I don't want it.* "Mariel was very young. Maybe she wasn't ready to be a mother."

"That girl, Glory . . . you sure about her? She's mine?"

"I looked into it . . . so, yes . . . biologically, she is," states Austin. He wishes he weren't sure. It isn't a truth he looks forward to sharing with anyone else, and he certainly doesn't want her dad to feel he has any claim to Glory.

"She looks like Mariel," Presley says with wonder.

A sound from the kitchen tells the men they aren't alone. *How could I have thought Glory would go to the car?* Austin futilely calls her name as he runs up the stairs. In the driveway he sees his empty vehicle. Panic sets in. How much did she hear? How much can one young woman stand? She knows someone wants her dead and then learns the someone is her biological father. Feelings of de'javu wash over Austin. He knows the betrayal the girl feels when she hears her whole life has been a lie. He remembers a period of time when he heard similar news about his past and went on to contemplate suicide. He must find Glory fast.

He asks himself where she'd go if she's seeking comfort. Elsa isn't around, and she must feel right now that Austin is part of a conspiracy against her. The only ones who've had her back through a lifetime are Mary and Steve. He makes tracks around the house. Sure enough, Glory is huddled against the female spruce. A pitiful sight. The few humans in her life aren't to be trusted, so here she is, hoping for honest affection from a tree.

Austin walks cautiously toward her, speaking in a gentle voice. "You are a glorious creation no matter who your real parents are. And Elsa loves you so much she gave up a normal life to raise you. She didn't know you were her grandchild, so she cared for you like you were her daughter. She and Burt gave you a lonely life, but it was only because they didn't want to lose you."

As he talks, Austin can hear Liz trying to reason with him in their last moments together in the old trailer. He'd been sitting on his bed reading her journal. Its entries had changed everything about his life. He didn't really listen to his biological mom's explanations at the time. Just as Glory is in her own world right now, not hearing a thing he's saying.

Words barely audible from her mouth are, "I'm the devil's granddaughter."

"Glory, you must know Presley isn't really the devil's spawn. That was just a figure of speech Elsa used to let you know he was a bad man. You aren't related to the devil described in the Bible, and that's a fact."

Speaking of the devil, what is Presley doing after learning he's a father? Austin is glad he removed the keys from his car. Presley still doesn't seem to possess transportation, so he's probably escaping on foot about now. Not daring to leave Glory alone, he has allowed the broken man from the basement to make a get-away. Calling 911 is the best Austin can do at the moment. He tells them to send officers to the Becker farm and nearby grounds.

Before going home, Austin returns to the basement to retrieve the jacket. Glory might want it later after she's at peace with her past. A quick search tells him the coat is gone. After twenty-one years of hanging unnoticed. On the positive side, it shouldn't be hard for police to spot a man running with a plaid coat over his arm.

He reminds himself that only last week, he and Glory returned Presley's old bike to the barn. A check of the junk pile in there reveals it has once more been removed. Austin must notify the police they should look for tire tracks in the high grass. Having no basket, hauling a coat while riding a bicycle might be more cumbersome for Presley than making his way on foot. Either way, the guy doesn't have much chance of escape. Austin can look forward to meeting up with him again, probably in a court room.

THIRTY-TWO

The week following Rue's frightening adventure has been a whirlwind of interviews with the police and the press. Austin and Gray have made a point of keeping Glory's name out of their comments. Meeting Presley and hearing his story have been enough trauma for the girl. There's no need for her to be put through any more only to satisfy the public's curiosity. Knowing she was the person Presley was really after would probably do nothing toward his capture.

One evening after people have quit stopping by the house, Glory and Austin find themselves with a little time alone in his trailer. The girl has been understandably going over her whole family situation in her mind. "Presley didn't seem as mean as I expected. But then he did want to kill me. That's pretty mean. Do you think the girl in the plaid coat loved him?"

"I do, Glory. The janitor at the high school told me how happy they seemed when they were together. I'm sure it was really hard on him when he lost Mariel."

"My mother was called Mariel," she said in awe. I can't get used to that idea. But I like the name."

"A lovely name for a lovely person the way I heard it."

Glory thinks about that. Then, "I don't think lovely people throw their babies away. Even Anita didn't do that."

It seems Glory is much more perceptive than he's given her credit for, but she's being a little hard on Mariel. "She really didn't throw you away," Austin explains. "Elsa told Wilma she thinks she saw the mother looking around the tree to be sure her baby went to someone worthy. Think how Mariel felt when another woman picked up the bundle and walked away. It takes a lot of love to give up a child because you realize you can't care for it as much as somebody else can." He thought of Liz who never even had the chance to make that decision. Her mother made it for her.

"I reckon you're right. But if I ever have a baby, I'll find a way to keep it," Glory says with resolve.

After a few more minutes during which she seems to be turning over the knowledge she's gained about her circumstances, Glory asks, "How can I ever get used to the way things are? Presley never was my brother. He's my father. I'm not going to call him that! And Mama is really my grandmother. I'll never keep it straight! I don't *feel* like that's the way it is. It all feels like a bad dream where people have other people's faces."

Austin puts his arm around her. "You and I should form a support group. When I was your age, I found out the woman I loved was my birth mom. The woman I called Mom was just a nice Meskwaki woman who'd cared for me all my life. And the man I thought was only a football fan, is my natural father. Life is really confusing for some of us."

"I'm not going to learn you're my brother or something, am I?" Glory asks, partly in fun.

"Gosh, I hope not!" Austin said with a laugh. But he wouldn't want to put any money on it.

◆◆◆◆

The next day is a continuation of Glory's discoveries. Austin takes her to visit her birthplace. The first sight when they drive onto the powwow grounds is a huge oak tree, a "spreading oak". A beauty of a tree, in Austin's opinion, much more eye-catching than Glory's adored Mary and Steve. The whole area around the Iowa River is at its best right after the powwow. The trees and other foliage are leafed out and inviting. The oak is at the edge of the clearing for parking cars. It backs up to more dense growth. No one can view the large tree from one side.

"Is this big tree mine?" asks Glory. "I feel like it is."

"Your guess is as good as mine. You were born twenty-one years ago, so it wasn't as big then as it is now." Still, it must've had a large enough trunk for a slim young girl to hide behind. In fact, this area could very well be the scene of Glory's birth. The baby was unclothed when found, and Mariel hadn't had a chance to even find a blanket. Those facts indicate that Burt and Elsa happened along right after the blessed event. Perhaps Mariel felt pains and darted behind the tree just in time. No one has mentioned whether the baby was cleaned up when discovered.

Glory seems to have been transported back to the scene. "I wonder how long she had to stay there watching the coat before Elsa and Burt came along. She might've been scared nobody would see it. Do you think if she'd had to get home before anyone came, she'd have left me there to rot?"

Austin couldn't help but laugh. "Interesting description. No, I don't think she could've made herself do that. Could you?"

"Glory, no! I think after maybe an hour, I'd have moved me to a different tree or just put me on one of the bleachers or something where the coat would be more noticeable."

"Think about it. If you saw a coat lying on a bleacher, you'd think somebody was coming back for it, so you'd probably leave it alone."

"I think if I'd been laying out in the hot sun with people talking all around me, I'd have started crying, and somebody would've heard me. I'd almost like to cry right now." And, indeed, Glory was tearing up in sympathy for the newborn she once was.

"Hey! Don't waste your tears! You survived!" and Austin gives her a hug. "I didn't think coming here would be so depressing for you." He looks around at his beloved powwow grounds. "I think it's a nice place to start a life. You were delivered on sacred ground. This is part of the original eighty acres the tribe bought over one hundred years ago. What an honor for you." He thought of his own beginnings at Ruby's house. "As good as a basket on a porch and a lot better than a garbage can where some babies are found."

"Ew! I guess if that were the choice I had, this place would be my pick. I wonder if my mother left any milk for me."

"She probably did," Austin says. Heck, he'd have said anything just to make her quit worrying about her young self. "And anyway, the Becker's would've known to find you some. After all," he teases, "they'd already raised Presley. He seems pretty healthy."

"Don't remind me. I'm glad he was gone by then, or he'd have probably pulled my hair or thrown me in the fruit cellar."

Remembering their last trip to the Cassidy Care Center to see Elsa, Austin and Glory are apprehensive. They expect the signs of dementia to have worsened rather than improved. That condition won't push up the date of Elsa's death, but it could make it hard for them to learn any additional facts about Glory's life. No one else knows her history except Wilma, and she's in custody.

As soon as they enter her room, and Elsa looks up from her magazine, Austin can tell she's having a good day. Her eyes are clear and her smile genuine. "Hi there!"

"Mrs. Becker! You're looking great!" he tells her truthfully.

"Yes, I feel *with-it* today. Must have slept well. What's been going on since you were here last?"

Oh, I don't know. Your son kidnapped my sister Rue and tried to trade her for Glory whom he wanted to kill so she couldn't inherit the farm. Wilma actually performed the abduction, and now she's in jail.. I found Presley in your basement looking at the plaid coat and crying. Glory heard him and me talking and learned he's her father instead of her brother. He got away and took the coat with him.

"Not much," Austin says aloud.

"Me either," Elsa reports. "Life is pretty slow in here. I have a lot of time to think. How did you do with your search for my latest will?"

"Actually, Glory found it. It was in your recipe box."

"That's right! I remember clear as day now. What did you do with it?"

"Your attorney Bill Hogan is holding on to it, so you can forget about the will now. We hope nobody needs it for a long time."

"Sometimes I feel a little guilty about Presley," Elsa admits, "I should at least give him a headstone, I suppose. Otherwise, he'll end up in an unmarked grave like a vagrant. Not very Christian of me."

"We'll make sure he gets one when the time comes. That'll be no trouble at all."

"Does Mariel have a stone? I suppose her parents took care of that. She must be buried on Meskwaki grounds."

Austin and Glory look at each other. "Did you know Mariel?" Glory asks.

"Mariel Bluesong? She was Presley's girlfriend. I thought they'd eventually get married, but she drowned not long after he went to prison. She's probably just as well off, but I liked her. I think she could've made Presley a better person." Elsa looks at Glory. "If I ever make a mistake and call you by her name, it's because you look a lot like her. She was an Indian. Some of them are very pretty, you know."

THIRTY-THREE

Arriving at the Morgan's after work, Austin sees only one person sitting on the porch. Liz is doing some kind of paperwork and Murray is napping at her feet. Neka is doubtless at Gray's side, wherever he might be. Husband and wife aren't often in the same place lately.

"Hi! Kinda quiet around here today. Is something going on I don't know about?"

"Not that I've heard," answers Liz without looking up from her work.

It could be the first time Austin and his birth mother have been alone to talk since he's been back. "Do you mind if I sit with you for a few minutes?"

"No. I'd love it! Guess I can take a break, but only because it's you. How are you Austin? I feel like you've been involved in so much drama since you've been here, there hasn't been time for just catching up."

He pulls a lawn chair closer to Liz but resists the urge to try reading her papers. "Yeah. *Drama* is the word for it. Everybody in this sleepy little settlement seems to be having some kind of crisis. At least you and I are okay. Aren't we?" And he looks at her intently, hoping for a candid answer.

"As far as I'm concerned, we're great." Her smile is warm. "It means the world to me to have you here. I hope you know that."

"I do. It feels good to be part of your family." He's never meant anything more.

"Tell me the truth, Happy. Have you been able to let go of the feelings you had for me before? I know they were real, so I've tried to give you all the time you need before I said anything."

"I know. Thanks."

"We can talk about it or leave it all in the past. I'm okay with whatever makes you comfortable." Liz is trying hard not to embarrass Happy.

"It had to be a weird thing for you to learn your son had a crush on you. But you never did say anything to make me feel stupid or ashamed of my feelings. I mean, it isn't something most moms have to deal with."

"It never crossed my mind to make you feel bad. In fact, my only concern has always been your happiness. I was just so naïve not to realize I was leading you to think of me as a girlfriend. It was so far from my reality, I didn't—"

"You don't have to explain. You already did, five years ago. I just wasn't listening. I was so wrapped up in my own misery, I didn't think about your feelings at all."

"I've always prayed time would help you understand. Has it?"

"It definitely has. That and your journals. When I finally made myself read them, everything made sense. By the time I finished the last one, I realized I finally know you. Really know you. And I feel now like you're my mother. I don't think my other mom would mind me saying that, do you?"

"No, Austin. I don't. The more I've thought about things she said over that summer, the more I'm convinced Ruby knew you were my son. Even if she didn't, I still think she would've been happy for me to take her place. It's the Meskwaki way, after all."

"Right. At first, I was afraid the tribe would let you be adopted as my mom, and I couldn't have stood that. Were you hurt when it didn't happen?"

"No. Her sisters were all for it, but the council decided they couldn't go against tradition and adopt a non-Meskwaki into the family. That wasn't a surprise. I'm your mother, and nothing they say or do will ever change that."

Austin, never an impulsive guy, gets up from his lawn chair and walks over to Liz. "I love you Mom. Is that okay to say?"

Liz laughs out loud. "Is it okay? You have to be kidding! I thought you said you read my journals!"

The tall dark son bends down and practically picks up his petite blonde mother. The embrace contains all the love, all the apologies, and all the relief of twenty-five years.

When they separate, both look at the floor and see that Liz's papers are in a huge pile. The pages are numbered but now completely out of order. Liz is going to have a big job unless she lets him help.

"I think I messed up again," says Austin as he begins retrieving his mother's project. "Is this stuff important?" As he's asking the question, his eyes land on a name, *Skyler Morgan. I shoulda known.*

Liz is still so happy, she can't manage to get upset. "Oh, yes. They're important. Normally, I'd be all crazy about now, but I'm so happy, I just can't care. We do need to find every page though." So the two bend down and, as quickly as possible, scoop up the parts of some unidentified manuscript. Fortunately, it isn't a windy day. Murray is somewhat helpful. He crawls under the porch to grab the papers that have slipped through the cracks. The drooling dog is incapable of keeping the ink dry so some deciphering is going to be necessary.

Liz sees the rest of the family at the end of the drive, so she hurries inside with her arms full. "Please don't say anything about this," she begs Austin.

"Happy!" calls Rue. "We took a LONG walk. We saw a baby horse."

"Good for you!" he responds, thinking how much he appreciates their timing. He's been fearing he'd never get to resolve things with Liz. There is one other thing, though, he wishes he'd had a chance to ask her. *What's the reason for all the phone conversations with Gray's brother?* He can't help but believe there's more than just some manuscript she's helping him with. Unless those papers are classified government documents, there'd be no reason for such secrecy. He hates to be having doubts about Liz's character just when they're becoming real mother and son. He scolds himself for thinking the worst. He's sure to find out the real story soon. Hopefully, Gray doesn't stop trusting her before she gets around to explaining.

THIRTY-FOUR

Austin is awake before sun up. Glory is sound asleep. The only sounds of life are the hooting of the owls and the whir of the small fan on the bedside table. Another definite sign Austin isn't the only person awake on the Morgan property is a dim light shining through the front window of the house. Austin can picture Liz on the couch with her phone and computer. It's very early for her and Sky to be doing business. He never can keep track of time zones, but it's possible it's later where Skyler is. Or maybe Liz is still trying to put the pages in order from the spill they took on the porch. He feels bad knowing his clumsiness may have caused her to stay up all night.

He's seen Gray take some kind of sleeping pill before bed, so the effects of those must make it easy for his wife to carry on all kinds of activities without bothering him. The thought of his dad's vulnerability makes Austin's spying seem justified.

He watches the patch of light for another half hour, and then makes the call to go in. He tells himself he might be able to help out. The truth is, his curiosity is getting the best of him.

Since he doesn't want to appear sneaky, he should probably just burst in and identify himself, "Hi! It's me, Austin." But that would wake up Gray, so he opts to be quiet and stand frozen in the middle of the living room.

Predictably, Liz is on the phone. "Listen, Sky, it isn't easy for me to get work done around here. I'm never alone. That's why I'm still at it now. Dropping all those pages really set me back, but I've got everything in order now. Have about finished the changes and will email you before four this morning. You're good, you know. I love the voice. I don't know if you mean for me to cry, but I do, every time."

"What? She loves his voice and cries every time she hears it?" Austin is getting fed up with her sweet words to Sky. *It's nice if they're working on a surprise, but do they have to be so gushy about it?*

Austin sits at the kitchen table and contemplates his responsibilities. Liz was the one who asked for him to come home. He's sure she didn't want him here to tattle on her. Still, if he learned anything from his experience five years ago, it's that keeping important facts from a loved one to spare his feelings, usually backfires. If his mother and Liz had been straightforward with him, a lot of hurt and a lot of wasted years could've been avoided.

He goes back and forth in his head. The question is "To squeal or not to squeal?" He's leaning toward a *mind your own business* policy when he hears a sound that makes him pause in his thoughts and hold his breath. It sounds like bicycle tires on the gravel driveway. Glory? Can't be. She returned the bike. The sound quickly fades.

He is reasonably sure Glory's okay because Murray didn't kick up a fuss. Still, he knows he should be in his trailer watching over her instead of stalking his mother. He gets up fast, knocking over the chair. It falls on a rug which muffles the sound, but since Liz isn't asleep, she hears it.

"Gray? Rue? Who's out there?" She sounds frightened. Maybe for their safety or of being caught talking to Sky. "Have to go!" she tells her caller.

Nuts! How can I explain this? Austin needs to manufacture a plausible excuse for Liz when she switches on the front room light.

"What on earth are you doing out here in the dark?" Her voice has the same motherly inflections as if she were asking, "What is your hand doing in the cookie jar?"

"I was starving and kept thinking of the molasses bread you made today. Guess I'm not very good at finding my way in the dark."

She just looks at him for a moment, as though trying to decide whether to believe him. "I guess not! Why didn't you just take some this afternoon? I mentioned it."

"I wasn't hungry then." *I sound like a little kid.*

"Well, don't move. I'll get you some." Liz is talking softly not to wake the rest of the family. Rue will be all excited if she comes out and finds a party going on in the middle of the night.

Austin doesn't say anything more because he doesn't want to delay his exit. He can't wait to get to the trailer and check on Glory. The mysterious sounds on the driveway have made him nervous. Everybody in town seems to agree that Presley Becker is history, but Austin expects to be looking for that man's return far into the future.

It doesn't seem wise to awaken Glory before dawn, so he sits in a chair with his bread and takes up a vigil. It is a little like locking the barn door after the horse is out, but he wants to be alert if the tire sounds are repeated.

As soon as daylight allows him to see their surroundings, he makes a thorough outdoor investigation around the trailer and yard to learn what, if anything, was disturbed by the late-night caller.

There's no indication anyone has been in the vicinity. The noises must have been Austin's imagination or an animal scurrying home. Presley isn't likely to risk coming near Glory so soon after being the object of a manhunt. Also, it would be very surprising if the man continued his pursuit now that he knows Glory is his daughter. Even Presley can't be that callous.

The one place left to examine in the light of day is the taco trailer. As far as Presley knows, Glory still spends her nights there. At least, the guy hasn't tried to start any more fires.

After the sun is up Austin and Glory take Murray for his morning walk. The dog keeps trying to go into the woods. He hasn't been very interested in that area lately, so Austin is puzzled. Glory, too, notices his behavior. "I think Murray wants to go visit my trailer." And she follows the hound.

"I see what Murray wants," she calls back to Austin. "My coat! Presley brought it back!"

"What?" Austin dashes to the trailer and follows Glory's pointing finger. He finds it hard to believe even as he stares at the plaid article of clothing hanging over the outside door handle. "I'll be darned. That's what it is alright."

"Oh, I'm so glad!" She takes the jacket and slips it on even though the August temperatures are already climbing.

"Wait," Austin smells a rat, and his name is Presley. He was the last person to be seen with the jacket, so Glory is right about him bringing it back. Austin regrets not intercepting him as soon as he heard signs of movement last night. That coat seems to mean a lot to the guy, and he isn't the type to return it simply out of sentiment. If it were Presley who left it, there must be a bomb in the pocket. "Let me see that thing. I want to be sure it isn't booby-trapped."

"A trap? Do you think he put it here just so I'd come over and fall in a hole or something?"

Austin hates to hear that kind of talk from Glory. Since he's known her, she's seemed so unaware of the criminal ways of the world. Now she's thinking more like her corrupt father.

She hands the plaid coat over, and Austin examines it. No bombs are found, but, not surprising to him, there's an envelope in one of the pockets. Presley is good at leaving notes. Austin remembers the unforgettable, *Give me Glory.* But this time, there's no message. The envelope simply contains a curly black and white photograph of a teenage girl. She is dark skinned, slim and attractive. Her facial expression reveals her pleasure with the photographer. Austin looks on the backside and finds written in the girl's own hand, *All My Love, Mariel.*

Austin would've said the guy had no material possessions to give away, but Presley Becker has found a way to leave his daughter two precious gifts.

◆◆◆◆

For a couple of reasons, Austin doesn't report Presley's midnight visit to anyone. Knowing he came back onto their property would have stirred up more anger in Liz and Gray, and they seem to have enough personal battles at the moment. It appears obvious the coat was the ending punctuation on Presley's dealings with his family. That physical reminder of his old love is staying behind with everything else he ever touched.

Contrary to his earlier feelings, Austin is now satisfied everyone's heard the last from Presley Becker. Glory's natural father isn't even likely to come back when his mother dies. And no one wants her experience in Wilma's cellar to be something Rue is forced to keep reliving because people are repeating the kidnapping story. There's a lot to be said for staying quiet and moving on.

THIRTY-FIVE

On Monday Rue is to make her trip to stock up on the essentials for kindergarten at South Tama. Liz has a list from the school, and Rue has opinions about what needs to be added to that list. Austin begs off. Counting Neka, the car will be full, and big brother has no advice for purchasing classroom supplies. He's just glad he'll never need any of those things again.

The whole delegation waves to him and Murray on their way down the drive.

Austin has writing to do for work, but he needs to get online to do some research first. He probably should've asked to use Liz's computer, but she told him the first week he was here he could use it anytime. He's found internet reception among the trees very sporadic, but he hasn't heard Liz complain much about the connection.

Unfortunately, she hasn't left her laptop on the table. It's in her bedroom. Her relative accessibility to the family the past couple of days tells him she must have finished whatever she's been working on with Sky. Austin has already gone through a guessing game in his mind. Perhaps his most logical conclusion is that the two are working on a grant application for Gray. He knows Liz has written grants at work, and there're some good ones to apply for. Since Gray is both handicapped and Native American, he's an ideal candidate.

However, the more he thinks about it, the more that idea doesn't make sense. Liz has been clear they don't need money, and if she and Sky were working on a grant for Gray, he'd need to be part of the process.

Austin is disappointed to find the laptop has been turned off and is password protected. Nevertheless, he remembers seeing a piece of paper taped to the bottom of her machine. Could he be that lucky? Sure enough, the word *Happy1984* is taped there. His name. Pretty predictable from a woman who was always thinking of her lost baby. He quickly gets into the computer and continues to wonder why anyone uses a password at all if it's so easily found by another party.

Liz's desktop shows some shortcuts to commonly entered documents. One is called Skybook. So it *is* a book. A book about Skyler or written by him. Should Austin open it? His conscience says *no*. Invading his mother's personal files is almost as bad as breaking and entering at her home. He wouldn't go to jail, but he'd definitely mess up their newly repaired relationship. He inserts his own flash drive and brings up the newspaper article he's writing. *Stick to your own business, Austin.*

He finishes in an hour. Considering the time it takes to drive twenty-two miles to Marshalltown to shop, probably topped off with an ice cream cone at Dairy Queen, he knows he has quite a while left to entertain himself. He goes to the kitchen and takes a soda from the fridge.

Who am I kidding? he asks himself. *I'm an honest guy, but I'm human. It isn't like I'd be looking at anything dirty or illegal. Just a book. Maybe I'll just check the title. That should tell me something. And maybe the first and last lines. Those could be clues as to why they didn't just hand it to me to read. After all, I have a degree in journalism. I might have a few helpful suggestions.*

That last thought makes him a little irritated and insulted. It is enough to push him back to the bedroom and onto the computer. Skybook turns out to be a big file.

First to appear is a title page. It says RED EARTH GIANT by Skyler Morgan. Austin goes to the Dedication page. The book is dedicated to *Gray Morgan, my brother, my hero, a giant among men.*

Austin immediately becomes teary-eyed. According to Gray, Sky has always been the superior one, the man who wins the trophies for smartest, most accomplished, most talented, handsomest, sexiest, and most popular. Maybe he's also the biggest phony. Maybe he just wants to write a successful book. It's called a novel rather than a biography, so he can play with the facts all he wants. Sky might manipulate the story to actually cause himself to be the star. Some people are good at that. Austin can't wait to read the whole novel. However, noises from outside and Murray's wagging tail tell him he's out of time.

He closes down the computer and makes it to the living room in time for Rue to come bursting in with, "My pencils are yellow with suns on them. They're beautiful!"

Glory is nearly as excited as Rue. "I ate a *large* Dairy Queen cone. Chocolate!"

It seems to have been a good day all around. The jury is still out on Skyler's motivations, but Austin feels confident Liz hasn't been doing any cheating on her husband, and that's all he really cares about.

◆◆◆◆

As far as he's concerned, Austin has to be extremely worn out when he goes to bed beside Glory. Otherwise, his thoughts go to things he's put off-limits for now. An evening walk with her down their country road might make him ready to fall asleep.

Since the temperatures have gone down into the lower seventies, Glory feels justified in wearing the plaid jacket. Austin expects to be seeing a lot of that garment.

"I told the people at the Courier I'd start coming back to work full days by the end of this month. I'm not ready, but if I want to save my job, I can't keep making excuses."

"You don't have to worry about me. I'm a grown woman now. I can take care of myself." But she reaches for his hand and holds it tightly. Austin can tell she's nervous about being left on her own again. He is nervous for her, but at the same time, knows she must learn to adapt to her surroundings and interact with people even when he isn't a few inches away.

"Someday you'll get the farm and all the stuff in the house. You can sell it or live there. You'll have choices. You even have choices now. You can stay with Gray and Liz or take over my trailer. No charge. I'd be happy for you to have it. Or you can live safely in Toby's Tacos until the tribe makes you get rid of it. Even though we don't know where Presley is, I don't think he still wants to hurt you."

Glory looks up at the tall Indian walking beside her. "I'm not very good at making choices. All those places you say I can live won't have you, so I won't be happy. I need you with me. Can I move to Waterloo?"

"Well, I guess so, but now isn't the best time. Don't you want to be close to your mom in the Home? She may not have long left."

"I've been close to her every day of my life. Now I want to be close to you." She squeezes his hand tighter as though someone were trying to separate them.

Austin can feel her pain. He doesn't want to part ways with Glory either. But to ask her to live with him, he should get to the subject of marriage, and that's something he won't be doing within the next couple of weeks. He has a lot of self-talk to do on the subject, and Glory is simply not mature enough for such a step. He remembers Liz telling him that if she's the one, they'll get together when she's experienced a little bit of life.

They reach the end of the lane and automatically turn around to start back to the house. Ahead, they see that Gray, Neka and Liz are catching up to them. "I thought you might be out here," Gray says cheerfully. "Just thought I'd tell you our decision."

"You mean your decision." Liz corrects him.

"Well, it isn't what I want. It's what you want."

"You've got that wrong. I don't want any such thing."

"You do. You just won't admit it."

"I think I know what I want. Who I want. The same person I've always wanted."

By this time, Austin is nervous. It sounds like his fears about their marriage are coming true. At least from his dad's perspective. "You guys don't even seem to know what you're arguing about."

Gray tries to clarify. "There's no argument—just facts. You heard me tell the guys I'm going to try a prosthesis. One reason for that is you, Austin. You think I should do it, and I respect your feelings. I figure I'll give it a go. If it doesn't work, I won't be any worse off than I am now. If it does, I'll be more useful to the police, and I'll be more independent when Liz goes to Oklahoma."

"What? You're going to Oklahoma?" Austin is looking at Liz, wondering how he missed that news.

"No, I'm not going anywhere. This is my home. Gray is my wonderful husband, the love of my life. Who is talking crazy tonight. He's being paranoid about his brother."

Austin can't believe Liz is prolonging the big reveal. Gray's recent loss of confidence is causing him to be overly suspicious. In earlier years, he'd have joked away his wife's little project. If his mother doesn't come clean before he leaves Tama, Austin is going to tell Gray himself.

The whole situation doesn't seem like a topic for encouraging sleep, so he tries to speak about something positive.

"I'm glad you listened to my suggestion, even though I'd rather it was your own idea. From little things he said, I get the impression Sky thinks the prosthesis is a no-brainer."

"He told me he'd get one if it were him and, because we have the same genetic makeup, it could be someday. He thinks it'd be a kick if we had opposite prosthetic limbs. I got to thinking about it, and I know if he ever loses a leg, he'll just take it as a challenge. He'll probably win a marathon. I decided I should get a head start."

"What's a prosthesis?" asks Glory after trying to make sense of the conversation between Gray and his son. Evidently, the old Britannica encyclopedias didn't cover that topic.

"A fake leg," answers Austin. "He ought to have it working by the time anybody in the family needs him to do something like be in a wedding."

"Wedding?" Glory asks. "Who's getting married?"

"No one as far as I know, but you never can tell what might develop. It'd be nice to be ready."

"This is messed up," observes Gray. "You start hinting about a marriage just when we're seeing ours end."

"Would you stop saying that?" Liz shouts. "Just trust me for a couple more days. Then I'll expect flowers by way of apology."

Austin backs her up. "All I know is that none of us is going to let ourselves think about romance or any important life changes if there's a chance you two are separating." He gives his dad a pointed look. "You're just going to have to work things out. For your family's sake."

"That isn't fair, and you know it," said Gray.

"Probably not, but lots of things aren't. Ask Rue what's fair about *your* plans."

The mention of Rue silences Gray. The four reverse their paths up the country road and return home in silence. Each has enough going on in his/her mind to keep sleep away for hours.

THIRTY-SIX

"Guess what!" announces Liz when everyone is on the porch attempting to enjoy their daily time together. "Franny Pushetoniqua called this afternoon. She asked if I mind if the police wives hold a benefit for Gray!"

"That's good of them," Austin responds. "I know a lot of people really like him, and they want a chance to help."

"Help what?" asks Gray. "How are they going to help me get over my lost leg?"

"Well, they can't do much about that, but they can show their support," explains Liz.

"You mean they can show their pity."

Liz ignores his comment. "Franny mentioned an Indian taco supper for a free will offering. And maybe they'll auction off some crafts. All proceeds will go to you. I think it's really nice of them to think of it."

"I thought you said money isn't one of our problems."

"I did say that, but if your friends want to make a difference, that's about the only way they know how. I'm sure you can find some way to use it. It's going to take a lot of gas to go back and forth to the clinic to get your leg fitted."

"Can I cook? I make Indian tacos," offers Rue, trying to get into the act. If a party benefits her dad, she's all for it.

Speaking to Liz, Gray warns, "If you let them do this, you'll get roped into working on a supper for somebody else in the tribe. There're plenty of victims of one kind or another on this settlement. It's better if the police don't get personally involved. We can take care of our own problems."

"Speak for yourself. Besides, it's too late. I told Franny to go ahead with it. It'll be at the tribal center."

"Would think you'd have mentioned the idea before you told her it was okay." He continues to be stubborn. "Don't expect me to show up."

"I didn't hear you complaining when everybody pitched in to search for Rue. Friends are pretty good to have around sometimes. You're lucky. When I got sent off to prison at sixteen, I would've appreciated even one or two people standing by me."

The group is quiet then. Nobody likes to be reminded of Liz's twenty years as a lonely inmate. The idea of that wonderful person being treated like a murderer is too awful to think about. And it's worse after hearing nobody from the outside gave her any assistance.

"You can't compare the two things," says Gray. "I only had half my leg cut off. Pretty insignificant as tragedies go."

"The way you complain, you could've fooled me," Liz shoots back.

Austin can sense another quarrel coming on, so he changes the subject. "I've finished my homesick series and am trying to come up with another new feature story to write for the paper. What if I submit the idea of an in-depth look at how service dogs serve?"

Gray is quick to respond. "Do what you want, but don't include me. I don't have any quotes to give you and don't want my picture taken."

"Okay. I predicted that. I'll find somebody else around here to talk to. But do you think it's a good idea?"

"Good as any." Gray is being careful to appear uninterested.

"Can I practice Indian tacos tonight?" Rue is still focused on her plan to work at the benefit.

"I don't think they'll expect you and me to cook," Liz explains. "We'll be looked at as guests, I think. So you probably should just sit with Gray and me. And smile."

"I don't want to smile. I want to cook. Me and Glory can cook together!"

"I don't even know what an Indian taco is," admits Glory. "Nobody would eat what I'd fix. About the only things I can make are fried potatoes and Snickerdoodles."

"Tacos are fry bread with hamburger and stuff on them. But Snickerdoodles are good, too! Dad, can we have those for your . . . thing?"

As usual, Rue's enthusiasm softens her father. He speaks in a more pleasant tone than before. "The question is whether we even want a lot of people coming to the *thing.*"

"I want a million people!!"

It's becoming obvious Gray will be causing his daughter much disappointment if he continues to balk at the whole idea. "Whatever," is the closest he comes to giving his unneeded consent.

Saturday evening finds Gray sitting just inside the front entrance to the tribal center, looking uncomfortable in his wheelchair, an afghan thrown over his lap. Liz has tried making a mild protest about the blanket, but it is clear her husband doesn't want folks staring at the empty space beneath his knee. "I'm not a sideshow," he'd told her. Austin knows how he must feel. Normally, Gray is present at such an event in uniform, the guardian of his people. Now he feels like a beggar asking for alms.

"Everybody's here! I hope they like cookies!" Rue declares as people begin to arrive. Not only members of the tribe have come but also police officers and other citizens from the town of Tama.

"I hope they have enough tacos to feed them all!" says Liz. She, too, is out of her element. Usually, she's in the kitchen during any kind of big dinner and has some control over the quantity.

Austin notes that in spite of Gray's continual threats about a divorce, Liz is at his side, greeting friends with a smile that belies any conflict between the pair. He's always thought her a class act, and that hasn't changed.

As the minutes progress, Gray seems to loosen up. Neka lays at his feet, her post for the duration of the afternoon. Austin is pleased to see Gray's hand going to the top of the dog's head every few minutes. She receives a pat and a scratch and maybe a few words. In a short time the animal has become an extension of her master. She's proven to be the loyal friend who never provokes his anger. In spite of the official vest she wears, many of the guests speak to her and ask about her. Neka, though, has eyes only for Gray.

Austin looks at Glory. "We may as well get tacos. You and I aren't really needed here."

Glory, he observes, is looking pretty overwhelmed. This is the first time in her life she's been in a crowd. He won't be surprised if she hyperventilates. "Are you okay? Maybe you'd rather step outside for some air." He can imagine how hot she must be in the jacket she insisted on wearing. Austin is no fashion expert, but he can't help but notice the plaid doesn't go very well with the flowered dress Liz loaned her for the occasion.

Glory takes him up on the offer. They go out onto the sidewalk in front of the center. A large overhang provides some shade but the outdoor temperatures are well over eighty degrees. There's no cool breeze to be had, and the humidity feels like one-hundred per cent.

"Don't you want to hang your coat up inside?"

"No, I'm fine." Glory gives him a smile that says, "Don't worry about me. I'm hanging on. The coat helps."

"There're lots of people," comments Austin.

"Yes. It's scary. Rue says they're all friendly. I just don't want any of them to talk to me."

"I don't blame you. Folks ask a lot of questions, and most of them are none of their business. If it weren't for Gray, I wouldn't want to be here either."

An attractive blonde lady walks straight up to them. Her appearance stands out in this largely black-haired crowd. Austin tries to pin point who she is. She must work at the casino where he was employed during summers all through college. "Hello, Austin! It's been a long time."

"I'm sorry." He has to admit he can't come up with her name. "You're—"

"Mary Ann Davidson. I used to work in Personnel at the casino. Your moth ... Liz and I were friends."

"It's okay," Austin assures her. "I'm all caught up now. I know Liz is my mother."

Mary Ann chooses not to comment on his statement. "I live in Des Moines now, so I miss out on some of the news from here. I do take the Tama Herald though, and that's how I heard about Gray's amputation and this supper. I just had to come say hello."

"They'll love to see you." Austin remembers now that Mary Ann was a kind lady. Also, she was another white woman for Liz to confide in back in the summer of '05. No doubt Mary Ann knows the whole shocking history of Liz's problem with her son.

"I can't tell you how happy I am things seem to have worked out for you," Mary Ann goes on. "Is this your wife?" She is, of course, looking at Glory.

Glory looks over her shoulder expecting to see some other woman standing nearby. "No!" she says when she catches on the lady is referring to her. "I'm just Glory."

Mary Ann looks amused. "Okay. Should I know you?"

"You probably should," Glory answers. "I'm a pretty nice person. At least I try to be."

Austin grabs the girl's hand. "She's a friend of the family."

"Pleased to meet you," Mary Ann says and moves on. She must be eager to ask Liz about this girl called *Just Glory.*

A Meskwaki woman appearing to be around sixty is shuffling her way to the front door. Her wobbly gait can mean the woman is a little inebriated or simply that she has trouble walking in flip flops. Or perhaps she's only exhausted for some reason. Her overall appearance gives the impression life has beaten her down. At first, she keeps her head lowered. Then just before reaching Austin and Glory, she looks up. Her gaze widens, and the lady looks frightened.

"Hi." Austin thinks maybe, as part of Gray's family, he should be welcoming people, even if he doesn't know them. In the absence of any response from this visitor, he continues, "Thanks for coming. If you'll go inside, you can enjoy some Indian tacos." He doesn't recognize the lady so can't call her by name. She doesn't speak. She has simply stopped dead in her tracks, staring at Glory.

He wonders if Glory has some way to know the mystery woman. It's unlikely since one can count the girl's acquaintances on one hand. Glory stares straight ahead and avoids looking directly at the guest.

"Do you know Gray Morgan?" Austin asks. It's rare for someone to attend one of these events if they don't have any connection to the family. "Or Liz?"

She can't look at him when she explains. "Officer Morgan was good to me years ago. H-He's the best one of the police."

"That's nice of you to say. He'll be glad you came." Austin is going to have to ask Gray about this member of his fan club.

He thinks he sees tears in the woman's eyes, but she finally moves along. He watches her reach the front entrance where she turns back for one more serious gaze. The sun seems to be in her eyes, so she shades them with her hand in order to get a better view of Glory.

"Wow," thinks Austin. *"All kinds of people come out when there's free food."*

THIRTY-SEVEN

Back inside, the noise level is increasing and so is the temperature. Austin wonders if the air conditioner is turned on but can't find anyone to ask.

"Let's get some food," he suggests. Glory doesn't answer but willingly follows him. He looks for Gray, Liz and Rue. They haven't moved from their original spots by the door. He knows Gray must be getting tired. He probably hasn't had anything to eat, and that isn't good for him. Liz always tries to keep their meals on schedule.

Rue runs up to Austin and Glory. "I haven't had a taco yet!" she says as though it's a very serious matter.

"Well, you can come with us," says her big brother. "We don't want them to run out, but guess we aren't expected to starve. Go ask the folks if they want us to bring them something, too. I'll be at the serving table."

Rue flies away and immediately returns with the message, "You go ahead. They'll come in a minute."

"Tell them to find a seat. We'll bring the food over." Rue runs back to relay his message.

While waiting in line, Austin's eyes scan the large room looking for the nearly-wordless woman from earlier. Suddenly, she is standing nearby, her hand on Glory's arm. "This coat. Where'd you get it?"

Austin doesn't think Glory should have to explain anything to the stranger. "She bought it. At Goodwill."

"Are you sure?" she asks in an accusatory tone. "I think it's mine."

"I'm sure you're mistaken, Ma'am. Unless you donated yours." Austin moves with the line, pushing Glory ahead of him.

"I'm not mistaken,' the woman insists. "I made it for my daughter. I remember every stitch."

Glory's eyes get big, and she looks at Austin for an explanation. She must be remembering Presley telling them Mariel's mother made the coat. But to Glory the woman he spoke of then was more of an imaginary spirit, not this flesh and blood Meskwaki who is looking at Glory like *she's* the ghost.

Austin is reaching for a taco as he's trying to answer the woman. "Do we know you, Ma'am?"

"I don't think so. My name is Danee. Danee Bluesong."

Austin drops the plate, and the taco ingredients scatter beneath the feet of surrounding guests.

"Austin, is she Mariel's mom?" Glory asks.

"I don't know," he answers. "But this is Gray's day. I don't think we should get into it here." He looks at the Bluesong lady for a minute, then says, "We probably need to talk, but it will have to be later. Come see me at the Morgan place on White Tail Road. Tomorrow afternoon."

The woman appears reluctant to go, but does as she's been told. When she's gone and the food mess has been cleaned up, Glory gets a fresh taco, and they sit at a long table with the family.

"I reckon she's my grandma," Glory says before she takes a bite. Her voice holds no feeling when she declares, "I'm probably supposed to love her."

She slips the plaid coat off and hangs it on the back of her chair. "I don't want to get stains on it," she explains.

Gray is sitting across the table. His face is red, and he appears to be sweating.

"Pretty warm in here, isn't it?" asks Austin.

Gray doesn't respond. He just nods and closes his eyes. Liz knows what is happening when she hears Neka whimper and sees her lay her head on Gray's lap, grasping at him with her front paw to get his attention.

"Tell people to clear away and give him some air," his wife says. Neka is getting more persistent. She barks out loud and even nuzzles Liz's purse. As it turns out, that's where the blood sugar monitor is kept.

In a few quick moves, Gray's levels are checked, he's given five small gum drops from Rue's pocket, and his color and breathing begin to return. A crisis has been aborted in plain sight of many of his friends. Everyone present is convinced Gray has an ongoing problem, and that a service dog can be a hero. Even Rue gets to take credit for having a bag of gum drops at the ready.

◆◆◆◆

"I know we had a scare today, but otherwise, it was pretty good, wasn't it?" At home, after the big event, Austin is hoping to hear the day has been a turning point for his dad.

Gray lowers his voice as though mimicking someone. "Yeah, I know the patient died, but other than that, how did the operation go?" Austin can see the man's point but is happy to know he also can find the humor after he was so opposed to the whole benefit to begin with.

"If I didn't have Neka, I'd be looking at a pretty shaky future." Gray continues. He seems to finally be coming to grips with his circumstances. They could be better, but they could also be a lot worse.

Austin can't wait to ask about their mysterious Meskwaki guest. "Do you know the older woman who came by herself? She was wearing a long skirt."

"You mean the Bluesong lady? I was surprised to see her there. It's been a long time since she's been around the settlement. She used to visit the police station pretty regularly, and I guess she did even before I moved back."

"Gee. What for?" The woman didn't look like a criminal to Austin.

"It always had to do with alcohol. DWIs and public intoxication. She drank too much and sometimes it even made her forget she had a kid. I think she's actually a good person. She used to be nice looking, but she looks kinda worse for wear compared to the old days. I did my best to get her into treatment. Hopefully, she finally took my suggestion."

◆◆◆◆

After hearing her history from Gray, Austin only half-believes the woman named Danee Bluesong will find her way to their place. She didn't seem very competent somehow, but he could be wrong. Of course, he's been away, but judging from the lady's age, she should have been around this area before he left. Having only eight hundred tribal members, the Meskwaki Settlement is the equivalent of a very small town. Of course, before he met Glory, he probably wouldn't have been interested in the Bluesongs. Some people just keep to themselves. And as a teen, Austin was pretty wrapped up in his own little circle of buddies.

If Danee is the mother of Mariel and is the woman who made the coat, she is someone Glory should meet. The girl's paternal grandmother is nearing the end of her life, Glory's dad has moved to parts unknown, so that will leave Austin's new friend with no blood relatives, a sorry state of affairs for a Native American. Family is so essential that when a person passes, relatives usually adopt another member of the tribe to fill the vacancy.

At any rate, Glory deserves to become acquainted with her mother's mother, if doing so will fill a void for her.

THIRTY-EIGHT

Mariel gave birth at the age of seventeen, and from the looks of it, she was following in her mother's footsteps. In spite of the rough edges he noticed earlier, the Meskwaki lady who is stepping from an old Dodge looks surprisingly young to be grandmother to a twenty-one-year-old.

"Ms. Bluesong! I'm so glad you came!" Austin walks out to the woman's car. "Shall I get Glory or would you rather you and I talked first?"

Danee seems relieved to have an option. "Wait. Please."

Glory is in the back yard with Rue who is giving her dance lessons. "Come sit on the porch," directs Austin. He motions for the woman to ascend the ramp.

Since there are so many people living at the Morgan residence, they obey an understood rule. If someone has company, the others stay out of sight unless invited. Besides, Gray and Liz are recovering from the emotional fundraiser the night before so aren't tempted to emerge and make conversation.

"I'll be right back. I'll get us sodas." Austin races into his trailer and back, glad to see the lady hasn't disappeared.

"Okay. Is there anything you want to ask me?" He hands her a Coke, and waits for her to start the discussion. He doesn't want to give away the story of Glory's life to the wrong person.

"I guess I'd just like to know how the girl got the coat. I can't believe it came from Goodwill."

Austin is trying to decide if she's interested in Glory or just the coat. "The jacket you say you made . . . where did you see it last?"

"My daughter Mariel was wearing it. Over twenty years ago. I can't really remember the last time, but she used to wear it a lot, almost all year long until it was getting to be out of style. I figured somebody made fun of it, and she finally threw it away but didn't have the heart to tell me."

"Well, Ms. Bluesong, I think you've probably answered your own question. It was out of style, so she gave it to Goodwill. Glory likes retro fashion, so she bought it, and it's hers now." For some reason, Austin is hesitant to tell Mariel's mother about her daughter's illegitimate baby. If the girl went to such lengths to keep her pregnancy hidden, she must have known Danee wouldn't approve. "Is it important to you to have the coat back?" He doesn't believe Glory will go for the idea, and Danee would have to tackle her for it.

"No, it isn't the coat I miss. It's Mariel. She drowned when she was only seventeen. The young lady with you looks so much like her that when she has the coat on, seeing her makes me stop breathing." Austin feels sympathy for Danee. She seems very sad and very sincere.

Remembering the photo Presley put in the coat's pocket, Austin, too, sees the same resemblance Danee does. Glory is a clone of her deceased mother.

As he is contemplating where to go with the conversation, Glory and Rue come around the house. "Glory dances good!" exclaims Rue. "I showed her."

"That's wonderful. Say, would you ladies mind letting me talk to my company in private?"

"We'll go inside," says Glory. "Just remember, the coat is mine. It was giv—"

"Okay. See you in a little while," Austin says before Glory can say her father gave her the coat.

"Do you still think she looks like Mariel?" he asks Danee.

"Yes. It's like she's returned." Her voice holds wonder, reverence.

"I'm afraid this girl is a whole different person. Did your daughter leave a child behind when she died?"

"No, she didn't. Mariel loved only one boy, a white but they didn't have a child. I was glad of that. I didn't want a half-breed grandchild, and that's all they would ever have had."

That statement stopped Austin from spilling the whole story. If Danee had wished for a child from the young couple, he'd have told her there was one. There seems to be no reason now to divulge Mariel's actions. The girl might have given her baby away even if Presley had come up with some money. Family disapproval would be very hard for a seventeen-year-old to withstand.

"I'm really sorry to hear about your daughter, Danee. I wish I could offer you something to help, but I really can't." He stands up, a signal their talk is done. "Do you live on the settlement?"

"No, I'm visiting my sisters. I couldn't stand the memories, so years ago, I moved to Nebraska."

"Your husband?" Austin is wondering if there's yet another person waiting in the wings to claim Glory. For a foundling, she's amassing quite a family.

"He died real soon after Mariel passed. She'd been our perfect child, so she took all the light from our lives when she went." She brightens a little then. "At least we didn't lose her to a white man."

"Well, I'm glad your bloodline didn't get tainted," Austin says as he gets up from his chair. As far as he's concerned, their talk is over. The woman can leave without meeting her granddaughter. She doesn't deserve Glory.

Danee is turning slowly toward her car. "Can I have your phone number?" Austin makes himself ask. If Glory ever decides she wants to contact her maternal grandmother, he can't deny her that chance. There are probably things the girl will want to know about her bloodline that even Gray can't help with.

The woman seems puzzled but takes a notepad from her purse and writes her number and address on it. "I like to look at her," she says.

Austin senses she might know the truth deep down. Otherwise, why would she have come? He's beyond thankful that his Meskwaki mom didn't have the same prejudices. She'd loved him regardless of his mixed heritage.

The car pulls away slowly, hesitating at the end of the drive as though the driver might change her mind. In spite of himself, Austin can feel the woman's pain. To her, it must be like driving away from her Mariel.

"Is she gone?" asks Glory when she comes out of the house a few minutes later.

"Yup. I doubt you'll see her again unless you want to."

"And she won't take my coat?"

"No. She said she isn't interested in doing that. She just wanted to know how you got it."

"She probably thinks I'm a thief."

"No way. She's still grieving for her daughter, and likes to hear anything connected to her. She doesn't seem to think much of Presley though, mostly because he's white."

"That's the only part about him I *don't* mind. He can't help his color."

"Danee might have been brought up to feel the way she does, so we can't blame her. She seems like a nice enough person otherwise."

"Well, she didn't say much to her own granddaughter. She can't be that nice." Once again, Glory is showing remarkable perception for a girl who hasn't had experience with people from any nationality. She spends a few moments mulling over what she's learned about her beginnings. "I guess I understand why my mom didn't want anybody to know about me. She was ashamed my father was white and creepy."

"I don't know if she was ashamed or just afraid. Of what her folks would do. A well-behaved girl like Mariel probably tried to please her parents. So sad that both of those women missed out on knowing you."

Austin and Glory start up the ramp to the house but turn around when they hear a car on the drive.

"It's her again! Did you say something to make her mad? She might be coming back to take the jacket after all!"

Austin grabs Glory's arm. "Don't run away. We'll stand our ground, whatever she's after."

Once again Danee Bluesong gets out of her car. "I couldn't leave without meeting you," she says to Glory. "It would bother me forever."

Glory doesn't know how to reply. She looks helplessly at Austin. On impulse, he decides to be truthful. "Well, then . . . let me introduce you to your granddaughter, Glory. She just turned twenty-one."

Glory tries to smile and folds her arms across her waist protectively. The coat isn't going anywhere if she can help it. She measures her grandmother with her eyes. They seem to say, "I can take you on if I have to."

"Hello, Glory," Danee says shyly as she gives the girl an unreciprocated hug. "I hope you've been having a happy life. We adopted Kayla Summer Chaser as our daughter after Mariel died. She's your mother now if you want to go live with her."

"Sorry, Danee," interrupts Austin. "I know how that works, but Glory's an adult and doesn't need to meet any more family. At least not now. Maybe someday she'll contact you."

"Whatever's best," the woman responds, her sober facial expression showing both disapproval and disappointment.

Austin feels no blame for not encouraging Glory to meet her mother's replacement. None of the family have missed her up until now, so they're apt to get along just fine.

"Have a nice trip back to Nebraska." are Austin's parting words to their visitor. "Stop and see Glory any time you're on the settlement."

Danee tentatively touches her granddaughter's cheek. "Yes," she says.

"Okay," says Glory as she draws the fabric belt more tightly around her waist. "I'm sorry your daughter drowned."

"I thought I should say something like that," she tells Austin after her grandmother is gone. "I feel sad about Mariel, and I never even met her, so I know it's worse for her mom who knew her for years."

THIRTY-NINE

It's been several weeks since Liz has allowed herself the luxury of television. Her presence has been very much missed while she's been hidden away behind one or the other of the bedroom doors. The family has pictured her at the computer during those hours, working on her mysterious project or communicating with her brother-in-law.

Sometimes when things are quiet, she can be heard talking softly on the phone. Everyone has pretended not to notice, except Rue who periodically hollers, "Mom, who you talking to?" Liz only replies, "Nobody." It's been like living with a reclusive teenager.

Tonight she's emerged to sit casually on the couch during *RANGO*. Rue curls up next to her mom the way she did before Liz became involved in secret matters. Gray has been ignoring them all. He simply scowls and remains mute. Austin can tell he isn't watching the movie. Obviously, he is in mourning over the death of his marriage. *It would be understandable*, thought Austin, *if Liz had actually said she's leaving. But she never has. Gray is making himself miserable over something imaginary.*

Now that he has some idea of what Liz has been doing, Austin doesn't worry as much about her puzzling actions. Tonight she's being the Liz he knows, even popping popcorn for them. She carefully measures out the allowable three cups of low-fat microwave corn for Gray, but he loses interest after two bites. Rue tries all her tricks to get her dad to laugh, but he isn't having any of it. Liz snickers at the animated comedy and seems unconcerned about any pending divorce. In fact, Austin can sense a certain peace about her that says *all is well*.

Every day, Liz has been telling whoever is listening that Gray will be his old self soon. But Austin thinks there's a possibility whatever she has been doing to surprise her husband is going to fall just as flat as Rue's jokes and the movie. By the time the secret comes out, he'll have conjured up dozens of dire suspicions. It will be just as hard to change his thinking as it has been to convince Glory she doesn't have a contagious disease. Austin has learned that facts don't always play a part in what people feel.

Just when it seems like the so-called comedy can't get any less funny, there's a knock at the door. Rue flies to answer it with Murray at her heels. Neka perks up but doesn't leave her place at Gray's feet.

The subdued movie watchers are greeted by Skyler Morgan's million-dollar smile. "I'm back! Where's my old friend Neka?" Neka's tail gives several loud thumbs, but she stays put.

Sky becomes a bit self-conscious when even the dog doesn't come to greet him. "Glad to see she's settled."

"Come on in, Sky! How was the powwow?" asks Liz. She rushes to pull out a chair and fetch him some popcorn. Gray sits in detached silence. Austin raises a hand to acknowledge the man who's caused him so much worry.

"It was great. They really know how to do things right down there. You should see the crowds they get."

"Well, if you'd ever grace the Tama powwow with your presence, you might find out it's just as good." comments Gray dryly. Austin, too, is tired of hearing how things are so much better somewhere else.

"You forget Tama's where I got my start," replies Sky, the smile still in place.

"Mom made me a new dress for the powwow," Rue informs him proudly.

Austin is hoping his sister won't go on to tell the story of her abduction. There isn't enough time this evening to get into that saga.

"That's great, Rue. Wish I could stick around and have you dance for me, but I've got to start a new job. Gonna be a trainer at a new gym back home."

Gray doesn't mention he's all the way up to forty-pound weights now. "Guess you have a lot to get back to. You and your new girlfriend."

Sky hesitates, confused. "No girlfriend, now that you took Neka away from me."

Gray rolls his eyes at his brother's attempt to dodge the topic. There is another quiet interval, so Liz saves the stalled conversation. "Did you find time to do any writing while you were gone?"

Sky looks mischievous, like he and Gray's wife share a confidence. "Not really. I've been having my last book printed, so I've been taking a break."

"Listen, Sky. There's something you should know." Gray manipulates his wheelchair to get closer to his brother. "My wife and I are separating. I know about you and her."

Austin is stunned that Gray has come right out with such an announcement. He whispers to Glory to take Rue in the other room. There's no reason for her to hear such talk.

"Sky, don't listen to him," says Liz. "He's delirious. Nobody is separating. And Gray, if you weren't in such a hurry to jump to conclusions, you might save yourself a lot of embarrassment."

"Why should I be embarrassed?" he responds loudly. "I'm not the one who's been courting my brother's spouse."

Sky keeps his volume under control, but is clearly upset by the accusations. "Come on, man, you know that's not true. It wouldn't do me any good if I tried. And how have I been chasing Liz when I've been hundreds of miles away?"

"It's the technical age. Phones, computers, all kinds of ways to keep in touch with somebody who's vulnerable."

Liz is quick to squelch that description. "What do you mean, *vulnerable*? What kind of helpless, mindless female do you take me for?"

Austin has been trying to stay out of things but senses his mom could use his support. "Now, Gray, don't be accusing anybody until you know the facts. I found out a little about what's been going on, and it isn't anything you'll be bothered by once you hear it."

Sky jumps in before Gray makes another of his wild allegations. "Liz, maybe we'd better explain ourselves . . ."

"Yes. I see what's happened, and it's my fault. I haven't been very sneaky. We live in close quarters around here, so it's been hard."

"Will you two stop carrying on in code while I'm sitting right here? My leg doesn't work, but my ears are fine!" Gray's face is growing red, and he seems to be having difficulty speaking. Neka is vigorously slapping at his hand with her paw.

"Oh, my God!" Liz exclaims as she runs for the bedroom and comes back with the glucose monitor. She quickly checks Gray's levels while Rue waits with a glass of juice. The little girl must have gotten it ready as soon as the dog touched her dad.

Silence has taken over the group. Everyone is watching Gray try to push Rue away. She is persistent, however, and finally gets him to take a couple of sips. Neka is calm but sits very close to her friend, alert to any changes.

In a short time, it's clear Gray's levels have normalized. But the overall strained feeling is still in the room. They all know stress isn't the sole cause of hypoglycemic attacks but have been told it's a contributor. No one wants to trigger anything.

Skyler stands. "You know what, Gray? I think my timing is pretty terrible. I should just drop off this package for Liz and be on my way. We'll have another chance to talk when life straightens out."

Gray doesn't answer, but nods his head. The man he usually is knows he's just behaved badly, that Sky isn't his enemy, but he isn't ready to express those thoughts to his brother.

Skyler hands the sack to Liz and turns to go. Rue rushes to him and hugs his legs.

"You're the best, Rue," says Sky. "They are so lucky to have you and your brother. We'll have some good times later." He turns to go, then adds, "Liz, thanks so much for your help. You'll be paid later. Now everybody, get back to your movie!" He scratches Neka's and Murrays ears and takes off.

"Aren't you going with him?" Gray asks Liz.

She walks over to Gray and puts her arm around him. "No, you can't get rid of me that easy. I'm in this for the long haul."

"But there's no end. Life with me isn't going to get better."

"Oh, yes it will. When I can look in your eyes and see my husband, things will be way better."

After Rue has gone to bed, Liz, Gray and Austin are still in the front room. The TV is turned off but everyone seems nervous about Gray.

"How are you doing? Feeling okay?" asks Liz.

"No, I feel pretty terrible."

"What is it? Should I call a doctor?" his wife is frantic to think she's taken his recovery for granted. Neka, who's supposed to know these things, seems quite unconcerned.

"Do we need to check his levels again?" Austin asks.

"No reason to get excited. I'm okay physically, but I don't feel very good about letting Sky go like that. He gave me the dog who saved my life and probably will again. What an ungrateful jerk I've turned out to be."

"You aren't *that* big of a jerk," Liz says and kisses him on the forehead.

"That's right," says Austin. "You're an especially kind man who's learning how to cope with the unlucky hand he's been dealt. Sky knows that, I think."

"But, heck, I accused him of having an affair with my wife. That's not very brotherly of me." He looks at his wife. "It's starting to seem like I was way off base."

"Actually, to use another baseball term, you're off in left field." Liz is smiling affectionately at Gray.

"By the way," inserts Austin to Liz, "what did Sky give you?" He has some idea what it is, and thinks it could help convince Gray of everyone's innocence.

"Well . . . let's find out!" Liz is enjoying herself now. She reaches in the bag. "Goodness! It looks like a book. Are you up for reading one of Skyler's novels?" she teases her husband. She doesn't need to remind him of how he's always poked fun at his brother's writing efforts.

"Not now. I'm trying to feel better toward him. Something tells me that book will make it harder."

Liz hands him a hard-backed novel with an eye-catching cover. RED EARTH GIANT shows a water-color of a man standing on a hill looking strong and commanding. *The journey of a Meskwaki man who knows how to live.* Whoever did the artwork has totally captured the look of Gray Morgan— standing on two legs. A reader can't tell if one of the legs is a prosthesis or not. In spite of certain features in common, any reader who knows him will not mistake the portrait for being his look-alike brother Skyler.

"Wow," breathes Gray. "This never crossed my mind." Unable to look at Liz just then, he asks her, "Did you have something to do with this? Is this book what you two were talking about all the time?"

"Guilty," she replies. "The book is fiction, written totally by Sky. But you'll recognize who he's channeled for his hero. I only did the editing. I think this copy is just a proof, so you can point out any inaccuracies, and we'll fix them before the book's published."

"I don't care if it's accurate. I just can't get over that he'd ever want to write about me. His life is a lot more interesting."

"He doesn't think so. Read the Dedication page." She helps him find it. "This will blow you away."

Indeed, Gray is blown away. Liz and Austin watch him straighten in his wheelchair until he seems to grow several inches. "Bring me my cell phone. Please."

Austin looks at his watch. "It's after eleven. And Sky is driving. Can't it wait 'til tomorrow?"

"It can't wait." Gray dials but apparently gets voice mail. "Hello, Skyler! It's your scumbag brother. I want to say I'm so sorry…and so humbled…"

FORTY

Gray's attitude has done a dramatic upswing following Sky's return visit. In fact, the next phone conversation Austin is privileged to overhear is his dad calling Tama County Florists. "A dozen roses, please. Delivered to White Tail Road for Elizabeth Morgan. Sign a card *Together Forever, Gray.*"

Having shed the weight of suspicious thoughts, he's feeling friendlier toward his family and the world. Austin has even heard notes of excitement in his father's comments about his future. "The department has several new cases in the works right now. Sure is good timing that I can give them some serious hours now. I think Neka's looking forward to getting out more, too. Maybe they'll let her join the force."

◆◆◆◆

Two weeks after the last visit to his prosthetist, Austin and Liz go with Gray to Marshalltown so he can pick up his new leg. The ride there is a quiet one. Everyone is nervous about what to expect from the anxiously-awaited limb. Will it be the answer Gray seems to be expecting or a dismal disappointment? Dr. Patell has made no promises.

There's a collective intake of breath in his office when the bionic leg is revealed to Gray, Liz and Austin. They've seen photos so aren't shocked at its mechanical appearance. The more lifelike covering will be added later when any adjustments have been made.

Everyone breathes easier when the leg is attached, and Gray seems comfortable. No obvious rubbing or pinching. At least not yet. Just seeing Gray stand tentatively on two legs is a thrill for the family.

The change in his facial expression indicates the man is feeling a surge of normalcy. Austin thinks he also detects determination in the set of his dad's jaw. The prosthesis is going to work because its owner has made up his mind. The Red Earth policeman has decided it will be man over machine. He will tame the blasted thing if need be.

"We'll keep at it," says his doctor. "I'll probably be seeing a lot of you for a while until we get it perfect, but I won't give up if you won't."

"Don't worry. I have a lot of years to go and a lot of things to do."

◆◆◆◆

For several days, Gray is like a child with a new toy, trying everything he can think of to test the leg's capabilities. He falls a few times right in front of everyone, but, just when they're waiting to hear a string of obscenities, he shocks them by laughing.

"Cool!" declares Rue. "Can I take it for show and tell?"

"Sorry," says her dad. "It's part of me now and has to follow me to work." Liz tries to be as confident as her husband about his chances for success. She has known friends who found it impossible to get a good fit and had to eventually give up hope of adopting their prostheses for the long term. Much has to do with the location of the amputation and whether a bone will be irritated by constant wear. Only time and regular use will tell.

◆◆◆◆

Austin is giving himself one more week before he moves out of the trailer. He dreads leaving everyone but is ready to live in more spacious quarters and follow a regular schedule.

Gray is already going to work two days a week. The first day reportedly went smoothly. "All the men try to be so darn helpful. They never were like that before I was one-legged."

"You probably just didn't notice," Liz points out. "You might've taken their helpfulness for granted before when you didn't need it as much."

Gray and Austin have been taking walks with Neka and Murray. "We have one more thing to do before I know you're going to be okay." Austin says on Friday.

"What's that?"

"You need to try doing something you haven't done in a long time. Didn't you used to play basketball?"

"You know I did. And I could outshoot you from the free throw line with one leg tied behind me."

"Maybe you still can, old man. Wanna find out?"

"Hey, slow down. I was kidding. If I get out on the court, I'll probably get twisted around and end up in a heap!"

"What if you do? It isn't like nobody ever falls down on a gym floor. We don't have to move fast. We'll just be two has-beens throwing the ball up. No pressure."

"Maybe later, but I don't think I have that much balance now. I'd have done better on crutches."

"Winning isn't the point. Maybe we can settle for a little game of catch."

"You're just afraid of me," says Gray with a laugh. He's relaxed a lot as far as what onlookers will think. To prove it, he actually positions himself on the free throw line. "Let's do this!"

And the shooting contest is on. The participants move cautiously, and it's good no one is keeping score because he wouldn't have much to do. But both men stay upright and, for Gray that's a victory.

As the two swish more and more baskets, the taunts they throw at one another get stronger and the cheering louder. When

Liz appears in the doorway with Glory and Rue, the three females aren't even noticed.

The men finally stop to rest, and the gallery makes itself known. "Yay!" says Rue. "Dad and Happy are stars!!"

Liz, too, is clapping, but Glory stands silently, mesmerized by yet another demonstration of how to have fun.

Austin throws her a ball, and she impresses herself by catching it. "I think I could get it through the hole, if you'll just move that net down a little lower," she suggests seriously.

"Right. And Rue could ride a bicycle better if it had four wheels. Some things just can't be made easier or it would ruin the challenge."

"But the hole is so high! Maybe if I stood on something."

Rue feels obliged to show Glory how to play basketball. It quickly becomes apparent to the older girl that a person can enjoy the game without ever making a point. The friends laugh and run around while Gray holds down a bleacher. Liz joins in by chasing down loose balls and gets the giggles when she slips and falls.

Watching the three girls, Austin realizes he loves them all. Just a few weeks ago, he didn't think he and Liz could ever be comfortable around each other, and he didn't even know the other two. Now he can't imagine life without any one of them.

At his lowest point five years ago, Archie told him things would get better. Archie isn't often right, but that time he nailed it. Things get better if you can just be patient.

FORTY-ONE

"Mama?"

The elderly woman in the bed looks toward the open door of her room. "Who is it?"

"It's me, Mama, Presley."

"Presley? Are you sure? "

He walks over to the bed so she can get a good look at his face. "Yeah, Mama. I've been in jail for a long time, but I'm out now. Gonna be leaving town again, but I just had to see you once more. I've missed you." He takes Elsa's hand, and she doesn't pull away.

Tears come to the old eyes. "You look thin. Haven't you been eating?"

Presley laughs bitterly. "Oh, yeah, but the food wasn't ever good enough that I'd want seconds."

"You never said why you did it. The Presley I raised wouldn't have held up a business."

"I didn't want to, Mama. I knew you'd be disappointed in me. But I was desperate. Mariel was planning to give away our baby because we didn't even have money to pay for a hospital or anything it would need. I had to do something. I just messed it up like I do everything."

There is silence in the room. A nurse's aide enters. "Is everything okay in here?" She gives Presley an accusatory look. "Do you need anything, Elsa?"

Elsa's mind is elsewhere. "I need to go back to when Presley was little. I'd try harder."

After giving the male visitor a warning glare, the aide slips out of the room.

"Please don't blame yourself, Mama. I was a grown man when I got arrested. And it was better I was sent away. I'd have been a worthless father."

"I think she's yours. Glory, I mean."

"Really?" Elsa gets to see her boy smile. "Glory's friend told me she is, but I didn't know if I should believe him."

"Austin is an honest man. If he told you, you can believe him."

"Wish I'd known sooner. I heard some girl was living with you, and I thought she was an imposter, just after your money. I kept thinking I should run her out of town."

"She was a life-saver for your father and me after we lost you."

"I'm real glad to know that. And I'm happy she got to have a life. She should've been my responsibility, and I blew it. I thank you for taking care of her for me." He lifted her hand from the covers and gently kissed it.

"Didn't do it for you. I didn't know she was yours."

"That's okay. Thanks anyway. Is she a good person?"

"Oh, yes. She's an angel." Elsa pulls herself up and speaks more loudly than she has been. "But please don't take her away!"

Presley sits beside his mother on the bed. "I won't. I can't do anything for Glory. Don't even know how to take care of myself." He hesitates, a little embarrassed to ask, "Do you have a picture of her I can take with me?"

h

"Just this one." Elsa points to her night stand and an image of Glory at about twelve years old, standing between Mary and Steve. "Don't lose it."

He reaches for the framed photo and puts it into his backpack. "I'll keep it forever."

Elsa appears to summon courage for her next announcement. "You aren't in my will anymore, Presley. I'm sorry."

"I don't blame you, Mama. I never expected to be after I found out about Glory. I'll manage somehow. It's time I got a job. Now don't you worry about anything." And Presley bends down and gives his mother a big hug which she eagerly returns. They stay that way for several minutes.

The nurse's aide peeks in. Seeing mother and son embracing, she is curious. *"I wonder how many secret children that woman has!"*

FORTY-TWO

Austin's time away from the Courier is nearly over, and he has exerted any helpful influence he might have over his family and Glory. Intuition tells him today's stop at the Cassidy Care Center will be his last. Elsa's statement about having a bad ticker and his own indefinite plans for revisiting Tama are indications he should see her while he can. *That*, he thinks, *is true for anyone. You never know how things will be the next time you get around to making contact with the people you care about.* He never anticipated at their last meeting, that the next time he saw Gray things between them would be so very different.

Glory is naturally delighted any time he suggests a trip to visit Elsa. No matter how many people try to stake a claim to her, the person Glory is most attached to is the woman she's always referred to as Mama.

On their way to the care center, Glory voices her concerns. "I hope she doesn't call me Mariel today. Even though it's a nice name. I only want to be her Glory."

"Well, that's the name she's thinking, no matter what comes out of her mouth. Nice bright flowers. She should like those." He's noticed the bouquet in her hand since she got into his car.

"These are peonies. I hope Liz doesn't mind I took some."

"Oh, no. I don't even think she planted those. They grew in the yard on their own when I lived there."

"We have some at the farm, too, and Mama liked them. But she always made me pick the ants off. I've got this bunch all clean for her."

Inside, they ask at the desk whether Elsa is available. Sometimes she can be found having a snack in the TV room or the dining room. Austin thinks it nice the woman has finally been getting the chance to do a little socializing. She spent so many years hidden away with Glory, she must have been all but forgotten by her friends. "I know they think I've been dead for a long time. They'll be shocked when my funeral gets advertised."

The nurse's aide greets them. "Elsa should be in her room, but she could be sleeping. She had a visitor earlier who stayed several minutes. Having company usually tires out the residents."

On their way down the hall, Austin and Glory try to imagine who her visitor might have been. They haven't been aware of anyone else who's called on her since they've been coming.

Glory is walking slightly ahead and can't wait to open the door to Elsa's room. "It's me!" She stops in the doorway. Austin can't see what has blocked her entry. Perhaps a chair is in the way. "Oh, Mama!" she exclaims and starts to cry. She turns around and tells Austin, "She's on the floor! I think she fell trying to leave. We have to get help!"

Staff have already heard her cries and are at the door in an instant. "Please stay out in the hall, dear," they command gently.

Austin takes Glory down to a lounge area where they can be out of the way. Another aide joins them before he can prepare Glory for what is likely to come.

"I'm so sorry, sweetie," said the nice lady in the blue smock. "I just saw your mother this morning, and she seemed in good spirits. She was in no discomfort at all while her son was here. I think she must've felt so good, she thought she'd leave the room to do something."

"Her son?" Glory exclaimed. "I can't believe Presley came. It must've been someone else."

"Well, I don't know. It did surprise me, but when he arrived, he said he was her son. And I saw them hugging. His visit didn't seem to be a disturbing one for her. In fact, I got the impression she was delighted to see him."

Glory looks at Austin. "Mama hated Presley. She'd never forgive him unless her mind was all messed up again."

"Well, maybe you can just take it as a good thing," says Austin. "They say forgiving people brings you peace."

The nursing home administrator enters the lounge area wearing a grim expression. A name tag says he is Miles Conner. "I'm afraid Elsa is gone," he tells her two visitors.

Glory has to straighten the man out. "No, she can't be gone. She hasn't driven for a long time. And we just saw her. She was in her room, but she'd fallen and knocked herself out."

Austin hugs her tightly and tries to make her understand. "By *gone* they mean she isn't alive anymore. I'm so sorry, Glory."

"Are you sure? Sometimes she just dozes off, and I have to check her pulse, but she always wakes up!" Glory is trying to convince herself as well as the men. "Let me try!" And she gets up to go see what she can do.

Austin keeps his arm around her and smooths her hair, unconsciously trying to mimic a mother's affection. "I'm sure they've checked her pulse, Glory. They wouldn't tell us she's gone until they made sure. It's just her body in the room. Your mom isn't really here anymore."

Glory seems to remember something about what she learned from the Bible. "She's gone to Heaven, you mean."

"That's right." Austin is glad Glory already knows about Heaven. All the Bible reading has given her beliefs to hold on to.

"You can go in and see her," Miles Conner says in a kind voice. "They've laid her back on her bed for a few minutes."

Glory is shaking. Austin is somewhat at a loss. He remembers Liz trying to help him feel better when Ruby died. The circumstances between him and his mom's friend were so awkward at that time there was nothing Liz could say. In spite of all the relatives and friends who surrounded him for days after his mother's death, he'd felt terribly alone. It's probably much worse for Glory. Elsa was her only human contact until she became an adult. It's hard for Austin to comprehend the size of her loss.

They go back to room fifty-four and enter with reverence. Austin is grateful the Home hasn't hurried to remove the body. Elsa is lying on her back with a slight smile on her face. The woman died a natural death when her time came. He never felt that happened to his mother. She was taken violently in her prime.

"I hope they checked her for gun-shot holes," says Glory. "If Presley was here, he might've got mad that she didn't leave him anything. He pulls guns on people who cross him. Mama was always afraid he'd do that to her."

Austin was sure nobody missed any bullet wounds, but he did wonder if the son's visit had anything to do with Elsa's heart stopping when it did. The fact she'd been on her way to the door might be a sign she was trying to stop Presley from going somewhere or doing something. Or maybe she was hoping to persuade him to come back.

Aware there are things that should be taken care of, Austin understands he isn't the one to think of them. He knows only the ways of the Meskwaki which are much different at such a time. He takes out his cell phone. "Liz, I'm at the care center. Elsa has died. She was Christian, so we need you to come."

Austin's mother takes charge and arranges for the care of the body and the funeral. They ask to have a small service at the center with a minister the receptionist recommends. Gray and family and Glory make only five to pay their respects to Elsa. Wilma can't get away. Presley's where-abouts are uncertain.

During the discussion about her mother's service, Glory decides there should be music. "One of Mama's favorite songs was *I'll Fly Away.* I think it kind of fits, so I'll sing it if everybody promises not to laugh."

◆◆◆◆

The following day when the pastor begins the prayer, Austin looks toward the little alcove that leads to the main hallway of the care center. He thinks he sees a glimpse of a blue t-shirt move just outside the doorway, but he can't be sure. A glance at Glory assures him she's concentrating on the prayer. By the time the minister says "Amen", no outside guest can be seen, so Austin doesn't mention his hallucination to anyone. He may have only seen what he half-expected to see. He's glad Glory is preoccupied, because any hint of Presley, and she wouldn't have been able to go ahead with her planned solo.

Not a single individual in the room even considers laughing at Glory's lovely clear voice singing her mom to glory. In fact, when she begins, *"One bright morning, when this life is through, I'll fly away,"* Austin is in tears. He can't look at Liz. It is the same song they sang together during their afternoon in the high school auditorium five years ago. Before his other mother's passing.

Like the funeral service, the burial in the cemetery behind the care center is sparsely attended. Besides the Morgans, Austin, and Glory, there are two nurses and Administrator Miles Conner. Glory glances around. Her face is tear stained, but she manages a smile. "Ever since Daddy died, I've thought I'd be the only one left to mourn Mama. This looks like a crowd! I hope she's watching."

A spray of flowers Liz and Gray purchased earlier for the top of the casket has been transferred to the burial site. A fruit jar full of peonies sits at one end of the six-foot deep hole that awaits Elsa.

"Did you bring the peonies?" Austin whispers before the minister starts to speak.

"No. I wish I had. But the ones over there actually look like Mama's"

Austin quickly points out, "All peonies look alike, I think." He's glad when the meditation begins. Glory doesn't have time to wonder how Elsa's peonies got here beside her grave. Austin believes the answer is obvious. The flash of blue in the funeral home was, indeed, Presley, who risked arrest to pay his respects.

FORTY-THREE

Austin sits with Glory in the waiting room outside Bill Hogan's office. It is the scheduled time for Elsa's will to be read. As at the funeral, interested parties not present are in jail or at some unknown location. It shouldn't take long to dispose of the woman's lifetime assets. Everything goes to the one named heir.

Glory is restless. She keeps looking toward the door. Finally, she stands and looks out the window toward the front of the building. "Do you think Presley will come today? He might think there's a chance he'll get something from Mama."

"He knows there's a better chance he'll be captured and put in jail. We aren't going to see him here." Austin is remembering the blue shirt and jeans he caught sight of at the funeral. The guy isn't afraid to take a gamble, but today would be an unusually ill-advised one, even for a man of Presley's bad judgement.

"Good. But I'm so sad," declares Glory. "I feel like Mama should be here when we talk about her things. And I didn't even get to say good-bye."

"I know, but she went easy. That's something to be grateful for. And the last time we talked to her she seemed content."

Glory is still puzzled by the visit her "brother" supposedly paid Elsa just before she passed. "When the nurse said Presley stopped in, I wanted to believe her, but I didn't. He wouldn't do that, and if he did, Mama would've told him to go away."

Austin suddenly feels the need to defend Presley. After all, he's witnessed him sobbing over his deceased sweetheart. The man must have some emotions. "Well, I'm sure the nurse wasn't lying. Even people like Presley sometimes like to ease their consciences at the end. And he probably loves her. Who doesn't love his mother?"

"Well, I guess it probably made her feel peaceful if she thought they forgave each other." Glory was trying to convince herself. "Except *Mama* didn't do anything to be forgiven for."

"I think parents always carry some guilt when their kids turn out bad. They were too strict, they were too lenient, or they didn't give him a toy train for Christmas. There's always something the kid can blame his mom and dad for."

"Well, Presley better not do that," Glory declares. "If he had been nicer, Mama would've been sure to leave something in her will for him. But she knew he wouldn't take good care of anything he got."

"Yeah. Can you imagine him working on a farm?"

"The thing is, I can't imagine *me* working on one. I don't know anything about farming, and to tell you the truth, I don't think I want to live in that house ever again. It's nice, but I didn't know what I was missing. I'd rather live in town, around people."

"I can understand that." He thought of her old pink room. "You could redecorate, make it look like a whole different place."

"Maybe. But all those barns and grounds seem like a lot for just me."

"I suppose you can sell the place, but it's been in your family for over a hundred years."

"Do I have to decide today?"

"Oh, no. You can think about it. You might not realize now how much you'll miss the place where you spent twenty years."

"There're a lot of things I don't realize, I think. I have so much catching up to do. I bet Presley feels kinda the same way, don't you?"

"I guess he probably does." And, no doubt about it, Liz also must have felt that same sense of being behind when she came out of prison. *A chance for another support group, people who've been kept away from the world. Glory has had it the hardest.* Liz and Presley were in their teens when they were taken from society. Glory had no normal years.

"Do you think Presley knows we're here today?" she asks.

"I don't think so. He isn't listed as a beneficiary, so the court didn't have to notify him about the reading. Hopefully, he's working somewhere and wouldn't have been able to come anyway."

"It had to be hard for him to find a job. It was hard for me when I couldn't tell anybody who I really was. And didn't have a Social Security number."

Austin is impressed by her kind heart. She's worried about a man who may have wanted to kill her. At least that's what has been assumed. Austin's always heard that children love their parents no matter how bad they are. Maybe it's built into Glory to care what becomes of her natural father. Austin himself can't help wondering what would have happened if Presley hadn't tried to rob the gas station. Or at least hadn't taken a firearm with him. It still wouldn't have been good. He hated to think it, but some guys are born losers. No matter what they try, they can't make it work.

The receptionist returns from a short trip into Mr. Hogan's office. "He had an emergency interruption. He's going to be a few minutes late. I hope you can stay a little longer than you were scheduled."

"Sure," says Austin. This is all we have planned for today." They can hardly complain when Glory is going to be leaving the building later as a land owner.

The receptionist lays a newspaper on the coffee table in front of them. "Something to read." Neither of them are in the mood for reading. Austin is going to be back in the Waterloo newspaper office sooner than he wants to be, and the Tama News-Herald is only a reminder. Today could be his only chance to help this girl make future plans, so he should probably get started. He's a little worried because his ideas for her are going to include himself as well. He may be committing to a long-range plan. But, for some reason, he can't stop himself.

"Glory," he begins. "Since we have some time to kill, I'd like to run an idea by you. You say you don't want to farm. You say the buildings and the land will be useless to you. What if I thought of something you can do there besides farm?"

Glory thinks a minute. No ideas come. "Like what?"

"Well, you know how much we all love Murray and Neka. And you know how Neka is a trained service dog who can sense if Gray gets in serious trouble with his blood sugar?"

"Yes." Glory looks baffled.

"Service dogs save lives all the time. What if you and I set up a training ranch for those kinds of dogs? Your farm is the perfect place. Plenty of shelters, plenty of places for dog runs, and room to train. It's far away from town, so all the barking wouldn't bother anybody. We could advertise all over the country."

"You and me?" It seems Glory is fixated on those words. Suddenly she isn't in this by herself.

"Sure. You don't think I'm going to abandon you on that big farm, do you? It isn't Meskwaki land, so we wouldn't have to have the business approved by the tribe. You'd be the owner, and I'd be an employee. And I could still do some writing for the Courier if I had time."

Glory walks to the window and gazes out at Main Street. She appears worried. "I don't know anything much about dogs. And wouldn't I have to buy some to get started and learn to train them and . . .?"

"Yes and yes. But I've been wanting a place to invest the money my Meskwaki mom left me. That cash was her jackpot winnings from the casino on the night she died. This would be something she'd approve of. Something that would help people.

We could hire a couple of professional dog trainers to get started. It's a nice dream."

He knows his timing isn't good, and he's given her a lot to consider. She's sure to be feeling overwhelmed about now. And they still haven't heard the will. That might be emotional for her, even though she's had the unread document in her treasure box for several years.

Austin thinks of one more persuasive point he can't resist mentioning. Then he'll shut up. "The training farm would be a way for you to stay close to Mary and Steve."

Finally, she turns his way and gives him a smile. "I'll think real hard about it."

Bill Hogan enters the room. "So sorry to keep you waiting. Come on in."

The reading of the will goes very quickly. Glory is moved by her mom's words of love for her. She feels a little bad for Presley but continues to believe he brought on his own exclusion.

"I told Elsa you'd buy him a grave stone." Austin explains to ease her conscience.

"And if he'll say he's sorry for taking Rue, I'll give him a job caring for the dogs. Cleaning the pens and stuff."

"Good idea," says Austin, knowing her job offer will likely never be needed. He appreciates the generous spirit that thought of it.

Austin can't leave out his friend. "If Archie isn't too settled in Des Moines, maybe he'll come back and work for us. Don't know, though, if he'd be very easy to supervise. He's a little lazy."

"One other problem," Glory says playfully. "There might not be enough money for a trip to Alaska."

"If there isn't, we can wait and go there after we sell our first service dog."

Keeping the make-believe going, she asks, "Who will run the farm while we're in Alaska? Anita and her kids?"

"Yikes! We can't possibly go anywhere if Anita or Arch are the only backup we have. I'm afraid we're going to be stuck on that ranch forever."

Glory doesn't laugh at that. "Forever on the ranch with you? My dream catcher must be working!"

Bill Hogan walks them back out through the lobby. Austin is happy to see three more people have joined their little crowd. Rue is leading Liz and Gray. He is wearing his uniform over his new prosthesis and looking mighty handsome. Best of all, Austin notices, the couple are holding hands and wearing big smiles.

"Mr. Hogan," Austin says, "This is my family. My little sister, Ruby, and our mother, Liz and father, Gray." It feels good to at last put into words his acceptance of his parents. Austin can see the moment is moving for them as well. If nothing else good had come from his answering Liz's plea for help, her much deserved happiness would be plenty.

"I'm glad to meet you folks," says Bill. "I always liked Elsa, so it's nice to know fine people like you are taking over as Glory's family." He clears his throat as though trying to decide whether to bring up his next idea. "I'm aware of the circumstances of Glory's birth, and I'm afraid I've neglected something."

None of the happy people listening to him has a clue what he's referring to, so they simply wait in silence for him to keep talking.

"I know, Glory, you're working toward a GED, and I think that's great. There's just one more thing you need in order to move ahead in this world you just joined."

Austin is still puzzled. Evidentially, he's overlooked something.

"You need a birth certificate," Bill Hogan declares. "Unfortunately, you can't go back and reenact the scene in order to get a standard form. But it's possible to obtain what they call a Foundling Registration. It'll document for anyone who wants to know that Glory Dawn Becker was, indeed, born alive. It'll also serve just fine if you should want to get a marriage license." He smiles knowingly at her and Austin.

"What do you know," replies Austin. "I've never heard of a Foundling Registration."

"They don't issue many of them. Luckily, true foundlings are rare. This is the first time I've come up against a case. I had to look on the internet to find out how to solve the birth certificate problem."

"Is that something else I'll have to take a test to get?" Glory is catching on to the fact that few important certificates are given out with no strings attached.

Bill laughs. "No, it's real easy. Why don't you come back at ten o'clock Monday, and we'll start working on it. I think you've had enough for today." And the attorney shakes their hands and returns to his office.

Glory looks at Austin. "What's a foundling?"

"A baby who's found, and no one knows who the parents are."

"Except I know who mine were. They were Presley and Mariel."

"But no one knew that at the start of your life. I don't think Presley is going to be around now to sign anything, and you need this paper. Burt and Elsa should have taken care of registering you right after you were found, so now it's a little harder. We'll get it figured out."

"I hope so. I want to be a real person."

Austin smiles. "You already are. The paper is just a formality."

"If I ever have a baby, I want her to be real right away."

"Her?"

Glory smiles. "I can't imagine me being mom to a boy. I wouldn't have any idea what to do with him."

"Oh, you'd learn. Just like you've been learning everything else."

"He might turn out like Presley." Glory considers that possibility for a moment. "But if he did, I wouldn't give up on him. I think we need to let some folks start over."

Austin thinks about the improvements he's made in his own attitude over the last few years. "You're a smart girl, Glory."

PRESLEY

The scene is one of the taverns in downtown Tama. Several months have passed since the surrounding county was rocked by the abduction of little Ruby Morgan.

A bearded stranger wearing sunglasses and a green cap is sitting at the end of the bar, nursing a beer. "I heard this town had a kidnap attempt awhile back. Never heard how it all turned out. Anybody get arrested?"

"One person did. An old lady. That surprised everybody."

"How did they know it was her that did it? Don't seem likely. Did the kid identify her?"

"No. Wilma Watson actually drove up to the town hall and turned herself in to authorities, hoping they'd go easy on her. She claims Presley Becker forced her to lure Rue Morgan away from the powwow. Pres wasn't even at the powwow. He had an alibi. Austin Wapiti didn't buy Wilma's excuses. He was inclined to believe she was caught up in Pres's promise to share his inheritance with her."

"That sounds about right."

"Wilma was so sure she was entitled to something from Elsa, she didn't even feel like she was doin' wrong. Not a bad woman, just money-hungry like a lot of people. Most I know would sell out their grandmothers for a promise of wealth. Maybe Presley would've given her a little something and maybe not. In most folks' opinions, the woman risked too much for too little."

"Will she have to serve any time?" the stranger inquires.

"Don't know until after a trial. Haven't heard if that will happen. Maybe she'll just get 'time served'. I'm thinkin' Bill Hogan will get the court to show mercy. The woman's in her eighties and probably not going to offend again."

"I don't know," Another customer joins the conversation. "Wilma's the one who snatched the kid. You do a crime, you should do the time. But the police have been so brain washed about Presley

Becker, they'd rather blame the whole kidnapping thing on him. Probably the way Pres's whole life has gone."

"I've heard that once upon a time, one of the prettiest girls in the high school loved him. Guess that was the best time of his life. It was all downhill for him after she drowned."

"Where is he now?" asked the stranger without taking his eyes off the Coors sign on the wall in front of him.

"Don't know. He just disappeared. When Elsa died and they had the reading of the will, people expected Presley to materialize right there in the judge's office and demand the farm. But he didn't show up. Stayed out of sight, and pretty soon the search for him went cold. Little Rue's healthy and happy, so people don't give him too much thought."

The other bar patrons start to get in on the rehash of an old scandal. Everybody adds his two cents. "Guess nobody cared enough about Presley to even chase him down."

"It don't matter to me where he goes, as long as he don't come back and make things hard for anybody on the settlement. Or in town."

"Don't think there's much danger. He knows better than to show his face around Tama."

"I hear Glory Becker's probably going to marry Austin Wapiti. So she's getting her happy ending, farm and all."

"I'm glad to hear it," the bearded man responds. "Seems to me that young lady should get everything." And he straps on his backpack, goes outside, and walks down the road headed out of town.

"Who was that masked man?" jokes one of the bar patrons.

"Nobody I know," says his buddy. The men order more drinks and move on to solve other world problems.

FOR DISCUSSION

1. Did you feel like Austin would have returned to the settlement even if Liz hadn't sent him the letter? Do you think sometimes we procrastinate doing what we want until something gives us a push?

2. How do you think the visit would've been different if Austin had gone to visit Liz and Gray three or four years sooner?

3. How was Rue able to make the reunion with Liz easier for Austin?

4. Can you understand Elsa and Burt's reasons for not letting the world know about Glory? Compared to what some abandoned children face, is she one of the lucky ones?

5. If you'd had a chance to talk to Elsa before she died, would you tell her how much she and her husband deprived Glory or let her die thinking she did her best?

6. Do you believe Glory will always be somewhat damaged by her beginnings? If yes, in what ways?

7. Is Presley a villain or just a guy who can't catch a break? Does it seem conceivable that he and Mariel could've had a good life together if he hadn't tried to commit armed robbery?

8. Does Gray's reaction to his disability seem understandable or weak? Does Austin's presence help him in any way?

9. Is Sky an egotistical jerk or a loving brother- or some combination? Do we see the real man or just the way he's perceived by others?

10. How did you feel about Danee? Did you want to see her become part of Glory's life?

11. Do you feel Austin and Liz now have a normal mother/son relationship? What things account for the change in Austin's feelings?

12. Do you think Austin loves Glory as a woman or as a child who needs his help? Can both be true? Can her feelings be taken seriously when she hasn't known any male but him? Would it be a bad idea for them to marry soon?

13. What do you imagine becomes of Presley Becker? Is it right if Wilma has to serve time, and he doesn't?

ACKNOWLEDGMENTS

Thanks so much to those who encouraged me while I was writing *Give Me Glory*:

Huge gratitude goes to Delinda Pushetonequa who shared many important facts about the Meskwaki culture. Linda Winter Chaser at the Health Center offered information about their diabetes program.

My beta readers Kristi Paxton and Suzanne Boldt, let me know I had a story worth developing. Super-proofer and cheerleader Jayne Parsons McKinley has, again, kept me excited and confident about my book-in-progress. I couldn't do without the feedback from these great ladies.

I'm thankful to my long-time friend, Norris Haner and to Stefanie Rash for unknowingly inspiring me to use amputation as the reason to bring Austin back home. Marty Sanders and Bud Blakely were kind enough to share some of their personal knowledge about diabetes. It is a touchy process, writing about serious problems I haven't experienced. I find real people are better sources than the internet, and I don't take for granted their contributions.

ABOUT THE AUTHOR

GIVE ME GLORY is Linda Wiges's third book. It is the sequel to her debut novel, the successful HAPPY DREAMS. Linda also authored the humorous work of suspense, WORTH THE WEIGHT. All three books are currently available on Amazon.com, on Goodreads.com, at the Hearst Center for the Arts, and at area libraries.

Previous writing experience includes full-length stage plays such as *Stressed to Kill* and *Best Seats in the House*. She's directed both locally.

Linda lives in Traer, Iowa with her husband. After careers as a high school English teacher and as an office professional at the University of Northern Iowa, she's been enjoying this creative way of using her writing skills.

You may contact her at linda.wiges@hotmail.com or on Facebook: Linda Wiges Author.

www.ingramcontent.com/pod-product-compliance
Lightning Source LLC
Chambersburg PA
CBHW061956170626
46813CB00006B/2659